Belinda in the looking glass...

"It appears I shall have to teach you how to accept a gift graciously," said Lord Kenmore. "Bend your head forward."

Belinda did as she was told. He drew the necklace around the base of her throat, the touch of his fingers sending little *frissons* of pleasure darting downward to her breasts.

"There now. Look in the mirror," was his command.

Belinda sat down on the gilt-legged stool to survey herself in the mirror. The jewels were perfect.

He leaned down, cupping her shoulders with his hands, to observe her in the mirror. "I vow my little jewels are quite outshone by the brilliance of your eyes."

She met his suddenly intense gaze in the glass and, recognizing his intentions, closed her eyes as his warm lips pressed against the nape of her neck...

➤   ➤   ➤   ➤   ➤

"Great Regency adventure...FIVE GOLD STARS [highest rating]!"
—*Barbra Critiques on The Elusive Countess*

An Amicable Arrangement

Also by
Elizabeth Barron

Miss Drayton's Crusade
The Viscount's Wager
The Elusive Countess

Published by
WARNER BOOKS

AN AMICABLE ARRANGEMENT

Elizabeth Barron

WARNER BOOKS

A Warner Communications Company

WARNER BOOKS EDITION

Warner Books, Inc.
666 Fifth Avenue
New York, N.Y. 10103

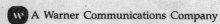 A Warner Communications Company

Printed in the United States of America

First Printing: May, 1988

10 9 8 7 6 5 4 3 2 1

For Pat Skurnik, my dearest friend,
and her family.

What a thing friendship is,
World without end!

—Robert Browning

chapter

1

The mansion of Denehurst had been built in a superior situation amidst the delightfully rustic woods and lanes of the County of Kent, yet conveniently close to Tunbridge Wells, the fashionable watering place.

By the second decade of the nineteenth century, however, the days of Beau Nash and the great Garrick had long since disappeared, and Tunbridge had declined to a town of sedate tea rooms and attractive villas. Only in its new theater did it recapture an echo of its former glory.

The resort's decline was mirrored by that of Denehurst. No longer did respectable people visit on the first Monday of the month to view its public rooms. Neglect had dulled its brocades and penury denuded its walls of the paintings that had once made it famous.

As the Blue Saloon was the smallest of the public rooms, and thus needed the smallest fire, it was there that the members of Sir Joseph Hanbury's family usually congregated on those rare occasions when they sat together. But when three members of the family gathered there one afternoon in March, after the coldest winter in memory, it was evident that this occasion was not a happy one.

"If you continue to insist that I marry Lord Winchell,

Papa, you leave me with but one alternative," declared Miss Belinda Hanbury, her face pale but resolute. "I shall be forced to run away!"

"Don't talk such fustian!" spluttered Sir Joseph, his face turning an ominous shade of purple. "You shall do as you're told, girl. Damme, it's a fine world we're coming to when a chit of nineteen can tell her own father she'll not wed the man of his choice!"

"Exactly, Papa. The man of *your* choice, not mine." Belinda sprang from the threadbare chair to pace about the shabby room, her dusky curls bouncing about her small, elfin face. "And the sole reason for Lord Winchell being your choice is that he is excessively wealthy, and your pockets are totally to let."

"Hold your tongue, Belinda," snapped Lady Angelica Hanbury, intervening from the depths of her fireside chair. "How dare you speak that way to your papa!"

Valiantly ignoring her stepmother, Belinda approached her father and grasped the lapels of his coat.

"How can you force me to marry such a man, Papa?" she pleaded, striving to keep her voice steady. "He's fifty— thirty years older than me! He reeks of brandy and, what is more, he has hands that wander all over me." She shuddered. "I cannot bear the thought of even being in the same room with him, never mind marrying him."

Gently removing her hands from his lapels, her father turned his back on her, clearing his throat before he spoke. "We all have to make sacrifices in our lives," he muttered, casting a look of desperation in his wife's direction.

"There's your brother Bertie's gaming debts to be paid, my dear Belinda," said Lady Hanbury, coming to her husband's aid. "And all the necessary repairs and renovations here at Denehurst. Your sister has grown out of all her dresses, and there is no money left to buy more. Not that she needs anything fancy, poor girl, in her predicament, but you—"

"I am to be the sacrificial lamb," cried Belinda. "Well, I won't be! This is 1814, not the Dark Ages. You cannot force me to marry that dreadful man against my will. Why can't Bertie marry some rich widow? Or, better still, let him find some employment so that he may pay off his own debts. And while we're speaking of Marianne's clothes," she added fiercely, "how is it that *you* are able to run up monstrous great bills with the dressmaker and milliner, Stepmama, when we are so much in debt?"

Belinda knew instantly that she had gone too far. Lady Hanbury's cold, pale eyes glistened in her plump face as she glared at her diminutive stepdaughter.

"You are a willful, ungrateful hoyden! Go to your room this instant, and don't you come down again until you are ready to apologize for your insolence."

Belinda bit her lip. She turned to appeal to her father, only to find that he had slipped out during the confrontation, no doubt having retreated to the stables, as usual, leaving his daughter to deal with her stepmother by herself.

"Forgive me, Stepmama." Belinda sighed and clasped her trembling hands tightly against her stomach. "It is only that I cannot bear the thought of having to marry Lord Winchell. Surely you, as a woman, can comprehend that?"

But although the appeal in her large blue eyes might have melted the hardest of hearts, where her stepmother was concerned she was up against granite; the soft, plump exterior was deceptive.

Lady Hanbury leaned forward to adjust the tapestry firescreen a little to shield her pink-and-white complexion from the heat of the fire. "You must remember that I, too, had to marry a man many years older than myself, and one with an almost grown-up family, to boot."

"Surely you cannot be comparing Papa with Lord Winchell!" said Belinda scornfully. "Besides, you were no more than ten years younger than Papa when you wed him. That's vastly different from the thirty or so years that separate Lord Winchell and me."

As Lady Hanbury had long since convinced herself, if no one else, that she was a young and beautiful woman of the permanent age of five and twenty tied to a very much older husband, Belinda's lack of tact did nothing to endear herself further to her stepmama.

"I don't wish to go on with this conversation," she said

frostily. "Go to your room and make sure Ellen does something about that wretched hair of yours. It looks like a bird's nest. I hope as you're not forgetting Lord Winchell is escorting us to the theater at Tunbridge Wells this evening?"

"How could such a treat possibly escape my mind?" was Belinda's response.

For once her sarcasm escaped Lady Hanbury's notice, which was, perhaps, for the best. To be in her stepmama's bad books meant that life at Denehurst could be extremely unpleasant for days, if not weeks. Although she had the appearance of being placid and indolent, Lady Hanbury's resentment could be harbored for a long period of time. To Belinda's relief, however, the thought of going to the theater had set her stepmother off on her favorite subject.

"It will be most delightful to visit the Tunbridge theater again," she was saying. "Your dear father hardly ever takes me, which is a great shame, for, as you know, it was at that very theater that we first met."

Belinda was determined not to endure yet another version of how, five years ago, the beautiful and distinguished actress, Miss Angelica Brown, had been courted by all the leading members of the Kent and Sussex gentry and aristocracy, only to choose Sir Joseph Hanbury, the recently bereaved widower, because she took pity on his three motherless children.

"Excuse me, Stepmama, but I think I should go and dress for the theater."

Lady Hanbury's plump fingers searched among the silver wrappings for another chocolate topped with sugared violets. "That's a good girl. Off you go." She waved a hand in Belinda's direction, scattering the wrappings about the hearth. "And don't you forget to come to my room before you go downstairs. I want to make sure you look just right for Lord Winchell tonight."

Belinda hurried from the room, the very sound of her suitor's name making her feel nauseous.

An hour later, she sat on the stool before her dressing table, peering into the tarnished mirror. A frown wrinkled the forehead beneath the dark curls with which, despite Lady Hanbury's admonition, Ellen had waged a losing battle. No amount of heated irons would straighten them.

Not even Marianne's nimble fingers had been able to curb their unruliness. The gold-spangled ribbon threaded through them probably would not last much more than fifteen minutes before it slid off, to be stuffed into her reticule like all the other ribbons and flowers and ornaments that her crisp curls had escaped.

Belinda flung down her brush. "Honestly, Bertie," she said, addressing her elder brother, Gilbert, who was staring gloomily out the window. "Angelica made me feel like some little—what is it you call them? Ladybirds?—that's it, a ladybird she was preparing to parade before Lord Winchell."

"Always said Angelica would have made a prime abbess in some select establishment if she hadn't married Papa."

"Oh, I wouldn't go that far, Bertie, for I've never heard a word of scandal about her. But I do wish she'd stop pretending she was once a great dramatic actress like Mrs. Siddons when, in reality, she was only a member of the chorus. But to return to the subject: there's no doubt that she and Papa are determined I shall marry Lord Winchell."

Bertie shifted his eyes to fix his gaze on a strip of wallpaper that was peeling away from a patch of damp on the wall. "Papa told me he'd been turned down by the moneylenders in London. Denehurst is mortgaged to the hilt. Something has to be done," he said in a hollow voice, addressing the rain-smeared window.

Belinda rose from the stool to survey her brother's slender back. "And I must be the one to do it, is that it?" she asked caustically.

Her brother turned around. "Oh, Lindy. I only wish . . ." He reached out to take her hands, but she slapped them away, her control shattered at last.

"I have to rescue you and Papa from dun territory, keep Angelica in frills and chocolates, and take care of Marianne for the rest of her life." Her eyes blazed so fiercely at Bertie that he recoiled. "And how is all this to be achieved, my dear Gilbert? Why, simply by selling myself, my body—oh yes, especially my body—to the notorious Lord Winchell!"

"No, no, Lindy," protested her brother. "Dammit, he's offering you marriage. There's no way Papa would accept anything less than an honorable proposal."

"Ha! An honorable proposal, indeed! Papa's honorable proposal is to sell his daughter so that his, and your, gaming debts may be paid off, accompanied, of course, by a handsome settlement upon you all."

Tears of anger sparkled on the ends of her long eyelashes, but she was determined not to allow them to spill.

Bertie ran his finger around his high, starched collar with its exaggerated points, as if it were about to choke him. "If there was any other way out, I'd take it, Lindy. You know that, don't you?"

She was sickened by his pleading and his cowed manner. "You are as weak as Papa, Bertie. Never fear. I have long since abandoned all hope of your bailing yourself, and us, out of this fix, so you may set your mind at rest. I shan't ask for your help."

Gilbert Hanbury's handsome face flushed beneath his sister's withering scorn. "If only I were able to settle all my debts, you'd see how I'd make a new start!"

She shrugged. "Yes, so you have said many times before, Bertie." She sighed heavily and then, summoning up a faint smile, stood on tiptoe to kiss his cheek. "Don't look so downhearted, brother mine. I'll soon have Lord Winchell twisted around my little finger, and no doubt he'll leave me alone and return to his former exploits once I have presented him with an heir."

She hurriedly dabbed at her eyes with a slightly grubby handkerchief and then spun around. "Come, tell me how I look. Will I do? I know Angelica is going to chide me for the state of my hair, but I cannot do anything more with it."

Bertie held up his preposterously long-handled quizzing glass to survey his sister's slight figure in the white cambric gown with sapphire-blue ribbons to match her eyes.

"You look stunning. I must say I'm surprised Papa was able to come up with the ready for all this new finery for you."

"Ready? You mean cash? You must be funning, dear brother! He has merely spread the word of my imminent engagement and as a result his credit in the village has been temporarily extended. Besides," she added, giving her brother a wry smile, "he says it's a good investment."

She drew on her white silk gloves and picked up her fan and reticule. "Will you not change your mind and come with us tonight, Bertie?" she pleaded.

"To the theater? Not I. Good God, Lindy. It's March. Everyone's in London, bar the few, like me, who are rusticating because they can't afford to go to town. No, I'm off to dinner with Charlie Warren and then to a cockfight in Chiddingstone."

Resigned to the fact that she and her stepmother would be escorted to the theater by Lord Winchell only, Belinda first ran into her sister's room to bid her a cheerful farewell, and then presented herself to her stepmother.

"Just as I thought," was Angelica's comment when Belinda entered the heavily perfumed room. "Your hair's a mess. Oh well, it's too late to do anything with it now."

Sorely tempted to poke her tongue at her stepmother's bare back, Belinda followed her down the staircase, feeling decidedly unwell at the prospect of an evening spent in the company of Angelica and Lord Winchell.

Her spirits plummeted even further when she entered the drawing room to find both her father and Lord Winchell wreathed in smiles. Indeed, they were positively wallowing in good humor.

Her father came forward to greet her. "My dearest daughter," he exclaimed, bending to kiss her cheek.

Thoughts of Judas rushed to her mind.

"Good evening, Papa, Lord Winchell," she said in a cool voice. She attempted to place a little distance between herself and her father, but he kept her hand in his, his grip tightening as he felt her efforts to withdraw it.

He cleared his throat nervously. "My dear Belinda, I have momentous news for you. Lord Winchell has asked for your hand in marriage, and I have gladly given him my consent."

"Oh, how splendid!" cried Lady Hanbury, clapping her hands. Then, perhaps realizing that this response might appear just a trifle too eager, she glided across to Belinda and, accompanied by an almost overpowering waft of Floris gardenia scent, enfolded her in her arms. "My dearest girl," she declaimed. "May you be forever happy." She released Belinda and hurried across to Lord Winchell. "You have made the Hanbury family extremely happy today," she told him.

Spoken with the utmost sincerity, thought Belinda. Someone placed her hand in the dry hand of Lord Winchell, and he bent to press his lips—alas, not dry—to it.

"My dear Belinda. I am a most fortunate man," said her corpulent betrothed, again kissing her hand with his moist lips. "You have made me the happiest man in the world."

An hour or so later, as she sat in one of the dress boxes in the theater at Tunbridge Wells, it occurred to Belinda that everyone concerned appeared to be happy except the one person above all who should be: herself. She had never before felt quite so alone, for she knew that she could not share the burden of her unhappiness with Marianne, who was her usual confidante and advisor.

This was no time to indulge in a fit of melancholy, however. What was necessary now was to muster enough strength to get her through this ordeal, for try as she might she could see no resolution to her dilemma but to marry Lord Winchell and make the best of it.

"Why so pensive, my love?" asked the object of her thoughts from behind her.

The proximity of his face to hers startled her. As she looked up into his eyes, she noticed for the first time their unusual color: the palest gray-green, as if they had been drowned in seawater. Indeed, what she hated most was their lack of expression, as if they were, in fact, the eyes of a drowned man.

"Oh, I was merely thinking about the play," was her belated response to Lord Winchell's enquiry.

Belinda became aware that the curtain had come down on the first act of the melodrama. People were milling about, visiting each other in the boxes on both sides of the theater. Food and flower sellers cried their wares in the pit and galleries. An aromatic mixture of oranges and pickled onions hung in the air.

"Where is Lady Hanbury?" she demanded, with some

anxiety, when she saw that her stepmother had left the box.

"She has gone backstage, apparently to visit some of her former colleagues." Although his expression was urbane, there was no mistaking the sneer in his voice. "A glass of champagne, my dear? I arranged for some refreshments to be brought here, so that you might join me in a toast to our future together."

She sprang to her feet. "I think not, my lord. I intend to join my stepmother." Her eyes sought the door, but Lord Winchell's substantial figure stood between her and it.

"Come now, sweetheart." He slid his hand up and down her bare arm. "This is the first opportunity we have had of being alone together since your father consented to our marriage. Surely I deserve just a little more from my pretty fiancée than a mere kiss of the hand?"

His tone was silken, but his grip was like steel as he drew her to the dark recess at the rear of the box.

"Let me go, my lord," demanded Belinda in a haughty tone that belied the wild hammering of her heart.

His response was a dry, mirthless laugh. She found herself crushed against his body, her face buried in his waistcoat, which smelled most abominably of snuff.

As Belinda struggled to get her hands between them so that she could push him away, his left hand gripped her hand, painfully dragging her head back so that she was forced to look up at him. To her horror, he kissed her, his tongue against her mouth, trying to force it open. Waves of nausea swept over her. She felt so faint that her ineffectual struggles served only to increase his demonic amusement.

"I shall be paying dearly for you, sweet Belinda. I expect ample recompense in return," he whispered against her mouth. "So fight away, my little wildcat. There's nothing I enjoy more than a spirited chase. It makes the surrender all the more worthwhile."

Belinda drew in a sobbing breath. "I shall never, never marry you, you loathsome man."

Laughing, he began to fondle her breasts, his expressionless eyes never leaving her face as he did so.

* * *

"I say, Gillridge," drawled Lord Francis Kenmore. "Didn't I hear you say that the little girl with Winchell in the box across from ours was the daughter of Sir Joseph Hanbury?"

Sir Ronald Gillridge tilted his chair back and eyed his cousin over a full glass of glowing bordeaux. "That's right. Not Winchell's usual style, of course, but they say Hanbury's trying to trap him into marrying the girl. Denehurst is mortgaged to the hilt, apparently."

Lord Kenmore put his quizzing glass up to his eye to examine the opposite box more closely. "Well, well," he drawled, raising his dark eyebrows. "Although Winchell's friendship with Prinny has made him acceptable in society I, myself, have never considered him quite the thing; but I'd wager the Prince Regent himself would not condone Winchell's present conduct."

"What the devil do you mean?" Gillridge almost tipped his chair over in his eagerness to peer across at the opposite box. "Can't see anything at all," he muttered.

"Just so." Lord Kenmore opened the baize-covered door of his cousin's box. "I think I shall stretch my legs. Care to join me?"

"Not I. I'll not meddle between a man and his future wife, especially not when it's Winchell. He's a bad man, Francis. Leave well alone. In any event, since when did you take to playing Sir Galahad? In the old days it might well have been you in that box."

"Me? Molest a well-bred young girl? My dear Ronald, you insult me!"

"Ah, I forgot that you confine your *affaires* to ladies of the stage. But I still say that it's not like you to gallop off to rescue ladies in distress, like one of those demmed energetic knights of old."

"Ah, my dear coz, I am a man of many parts. You would be surprised to learn what I get up to when the mood takes me."

Francis stepped out into the crowded passageway behind the boxes. He began to elbow his way through the crush of people, spurred on by his memory of the brief glimpse of a girl's terror-stricken face he had caught through his quizzing glass.

chapter
2

When he reached the closed door of Winchell's box, Francis hesitated, momentarily wondering what his excuse for being there might be, considering he and Winchell were barely on nodding terms.

He decided that he would think of something when the time came. He was about to rap on the door when it was flung open and a small form precipitated itself against his chest.

"Oh!" gasped the form, which resolved itself into the girl he had glimpsed through his glass.

Miss Hanbury, for Francis took for granted that it was she, was an elfin-faced, diminutive creature who appeared to be no more than fourteen. This, surely, was unlikely, for although he would not put it past Winchell to be chasing pubescent females, he could not imagine any parent casting his child into the toils of such a man. Fifteen bordering on sixteen, perhaps? Even that was hard to believe when he looked at the tiny creature.

A gold-spangled ribbon dangled from her tousled dark curls. He reached down to remove it and presented it to its owner, but, as she chose to ignore it, he tucked it into his sleeve.

"Oh, please, sir, you must help me," she cried, clutching his arm as if she feared he might run away.

"Of course," he said soothingly. "You are perfectly safe now."

The guileless blue eyes widened. "You don't understand," she hissed. "I think he's dead."

Francis began to wish he had stayed home for a quiet evening of *vingt-et-un*, as Gillridge had suggested. The play was, as he had suspected it would be, appallingly bad, and it was also damnably cold in the theater. It was just his bad fortune to have returned from an extended sojourn in the West Indies to the longest and most severe winter in memory. Even the Thames had frozen solid. Unfortunately frost fairs and skating were not in his line.

"Will you help me or not?" cried the girl.

Dragging his thoughts back to the present, Francis put a protective arm about her. "Calm yourself, child," he said, employing the tone of a father reassuring his infant. "What do you mean, you think he is dead?"

"What I say!" Her sapphire-blue eyes darted fire at him, and she stamped her foot in exasperation at his stupidity. "I think I have killed Lord Winchell." Without even a "by your leave" she dragged him into the box and slammed the door behind them.

Francis had to adjust his eyes to the darkness before being able to make out the body of a man sprawled facedown on the carpeted floor.

"I hit him with a champagne bottle," explained Miss Hanbury.

"Good Lord! Bring that candle over here, would you, please?" Francis knelt down by the inert figure and turned it over, pressing his hand to Winchell's chest to feel for a heartbeat. "He's not dead," was his pronouncement.

"Oh, thank heavens for that." With a flurry, she knelt down on the other side of Winchell. Francis caught a subtle waft of some woodland fragrance from her as she did so.

"Where did you hit him?"

"On the side of the head. He was trying to—"

"Yes, I know. I saw what was happening from the box across from this one."

"Oh." Tilting her head to one side, like some small inquisitive bird, Belinda examined him.

In her panic she had not registered the gentleman who had appeared so opportunely. Now she saw that he was singularly handsome, with dark—almost black—waving hair, dark brown eyes beneath slanted eyebrows, and a mouth that slid into a crooked smile as he observed her observing him.

"I should introduce myself," he said. "Kenmore. Lord Francis Kenmore."

"Miss Belinda Hanbury." She held out her hand and his fingers clasped hers above the recumbent figure of Lord Winchell. "How very kind of you to come to my rescue, sir."

"It appears that you were quite capable of rescuing yourself, ma'am." He ran his hands over Winchell's head, then wiped them fastidiously on his handkerchief. "Pomade," he explained.

"Yes, I know. Horrid, isn't it? I must reek of the stuff."

"He has a lump as large as a pigeon's egg behind his ear."

"Do you think he will live?"

"I am certain of it." She did not appear particularly pleased by this news. "But he will have a nasty headache for a day or so, I should imagine." Francis loosened Winchell's neckcloth, while Belinda disposed his head more comfortably upon a cushion.

"There's nothing more we can do for him at present." Francis stood up.

"You won't leave me alone with him, will you?" pleaded Belinda, scrambling to her feet.

"Certainly not. But surely you cannot be here with Lord Winchell by yourself?"

"Oh, no. My stepmother is visiting friends backstage. She was an actress here once, you see."

"Ah, I understand." Not that he really could comprehend how any chaperone, even one who had once been an actress, could leave this child alone with a devil like Winchell. He ran his eyes over her. "Have you a pin?"

"A pin? What on earth for?"

Without actually touching her, he indicated the torn bodice of her dress, which revealed more than was proper of her rounded young breasts.

She hastily dragged the flimsy fabric together across her chest. "Damn him!" she muttered, her face fiery red with embarrassment.

She turned away to scrabble in her reticule, and then turned back again. "I haven't got one." Her face puckered up as if she were trying hard not to cry.

"Never mind," he said cheerfully. "I believe this will do the trick." He drew out a sapphire-headed gold pin from the immaculate folds of his white neckcloth. "Stand still a moment and we'll soon have you set to rights."

Belinda did as she was told, and he deftly fastened the two torn sides of the bodice together. A strange trembling sensation ran through her when his fingers brushed her breasts. But it was not at all like the feeling of revulsion she had experienced when Lord Winchell had touched her there. Her breathing quickened, but even as she began to wonder if she should be permitting him to do this, particularly as she was finding it so intensely pleasurable, he stepped back.

"There. Matches your beautiful eyes. All it needs now is your shawl or wrap. I take it you have one?"

Feeling decidedly shy with this elegant stranger, Belinda was glad of the opportunity to turn away to seek her shawl. She found it on the back of her chair. He took it from her and placed it about her shoulders, giving them a reassuring squeeze as he did so.

Her racing heart having quietened a little, she felt able to face him again. "What are we to do about—about him?" she asked, nodding at Lord Winchell, from whom loud snoring sounds were now issuing.

The strident clang of the bell, warning patrons to return to their seats for the second act, sounded through the theater. Belinda clutched Lord Kenmore's arm. "Oh, my goodness," she breathed. "Now Angelica will be returning. What on earth will she say?"

As if in answer to her question, the door swung open and the majestic figure of her stepmother sailed in, accompanied by an almost overpowering wave of expensive scent.

She must have positively bathed in the stuff, thought Francis.

Lady Hanbury did not progress very far into the box, her way being somewhat impeded by Lord Winchell's body stretched across the floor. She gave a little scream. "Lord!" Her eyes narrowed as she searched for her stepdaughter. "Belinda! What have you been up to?"

Francis could feel the girl beside him tremble, but before he could say anything she moved forward. "Stepmama, I should like to present Lord Kenmore. He has been vastly kind, coming to my rescue when that wretched man— Oh!" Her exclamation was caused by Lord Kenmore's having pinched her arm. She was about to turn upon him and indignantly demand what he meant by it, but he was already bowing low before the bemused Lady Hanbury.

"Forgive my intrusion, ma'am, but your stepdaughter appealed to me for assistance when Lord Winchell tripped over a chair and struck his head against the marble-topped table."

"He did—" Belinda encountered a crushing glance from Lord Kenmore and promptly closed her mouth.

"How excessively kind of you, Lord Kenmore," gushed Lady Hanbury. "But how in the world could such a dreadful thing have happened? Poor, poor Lord Winchell. What on earth shall we do?"

"Did you travel here in his carriage?"

"Why, yes, we did."

"Then perhaps it would be best if—" A loud groan interrupted Francis. "Pardon me." He went to kneel on one knee beside Lord Winchell. "He's coming to."

Another loud groan turned Belinda's stomach to water. Dear God, what would become of her when the truth was revealed?

"What in hell's name is going on?" were Lord Winchell's

first words, spoken in a thick, slurred voice. He struggled to sit up, grabbing at Lord Kenmore for assistance. "Who the devil are you?"

"Kenmore. Don't try to stand up yet. Better if you prop yourself against the wall for a while. Fell and hit your head."

"The devil I did!" Lord Winchell ran his fingers over his head, wincing when they encountered the lump. "Feeling devilish queasy, I know that."

From the neighboring boxes and the circle above came hisses for them to be quiet, indicating that the play had begun again.

Francis got to his feet and looked down at Lord Winchell. "Might I suggest that I make arrangements for you to be conveyed home immediately by your servants? I shall undertake to drive Lady Hanbury and Miss Hanbury home myself."

Lord Winchell closed his eyes and wrapped his arms about his protuberant stomach, groaning so horribly that Belinda began to look around for a suitable receptacle, just in case.

"You have had a very nasty fall," said Lord Kenmore. "Your physician should attend you as soon as possible."

The older man's pallor grew even more pronounced. "Yes, yes. You are right. I beg you, Kenmore, have my servants sent for." He looked up at the ladies. "My humblest apologies. Can't think how. . ." He shook his head in bewilderment, wincing with pain again as he did so.

Taking her cue from Lord Kenmore's explanation of how he had received his injury, Belinda bent down to Lord Winchell. "I trust you will soon be feeling very much better, my lord."

He grasped her reluctantly proffered hand, kissing it repeatedly, so that she began to think that it was *she* who would be in dire need of a basin.

"My little angel," he whispered. "I give you my word I shall make this evening up to you."

Disgusted by the sight of the lecherous old satyr and the shrinking young girl, Francis drew her away. He then addressed Lady Hanbury. "If you and your stepdaughter would kindly remain with Lord Winchell for but a few minutes, ma'am, I shall make all the necessary arrangements."

As these arrangements entailed sending for Lord Winchell's servants to carry him down to his carriage—no easy task—and also persuading an amazed Ronald Gillridge to lend him his carriage and servants so that the Hanbury ladies might be conveyed home, it was in excess of forty minutes by the time they were toiling along the Ashurst road.

The road was so deeply rutted, as a result of the heavy snows that had melted only recently, that Francis soon resigned himself to the fact that he would be lucky to see the end of the farce, never mind the play. He also resigned himself to having to listen to Lady Hanbury's vapid comments on the play, Lord Winchell's accident, and his own gallantry in having come to their rescue.

Belinda closed her eyes and leaned her head against the squabs. The rather one-sided conversation between her stepmother and Lord Kenmore drifted in and out of her consciousness, while she tried to concentrate on working out all the likely repercussions of all that had happened at the theater.

For now, at least, it appeared that Lord Winchell believed the story that he had fallen and struck his head. Unfortunately, that probably meant that he would still wish to marry her. On the other hand, at least she would not be charged with attempted murder.

She gritted her teeth. Heavens, what wouldn't she give to have murdered the horrid man in truth! He was a—a beast, an animal! She thought again of his expression when he was fingering her, and shuddered.

Squeezing her eyes more tightly shut, Belinda forced her mind to dwell on more pleasant thoughts. Her mind, having a will of its own, chose to dwell on the memory of the fleeting touch of Lord Kenmore's long fingers.

Those memories, however, were disquieting in their own way. They conjured up new feelings which, even now, were spreading warmth throughout her body. Too weary to discipline her mind, she permitted herself this indulgence, and drifted off on a blissful cloud of warm, pleasurable emotions.

The carriage jolted to a halt. She opened her eyes with a start to find Lord Kenmore watching her with an amused glint in his eyes. For a horrid moment she wondered if he possibly could have read her mind, and decided to give him a haughty glare to squelch any ideas he might be harboring concerning her.

He raised his eyebrows in a quirky, questioning response and then descended from the carriage, so that she was left wondering if she had betrayed her thoughts to him in some way.

Slowly she got down from the carriage, ignoring his outstretched hand. She was immensely relieved to be home. It had been an extremely trying evening.

"If you will excuse me, Lady Hanbury, I shall not come in," said Lord Kenmore in response to her invitation. "I gave Sir Ronald my word that I would return before the end of the play." He turned to Belinda at the foot of the steps. "Good night, Miss Hanbury."

"Good night, my lord." She slipped her hand out of her muff and shook hands with him. "I cannot thank you enough," she whispered. After all, even if he did treat her like a child, he had most gallantly come to her aid.

"Always at your service, ma'am," was his formal, yet quizzical, reply. She found his teasing manner vexatious in the extreme.

He turned away to walk back to the carriage.

"Come along, Belinda," snapped Lady Hanbury. "It is freezing cold out here."

Belinda began to mount the steps when she suddenly remembered his sapphire pin. "Sir," she hissed at Lord Kenmore's back.

"What is it?"

"Your pin."

"What? Oh, keep it as a memento."

"Don't be so ridiculous. I cannot possibly keep such a valuable thing."

"Belinda! What are you about?" demanded her stepmother's voice from the doorway.

"Then we must find another way for you to return it," said Lord Kenmore in his infuriatingly condescending tone.

"I could take it out now."

"No, no. Your stepmama might notice your torn dress and perhaps put two and two together. Send it to me. I am staying with Sir Ronald Gillridge; Bedford Terrace."

"Very well. That is what I shall do."

Something in the girl's voice tugged at Francis. She sounded as if she was disappointed.

"Or perhaps we could contrive some sort of clandestine meeting," he added, sotto voce, thinking this might appeal to the chit's evidently romantic imagination.

"Oh, yes. I think that would be best," was her disquieting response. "I shall send a message to you within the next few days."

As he sprang onto the box, taking the reins himself for the return journey, Francis cursed his glib tongue.

He had the uneasy impression that he had not seen the last of Miss Belinda Hanbury.

chapter

3

Still shivering from the cold, Belinda relinquished her bonnet, muff and cloak to James the footman and then, avoiding her stepmother, darted up the stairs.

"I wish to speak with you, Belinda," Lady Hanbury yelled after her in a most unladylike fashion.

Belinda poised in flight, but did not turn around. "Pardon me, Stepmama, but I must go and see Marianne." She ran lightly up the remaining stairs, ignoring the splutters of exasperation from below.

As she had anticipated, Marianne was still up. Wrapped in her favorite blue India shawl that covered her from head to toe, she was huddled by the fire, immersed in the book she was reading.

Upon Belinda's entrance the book was tossed aside. "Oh, my goodness! Is it that time already?" Marianne's eyes flew to the tortoiseshell clock on the mantelshelf. "But surely you are home very early, dearest? It is only a little after nine." She jumped up to embrace Belinda. "Oh, you poor soul, you're frozen. Come and get warm."

Belinda allowed her sister to draw her to the fire. By now her teeth were chattering with both the chill and a delayed reaction to the evening's events. She knelt before the meager fire, holding her hands out to its warmth and rubbing them. She was acutely aware that her sister's brilliant blue eyes were fixed upon her, that she was awaiting an explanation, but she wished to arrange her thoughts into some semblance of order before she spoke. It would never do to alarm Marianne.

But it was too late. "Something dreadful has happened," said Marianne, her eyes like saucers. "I can tell." Kneeling down by Belinda, she took her cold hands in hers. "That horrid man did something to you, didn't he? I beg you, Lindy, don't leave me in suspense."

Belinda flung her arms about her oversensitive sister and hugged her. "You are right, something did happen," she said gruffly, and there, seated on the hearth rug, she gave Marianne an expurgated version of what had occurred that evening. No amount of expurgation, however, could explain away her torn bodice.

"Lord Winchell ripped your dress!" exclaimed Marianne. "Oh, Lindy."

"Well, you see he—he grabbed at my dress as he was falling," hurriedly invented Belinda. "That's how it happened."

Marianne's beautiful eyes filled with tears. "Oh, Lindy, to think that you have to endure that horrid man for us, for *me*, especially!"

Belinda sprang to her feet. "Faradiddle! And you may stop crying this instant, for you know how I cannot bear to see you cry. I am well able to deal with Lord Winchell, I can tell you. Just you wait and see. He'll soon be saying: 'Yes, my dear. No, my dear. Anything you say, my dear.' Our ears will be filled with the creaking of his corsets as he bows to my every command."

Her exaggerated imitation of Lord Winchell's unctuous speech and old-fashioned bows turned Marianne's tears to giggles. "But this Lord Kenmore, Lindy? You haven't told me how he looks. Is he handsome?"

"Yes, extremely so," growled Belinda. "Knows it, too." She said no more, not wishing to discuss Lord Kenmore, least of all with Marianne. Her sister was capable of reading her face and thoughts as easily as she conned the pages of one of her favorite books.

"Is he tall?" prompted Marianne. "Dark or fair?"

"Everyone appears tall to me, you know that." Belinda plumped herself down in Marianne's rocking chair to set distance between them. "He's about the same height as Bertie. About thirty or so, I should imagine. Dark hair and eyes. Very elegantly dressed. Bertie would have been pea-green with envy had he seen the fit of his coat and the elegance of his neckcloth." She dragged the heavy gold fringe of her shawl through her fingers and frowned. "He treated me as if I were a child."

"Perhaps he thought you *were* a child, dearest," said Marianne gently. "After all, he wouldn't be the first person to make that mistake, would he?"

The fringe-dragging became more vehement. "No. But he had no right to be so mocking and condescending."

Marianne studied her sister's averted face and then quickly changed the subject. "How will you return his pin without Angelica knowing?"

"Don't you worry your head about that. I shall find a way. Better you don't know about it, though," added Belinda with a grin.

Marianne sighed. "Oh, Lindy. Promise me you won't do anything rash."

"Do not worry, dearest. Have you ever in your life known me to do anything rash?"

This decidedly loaded question caused both sisters to dissolve into giggles.

"I must get this dress off before Angelica sees the rip in it." Belinda jumped up from the chair, greatly relieved that Marianne's questions about Lord Kenmore had gone no further.

She proceeded to strip off her dress, unaware that she had revealed far more to her perceptive sister by her unusual reticence than had she chattered on, nineteen to the dozen, about her new acquaintance, as she normally would have done.

* * *

A few hours later, the subject of the sisters' brief discussion was also warming himself before a fire, his feet propped on the hearth rail of the fireplace in his cousin's snug study.

"Gad, what an evening!" exclaimed Sir Ronald, eyeing his cousin over a large glass of cognac. "I tell you, Francis, that's testin' friendship too far. First you drag me off to the theater 'gainst my will. Then you dash off to rescue some chit, like a deuced Saint George. And you end up drivin' her home in my carriage, leavin' me on my own to watch the most damnably borin' play I ever hope to see. I wouldn't mind if I'd been in the pit, old man, but from where I was I couldn't even see the dancers' ankles, let alone their knees."

Francis held up his glass to examine the pale gold liquid against the light of the lamp on the table beside him. "Accept my humblest apologies, coz. I am forced to agree that mine was, quite definitely, the vastly superior drama."

"What's she like, the Hanbury female? Not out yet, is she?"

"I shouldn't think so. She's not even old enough to be termed a female. Looks about fourteen, but I daresay she's nearer sixteen. Spirited little thing. Like a little wood nymph. Bit of a handful, I should imagine. Make a perfect Ariel in *The Tempest*—or perhaps a female Puck." He smiled to himself. "Now there's an idea!"

"For God's sake, Francis. Must you always be thinkin' of people in theatrical terms! And that reminds me. What the devil do you mean by refusin' to come to the green room with me after the show was over? You knew very well I'd laid on a special dinner, thinkin' we'd bring home a few delectable beauties for our night's entertainment. And what happens? The notorious Baron Kenmore of Luxton, famous for his infamous after-theater parties, says he's weary and would prefer to sleep alone tonight!" Sir Ronald's face had grown ruddy with indignation. "What the devil's happened to you, Francis? You thinkin' of taking holy orders?"

Francis shot him a speaking glance. "Hardly," he drawled.

"Don't tell me you lived a life of celibacy in the West

Indies with all those dusky beauties and that heat, for I won't believe it.''

"Then I shan't tell you. Not that it's any of your business,'' Francis added with a sweet smile.

"Dammit, Francis. You've changed since you went to Jamaica. Don't deny it. And now I come to think of it, been meanin' to ask you why you chose to stay there more than a year.''

"You know why.''

"Because you killed that scoundrel Prescott in a duel? From all I've heard of him you did the world a great favor by doin' so. But why a year? Why not just the obligatory few months to avoid the law, and then return to England?''

"You're in a damned inquisitive mood tonight.''

"You owe me an explanation,'' insisted Ronald.

"I do?''

Ronald quailed beneath his cousin's searing look. "Cousin. Family, y'know,'' he stuttered. "Concerned for your welfare.''

Francis smiled, his eyes glinting with mockery.

Recognizing that look, Ronald was aware that he was perilously close to deep water, but emboldened by a vast quantity of wine and spirits he waded in even farther. "Still don't know why you fought Prescott. What was your quarrel with him? Hart said it was over the Countess of Beresford, the beautiful Rosaline herself, but she's married to that nobody, Courtenay, so perhaps it ain't so.''

This time he had gone too far. In one graceful movement Francis rose and walked to the table behind the sofa, which was laden with bottles.

"'Night, Gillridge. I'm taking this, if you don't mind.'' Bearing the almost full decanter of brandy and his glass, Francis walked out on his astonished host before he had time to say another word.

"God damn him,'' muttered Francis to himself, as he mounted the stairs. God damn them all to hell, with their questions and innuendoes. He frequently wished he had remained in Jamaica. After the vibrant heat and colors of the West Indies, and its primitive quality, the artificiality and narrowness of society life in England seemed to him empty and stifling. Even his passion for the theater in all its forms had lost its power to inspire him, leaving him unutterably bored with life.

His valet, Carter, awaited him in the guest bedchamber. As soon as he had assisted his master in removing the dark blue coat, which fitted his fine figure like a glove, and his gold-tasselled hessians, he was summarily dismissed.

"But, my lord, you cannot undress yourself," protested Carter, an expression of pain creasing his smooth face.

"I said, that will be all," repeated his master.

Recognizing that his lordship was in one of his dangerous moods, Carter decided that it was best to retire discreetly. Tiptoeing from the room, he pulled the door to with a gentle click.

As he took one pace from the door, Carter heard the sound of a thud from inside the room, and winced. Lord love us, he thought. One minute more and that would have been his head, not the door. Shaking his head, he went down the back stairs to the laundry room to press his lordship's coat. Couldn't hang it up all wrinkled. Gawd Almighty, where was it all going to end?

The object of his concern, having vented his spleen by hurling the second boot at a garish hunting scene on the far wall, sat on the edge of the bed with his head in his hands, his thoughts much the same as those of his faithful valet. Where was it all going to end?

It was almost two months since he had invited Rosaline and her husband, Richard Courtenay, to Edmund Kean's sensational debut in *The Merchant of Venice*. Two months since he had proposed that ridiculous wager and accepted Rosaline's even more ridiculous provisions. Yet he was not one jot closer to winning it.

Why the devil should he concern himself with such a preposterous wager, anyway? To win it, he must marry within four months—within less than two months if he wished to stand as godfather to Rosaline's first child. And then there was Rosaline's additional provision to be considered: That he must be truly in love with his bride, and she with him. What ludicrous claptrap!

Of course, all that flummery about love had come from Rosaline's desire to see him settle down and put an end to his aimless wandering. Only that way could she entertain the thought of his being her child's godfather. "And salve her own conscience for having spurned my love," he informed the bedpost.

Why in God's name had he made a fool of himself by accepting the wager? I must have been out of my mind, he thought. It was certainly not for the money. One hundred guineas; what did that mean to him? What was the adage? "Lucky in money; unlucky in love." That certainly was true in his case. His sojourn in Jamaica had served only to increase his massive fortune. Striving to forget Rosaline, he had immersed himself in acquiring sugar plantations and the numerous slaves that went with them. All had prospered beyond belief.

"Yes, my dearest Rosaline, it would please you to think that I no longer wore the willow for you, that I loved another woman," he told his glass before draining it.

A wry smile twisted his lips. Alas, it needed stronger physic than a wager to purge him of his love for Rosaline. The knowledge that, but for his own lechery and stupidity, she could have been his, burned inside him like eternal hellfire. Now he tortured himself further by remembering her as he had last seen her, in January, her astonishingly green eyes gleaming like emeralds, her dark auburn hair in coils about her radiant face, more beautiful than ever with her rounded belly carrying Courtenay's child.

Her confinement was due in a month. The christening doubtless would follow less than one month later. Therefore he had a period of not even two months in which to find a suitable bride: a bride who must appear to be head over heels in love with him and, moreover, of whom he must appear to be equally enamored.

In six weeks? Impossible!

Yet it was the only way in which he could win the wager. He paced about the room like one of the caged tigers in the Tower of London menagerie, his breath coming fast. Then he halted, staring out the window at the rain-swept street below. His eyes narrowed. By God, he would win this wager, whatever else happened. He would act the love-sotten, contented husband, and stand at the font for the christening of Rosaline's firstborn . . . and when it was all over, he would turn his back on the lot of 'em and bury himself in Jamaica, where he would die at an early age of an excess of rum and whoring.

Feverishly he dragged off his clothes, tossing them onto the floor, and stood naked before the fire, the firelight giving his slender but broad-shouldered body a ruddy glow.

He'd had more than enough of Tunbridge Wells. The place was like a museum, full of antiquities. Tomorrow he would leave for London. It was the start of the Season. He was an eminently eligible bachelor. Within two weeks he would have found himself a suitable bride, one who could pass even Rosaline and Courtenay's eagle-eyed inspection. With his wealth, position and looks he would have his pick of eligible females, particularly if he set out to be charming. Once he had found the right one, it would be easy to make her fall in love with him. His talents as an actor were about to be put to good use.

"And you're about to lose your freedom, Francis, old fellow, but only temporarily," he told his reflection in the full-length mirror, which hung in a stand of polished walnut. Reluctantly he pulled on his nightshirt of embroidered fine linen. Too damn cold to sleep *au naturel* as he had done in Jamaica.

His announcement at eleven the next morning that he intended to drive to London that very day did not in any way dismay his good-natured cousin.

"Come with you, if I may," responded Sir Ronald. "This town gives me the creeps. All dowagers and senilities. Think I'll put this house on the market. Can't stand another day rusticatin' here."

As the elegant town house, with its delicate wrought-iron railings and balconies, was less than one day's drive from

London, it was not exactly Francis's idea of rusticating, but he was not about to waste his breath in arguing with his cousin. He intended to concentrate his energies upon making a mental list of possible brides and planning his strategy.

He had just completed a hearty breakfast of grilled tomatoes, bacon and kidneys, when his cousin's butler entered, bearing what appeared to be a rather crumpled piece of paper on his salver. "This note has just been delivered, my lord," said the stone-faced butler. "The bearer awaits your reply."

Francis took the note and found it to be a torn scrap of lined schoolroom paper covered with a few hastily scrawled words. As he scanned them, he felt a spasm of foreboding.

> *I am in desperate need of your assistance. Please meet me at Number 11, Chapel Yard, near the Pantiles at noon. (I shall be sure to bring your sapphire pin.) DO NOT FAIL ME, I BEG YOU. Yours in haste, Belinda Hanbury.*

"Who's it from?" asked his insatiably curious cousin.

"That wretched Hanbury chit. Wishes me to meet her so she may return my sapphire pin."

"Your sapphire pin? What in the devil's name is Miss Hanbury doing with your sapphire pin?"

"Never mind." Noon, she had written. Ha! It lacked but twenty-five minutes to noon, and he wasn't even dressed. "She asks me to meet her at noon. I've a good mind to send word to her that I've already left for London."

A vision of a small, ashen face with large innocent blue eyes entered his mind, and he sighed resignedly. "Bring the messenger in here," he ordered the butler.

The messenger was one of Sir Joseph Hanbury's footmen.

"Where is your mistress at this moment?" Francis asked him.

"She's visiting 'er old governess 'ere in Tunbridge, m'lord."

"Ah, so she is already in town?"

"Yes, m'lord."

Francis sighed again. "Very well. Tell Miss Hanbury that I shall meet her at Number Eleven Chapel Yard at a quarter to one, and no earlier."

He cast his eye over the young footman and came to the conclusion that as he had been chosen to convey the girl's message, he probably could be trusted to keep his mouth shut. "What is your name?"

"James, m'lord."

Francis leaned back in his chair, his thumb and one long finger stroking his chin. "Well, James. Can you tell me what might have occurred in the household this morning to cause your young mistress to send me this note?" The footman was sure to have read it, considering she hadn't even thought to seal it.

James grinned. "Oh, yes, m'lord. Lord Winchell called early this morning, demanding to see Miss Belinda. Mad as fire, 'e was; closeted with 'er more 'n 'alf an 'our."

"I suppose you wouldn't have any idea as to what passed between them?" asked Francis.

James grinned again. " 'aven't I just! It so 'appens I was on duty in the 'all, so I 'eard bits and pieces."

"Would it be at all possible for you to share some of these bits and pieces with me, James?"

James winked, in the style of one conspirator to another. "Lord Winchell told Miss Belinda unless she agreed to wed 'im, 'e'd tell the world what she did to 'im last night. I could 'ear Miss Belinda yelling at 'im, and then crying, poor mite. It was all I could do to stop meself from going in and whomping 'im. After Lord Winchell left, Miss Belinda ordered the trap to take 'er into town to visit Miss Pettivale, 'er old governess that was."

"And while she was there she sent you here with the note for me, is that correct?"

"Yes, m'lord. Got a bag with 'er, she 'as. Aksed me to stow it in the trap without anyone seeing."

Francis groaned inwardly. This was all he needed to scupper his plans: to become embroiled with a runaway chit of a girl!

Having sent for his purse, he gave James half a crown to

keep his mouth shut. To his surprise the footman had to be persuaded to accept it.

"I'd do anything to 'elp Miss Belinda, m'lord," he protested. "She's by far the best of 'em. If any of us 'as troubles, it's always to Miss Belinda we turn."

Francis raised his eyebrows at this. Strange sort of household they must have at Denehurst, if the only person to whom the servants could turn was a child of fifteen.

"Give Miss Hanbury my message," he told the footman, and dismissed him.

"Gettin' in a trifle deep, ain't you, Francis?" was his cousin's only comment, when the door closed on the loquacious James.

"Not for much longer," said Francis, striding purposefully across the room. His grim expression boded ill for Miss Hanbury. "Winchell's excesses must finally have affected his brain. What in God's name he wants that rambunctious child as a wife for I cannot imagine."

He swung around at the door. "And you can damn well remove that grin from your face, Gillridge. Winchell or no Winchell, I fully intend to send the girl packing back to her home where she belongs."

chapter

4

When James returned to Miss Pettivale's cramped apartments in the small courtyard off Chapel Place, Belinda greeted Lord Kenmore's relayed message with a mixture of impatience and relief. She was terrified that at any moment her father would appear to drag her back to Denehurst. Every sound, every footstep on the paving stones outside in the courtyard made her start.

Eventually, unable to bear the strain any longer, she sent James out to stand at the end of the lane to watch for her father.

It was not like her to be stricken with nerves, but the entire situation concerning Lord Winchell had undermined her; so much so, in fact, that she had been forced to turn to Lord Kenmore, virtually a stranger, to seek his assistance and advice.

"I cannot consider it seemly for you to be meeting with a strange gentleman in such a clandestine manner, however obliging he might be," said Miss Pettivale, anxiously twisting her half-mittened hands together.

Belinda gave her a faint smile. "That is exactly what Lord Kenmore suggested: a clandestine meeting. He was not in earnest, of course. I wonder what he is thinking of all this—no doubt wishing he'd stayed home last night instead of going to the theater!''

"He will be thinking that you are a female of extremely lax morals, with no one to protect you," said her old governess in her most severe schoolroom tone.

"The former is untrue; the latter, alas, is not, insofar as Papa is insisting that I marry that evil man."

Miss Pettivale fell to wringing her hands again, her faded eyes brimming with tears. "Oh, I do so wish that there was some way out of your predicament, my dear Belinda. I cannot abide the thought of your being forced into a marriage with a man you despise."

Belinda darted across the room to hug her former mentor and then gave her a little shake. "You are not to worry your head over me," she commanded with an attempt at a sunny smile. "It will all work out, I promise you. Whatever happens, I give you my word that although I must marry someone, it shall not be Lord Winchell."

Again, footsteps sounded on the flagstones outside, this time striding up to the door itself. Belinda's heart pounded in her breast. "It must be Lord Kenmore," she whispered. Her face grew warm at the thought of seeing him again, this time in daylight, and suddenly she wished that she had not been quite so impulsive in writing that desperate note to him.

The knocker pounded impatiently on the door: one, two, three . . . at least six hard knocks.

"Go let him in, if you please, dear Petty, before he brings everyone out into the courtyard to see what is happening."

Her governess scurried to the door. She dragged back the velveteen curtains that shut out the drafts, and then set about turning all the keys and drawing back the various bolts, while Belinda and, it appeared—from the renewed application of the knocker to the door—Lord Kenmore stewed with impatience.

A shiver of apprehension ran down Belinda's spine upon his entrance into the little parlor. His expression was grim, his dark brows drawn into a frown above eyes that flashed with anger.

He was barely civil to Miss Pettivale, merely favoring her

with a curt inclination of his head upon being introduced, and then turning back to Belinda.

"What the devil is the meaning of this note?" he demanded, holding it out.

"Will you not be seated, my lord?" twittered Miss Pettivale, in a positive agony of apprehension.

Belinda could not blame her for her fear. In the small, cluttered room Lord Kenmore looked far taller and more forbidding than he had appeared last night in the theater. He was enveloped in a multi-caped greatcoat of white drab. Although he removed his curly-brimmed beaver and set it down on the floor, having found no other available space, he refused to relinquish his leather gloves or gold-knobbed cane.

His belligerent mood vexed Belinda, not because it offended her sensibilities—indeed, she could not, in truth, blame him—but because it was causing Petty such anxiety that the trembling of her little hands was visible from across the room.

Belinda took in a deep breath and folded her hands before her. It would not do for her to lose her temper, which she was perilously close to doing. "You have just cause to be vexed, my lord, but pray direct your fury at me, not Miss Pettivale. She is nervous enough as it is."

Lord Kenmore directed a searching look at Belinda, as if he were seeing her in a different light. The anger slowly faded from his eyes and, with a resigned sigh and a rueful smile, he turned to Miss Pettivale to bestow upon her an elegant bow that would have flattered even a duchess.

"I beg you to accept my sincere apologies, ma'am. It was not my intention to be uncivil. It was merely that Miss Hanbury's note caught me off guard. Not only was I about to leave for London, but I do not deem it advisable for a young girl to be sending notes to strange gentlemen, arranging assignations with them."

Miss Pettivale was utterly disarmed by his dazzling smile, which displayed even, white teeth and warmed his dark eyes.

"Oh, Lord Kenmore, that is my concern exactly. I dread to think what Sir Joseph would say if he knew."

Eager to break in on this strange new alliance, Belinda stepped forward. "What Papa would think is utterly beside the point," she blazed. "Forgive me, Lord Kenmore. I thought you my friend last night. It appears I was mistaken."

By God, the girl has spirit, thought Francis in reluctant admiration. She also had more poise than he had remembered from last night. Despite her tiny stature, she bore herself today with an air of pride which he found both intriguing and attractive. It was his turn to be disarmed.

"Why do we not all sit down and discuss this together in an amicable fashion?" he suggested, unbuttoning his greatcoat.

There was an audible sigh, like the gentle rustling of autumn leaves. "May I take your coat, my lord?" asked Miss Pettivale.

The coat was given into her care, but seeing her stagger beneath its weight, Belinda took it from her and laid it on a chair. It was warm from Lord Kenmore's body and smelled of the aromatic cologne he used.

Reluctantly accepting Miss Pettivale's offer of a glass of elderberry wine, Francis gingerly sat down in the only chair that looked as if it possibly might bear his not over-substantial weight. The parlor was filled with little chairs and little tables covered with little knick-knacks. He felt like Gulliver among the Lilliputians.

Having taken a few sips of the surprisingly good elderberry wine, he set his glass down on the minuscule table at his elbow. "Now, Miss Hanbury, let us waste no more time. Tell me what has happened to cause you to write that note to me. And pray be seated, or I shall be forced to rise, not wishing to be presumed uncivil." For she was pacing about the room, her small form circumventing the tapestried footstools and highly polished occasional tables.

Sick with apprehension, Belinda reluctantly sat down on the edge of the chair that faced his.

"Lord Winchell came to see me this morning. He told me that he now remembered exactly what had happened at the theater. He—he was extremely offensive. I told him that, considering his conduct, I could not possibly think of marrying him now. I also informed him that the only reason that I had entertained the idea before was because I had been forced to do so, on account of my—my father's financial difficulties.'' Embarrassed, she looked away from Lord Kenmore's dark, penetrating eyes. ''He told me that, despite the attack I had made on him, he still intended to marry me.''

''Decidedly odd fish, Winchell,'' drawled Francis. ''Hadn't realized, mind you, that one of his pleasures included being struck on the head with champagne bottles.''

Belinda choked back a giggle, but her face quickly resumed its former anxious expression. ''He threatened to lay a charge of assault against me if I refused to marry him.''

To her amazement she was interrupted by a crack of laughter. ''What a gudgeon he must think you! No, no, do not bridle at me, my dear Miss Hanbury. It is only that you are innocent of the ways of society. The Winchells of this world cannot abide being objects of ridicule. It is their greatest fear to be considered ridiculous. And Winchell would be laughed out of London if he ever were to let it be known that he'd been knocked unconscious by a chit from the schoolroom.''

''I am not a chit from the schoolroom!'' declared Belinda, her bright blue eyes flashing with indignation.

''No, no, of course not,'' Francis hastened to assure her. ''But not long out of it. Never mind that,'' he said, as she opened her mouth once again to refute this charge. ''What I should like to know is why the devil—begging your pardon, Miss Pettivale—Winchell wishes to marry one so young; one, moreover, who is so adamantly opposed to marrying him.''

Belinda blushed. ''I have the horridest feeling that it is my very reluctance to marry him that he finds so attractive,'' she whispered. She shuddered at the memory of the wolfish expression on Lord Winchell's face when he had touched her last night.

Francis was astonished to find such acute perception in

one so young. Yes, of course, that could very well be it. The idea of the chase and capture of this spirited child-woman was likely to excite Winchell's jaded palate to the point of offering marriage. His jaw tightened at the thought of the bloated roué and the innocent little Belinda Hanbury together.

"You were right to apply to me, Miss Hanbury. Winchell must be stopped—and immediately. But surely if you were to acquaint your father with your fears he would not force you into such a marriage?"

Miss Pettivale stirred uneasily in the small cane chair at his side, and he felt an almost tangible increase of tension in the confined room.

Belinda pleated the folds of her blue-and-white spotted muslin dress, avoiding his eyes. "I should not be telling you this," she said, "but having gone thus far, I suppose there is no point in holding anything back."

"Not if you wish me to be of some assistance to you," he said gently. "I assure you that whatever you tell me shall not be repeated outside these walls."

He was not at all sure that he wasn't dreaming all this. Certainly it had the semblance of some strange, convoluted dream. The spoiled and pampered Baron Kenmore was not famous for exerting himself in the service of unfortunates. Only once in his life, before last night, had he acted in the capacity of a Saint George, but that had been different; that time it had been for Rosaline.

"My father is in debt," began Miss Hanbury. "He has been trying for a long time to recoup our fortunes at the gaming tables—with no success, of course. Denehurst is mortgaged to the hilt. My stepmother runs up monstrous bills at jewellers, dressmakers, milliners, *everywhere* . . . as if we were wealthy beyond belief. Worse still, my brother Bertie is fast following in Papa's footsteps." She looked up, her chin raised, head thrown back with a daunting expression that rejected pity.

A low whistle escaped Lord Kenmore's lips. It was not an enviable burden the child carried. "And have you no other brothers or sisters who could help in any way? I take it that you are the eldest?''

Again Miss Pettivale stirred but did not speak.

''Bertie came of age this year. I have one other sister, Marianne.''

''Younger than you, of course.''

''No, Marianne is two years older than I.'' The skirt pleating grew more vigorous.

''Then why in heaven's name has the burden of bailing out your family been thrust upon you? Surely it is the duty of your elder sister to marry and save your home.''

This time, seeing Belinda's hesitation, Miss Pettivale intervened. ''That is not possible, my lord.''

''Why not?'' he barked.

Belinda held up her hand to halt Miss Pettivale's response. ''My sister Marianne can never marry, Lord Kenmore. Let us leave it at that.''

He was about to demand an explanation, but something in her eyes warned him not to question her any further on the subject. Lord, that was all the child needed: an imbecile elder sister. No wonder she felt duty bound to take all the responsibilities of her shiftless family on her tiny shoulders.

Compassion stirred within him, and he was surprised by it. Compassion was not one of his strong suits. But what the devil could he do about the girl's plight, other than assist her in running away, which he had no intention of doing? He shuddered at the thought of her fresh innocence on the streets of London.

''Your footman tells me you have a travel bag of some kind with you. Was it your intention to run away and seek your fortune in London like Dick Whittington?'' he asked, smiling.

Belinda sprang from her chair. ''Must you always address me in such a patronizing fashion, as if you were speaking to a child?''

''My dear Belinda,'' admonished Miss Pettivale. ''Lord Kenmore is only trying to help you.''

Belinda turned on her. ''It does not help me to be treated like an infant.''

Lord Kenmore tried to hide his smile behind his hand. "What age are you, O Ancient One: fifteen, perhaps sixteen?"

"Sixteen!" Belinda whirled around to confront him. "I'll have you know, sir, that I shall be twenty this August. *Twenty*, not fifteen or sixteen!"

Lord Kenmore regarded her with an expression of disbelief. Slowly he got to his feet. "Is this true?" he demanded of Miss Pettivale.

"Why yes, my lord, Certainly it is true. Belinda is nineteen and a half years old."

"Oh, why do I have to be so small," moaned Belinda. "Why, oh why? Did you in all honesty think that I was only fifteen?" she demanded of Lord Kenmore.

"Certainly I did, and could not imagine how any father could force a child of that age into marriage with Winchell."

Despite her exasperation, Belinda had to laugh. "Papa is not such a monster as all that, my lord. Indeed, he would not be forcing me to marry anyone were it not that Angelica's extravagances are driving him to distraction."

They all fell silent. The only sounds in the small room were the steady ticking of the long-case clock in the corner and their own breathing.

"So you see," said Belinda eventually, "I have no choice but to marry someone who is sufficiently wealthy to bail Papa out of dun territory; unless, that is, you can think of something else, sir."

Lord Kenmore responded to neither her words nor her shy smile. It was almost as if he had been turned to stone. Although his eyes were intent upon her face, his thoughts appeared to be miles away.

Belinda wondered if he had gone into some sort of trance. "My lord!" she said sharply.

He shook his head and came to, a faint, crooked smile touching his lips. "Forgive me. I was thinking what could be done. Do I understand you correctly, Miss Hanbury? Although you refuse to marry Lord Winchell, you would be willing to marry any other man whose qualifications were suitable?"

"That is correct," replied Belinda.

"You have no one in mind at present? No one for whom you hold a preference, who has captured your heart?"

She blushed, but met his eyes in a direct gaze. "No, sir. No one with whom I am in love, if that is your meaning. I have yet to meet a man I could love," she added, her voice touched with bitterness.

Her jaundiced view of the male sex was understandable, thought Francis, considering it was based most probably upon her father and brother.

He took out his slim gold watch from the pocket of his waistcoat. Thirty-five minutes past one o'clock. Ronald— and his horses—would be champing at the bit.

"Would you be prepared to marry me?"

His question shot like a bolt out of a cannon. Indeed, the effect it had upon the female occupants of the room was almost as startling as if a cannon actually *had* been fired in the tiny parlor.

"Marry *you*!"

"Good gracious me!"

The two ladies spoke in unison.

Francis chose to address the incredulous Belinda. "That is what I said. Would you marry me? I am, I give you my word, presently unattached and with no other prospects of marriage at the moment."

Or ever, he thought, a pain like a knife twisting in his breast.

"But you do not love me," said Belinda in an agitated voice. "You do not even know me." She raised her troubled eyes to his, and then looked away.

"That could soon be remedied," he said gently, tempted to take hold of her restless little hands.

He turned to address the governess. "Miss Pettivale, I recognize that my request is extremely improper, but I wonder in the circumstances if you could oblige me by leaving us alone together for five minutes?"

"Why certainly, certainly," she murmured, evidently overcome by the romantic nature of the situation, and hurried from the room.

"Pray be seated, Miss Hanbury," he said, indicating the narrow chaise longue.

As soon as she sat down, he seated himself beside her and took one nervous hand in his.

"You are unusually silent. Not quite the forthright Miss Hanbury of the champagne bottle whom I encountered last night," he teased.

Her sapphire-blue eyes met his, but this time she did not look away. "Do you truly mean it? You are not funning?"

"Yes, I mean it. And, no, I am not funning."

"Are you wealthy?"

"Excessively so."

"Then why haven't you married before now?" she demanded.

"Because I had no wish to do so. Hitherto, I have enjoyed the carefree life of a bachelor."

"Yet you are prepared to give up that life for an utter stranger, someone for whom you do not care two pins? Surely you cannot expect me to believe that!"

He gave her a rueful smile. "I have not had much time in which to perfect my plan, my dear Miss Hanbury. I must own, therefore, that it came to me in a flash and that the words were spoken spontaneously. Shall we examine the plan together?"

Her hand moved beneath his, but she did not draw it away. Taking her silence for acquiescence, he continued. "You are correct in stating that we are virtual strangers, with no desire to marry each other bar the pressing necessity that you marry someone. May I speak plainly?"

She nodded.

"There may come a time when you wish to marry someone else, someone with whom you have fallen in love. My suggestion is, therefore, that we marry, but that the marriage not be consummated. Then, after a suitable period of time, say, six months or so, it can be quietly annulled and we can part."

She pulled her hand away, and sat bolt upright. "But what about the financial settlements? You seem to have forgotten my chief reason for having to marry."

"That will form part of our agreement. My obligation to maintain you, however, will come to an end when we part, naturally."

"And you swear that you would not expect me to . . ." She floundered, not knowing quite how to go about discussing such intimacies with him. To her extreme annoyance, she knew that she was blushing so fiercely that he could not fail to notice it.

"The marriage will not be consummated," he repeated, fighting the temptation to smile at her naivete; in truth, it was deuced attractive. Confound it, man, he told himself. If you're not careful you'll be on the way to becoming another Winchell yourself!

"I cannot comprehend it," she said with a frown. "Why on earth would you do this for me? After all, you will be receiving nothing in return."

Won't I just, thought Francis. He was determined to ensure, however, that she never found out about Rosaline's wager. It was going to be difficult enough to persuade Rosaline and her husband that this was indeed a love match. His only chance of success was the conviction on the part of Miss Hanbury that he was marrying her for purely chivalrous reasons.

"Let's just say that it will amuse me immensely to deprive Lord Winchell of his sport."

Belinda eyed him circumspectly. How odd men were! To marry a woman one hardly knew merely to spite an enemy seemed decidedly peculiar to her. She looked up, and caught his rueful, almost abashed, little smile. Immediately she knew that he was making this enormous sacrifice solely to help her out of an appalling predicament, but being a man of sophistication was unwilling to admit to such a chivalrous impulse.

"You could call it an amicable arrangement between us," he suggested.

She was about to reply when they heard feet pounding across the yard. She sprang up to draw back the net curtain from the window. "It is James." She ran to the door to open it.

The footman stepped inside, closing the door behind him. "It's Sir Joseph, Miss Belinda," he announced, his face white. " 'e's just turning down the lane. I think 'e saw me."

"Miss Pettivale, would you kindly come in here," called out Lord Kenmore, instantly taking charge. "James, stand by the door and be ready to open it for Sir Joseph." He swung around to face Belinda, a strange, excited light in his eyes, as if he had been drinking. "Well, Miss Hanbury, what is your answer?"

She could hear her father's heavy footsteps on the pavement outside. Her eyes opened wide and she reached out instinctively... to find both her hands gripped in Lord Kenmore's.

"Yes, my lord. I shall be happy to accept your..." She paused, searching for the correct word. She could hardly call it a proposal. "... your offer."

"Capital! Ladies, shall we be seated? James, are you at your post? Good. Then I ask only one thing more: that—to begin with, at least—you will permit me to do the talking."

Belinda had the distinct feeling that she was involved in the production of some melodrama; the stage was set and the curtain about to rise. At the same time, she was aware of an overwhelming sense of relief. Although she would never be able to repay Lord Kenmore fully for all his kindness, she vowed to do everything in her power to ensure that he would never have cause to regret his offer.

At last she had found what she had considered to be the unfindable: a man who was not motivated solely by his own selfish desires!

chapter
5

Upon her father's entrance into the little parlor, Belinda was humorously reminded, despite her anxiety, of the proverbial bull in the china shop. Sir Joseph paused in the doorway, his corpulent figure filling the small space, his eyes raking the room until they fastened upon Belinda. "Aha!" he barked. "So, you *are* here."

Belinda lifted her chin. "Yes, Papa, I am here. Though why you should have thought otherwise I do not know, for I told you quite plainly in my note that I was coming here to stay with Petty for a while."

Sir Joseph shifted forward, and then paused, unable to find any more available space to move into. This time it was James who received a scorching look. "Outside!" he was unceremoniously ordered. Visibly relieved at escaping his master's wrath, the young footman sidled past him to wait outside.

Now Sir Joseph pinned his gaze upon Lord Kenmore's elegant figure. "And who the devil might you be?" he demanded.

Recollecting Lord Kenmore's request that they leave the talking to him, Belinda bit back a reply and waited, her heart pounding against her ribs.

His expression urbane, Francis ran his long fingers up and down the ribbon of his quizzing glass before he replied. "Kenmore. Lord Francis Kenmore. Your servant, Sir Joseph." He smiled his slightly one-sided smile and made a bow which, although suggesting extreme self-assurance, also contained just the right amount of deference due to an elder.

"Pray be seated, sir," he said, indicating the chair from which he had risen.

Miss Pettivale darted forward. "Oh, dear me, I am quite forgetting my manners. Yes, do pray be seated, Sir Joseph."

"Upon what?" barked her former employer. "Dammit, woman, you don't think anything here would bear my weight, do you?"

This time Lord Kenmore's smile was one of genuine amusement.

It was not appreciated by Sir Joseph. "You may be smiling on the other side of your face, sir, by the time I have finished with you. What the devil have you to do with my daughter?"

"Papa," began Belinda, to be stopped short by an almost imperceptible little frown from Lord Kenmore.

"I realize that all this must appear highly irregular to you, sir. Will you permit me to give you an explanation?"

Belinda's father shifted his weight. "It had better be a good one," he growled.

Lord Kenmore stood in the center of the room like an actor at center stage, his self-assurance bolstering Belinda's courage. "For a long time I have loved your daughter," he began.

Belinda blinked at this startling assertion, but remained silent.

"I frequently visit my cousin, Sir Ronald Gillridge, here at Tunbridge," Francis continued. "Although I have encountered your daughter on only a few occasions my love for her dates from the very first time I met her."

He turned to Belinda. She was amazed to see that his face was suffused with an expression of such tender affection that her head whirled. For one heart-stopping moment she forgot that this was all pure invention and responded with a tremulous, but equally warm, smile.

This exchange of looks was not lost upon her father, who loudly cleared his throat. "That is all very well. But can you explain to me why I, Belinda's father, have never been informed of this attachment?"

"It was your daughter's wish, Sir Joseph."

Belinda shot Lord Kenmore a look of startled enquiry. She began to fear that at any minute his exceedingly fertile imagination would land them in hot water.

"She knew how much you desired her to marry your friend, Lord Winchell," continued Lord Kenmore.

"Humph! And am I to understand, girl, that you have for a long time been harboring a secret affection for this gentleman?"

"Yes, Papa," whispered Belinda, her eyes filling with tears. "But I could not bear to go against your wishes."

"Why not? You've been going against my wishes ever since your mother died, so why not in this instance?"

It was a good question, and one that Belinda found hard to answer, but, encouraged by Lord Kenmore's prowess at invention, she plunged in.

"I could discover nothing at all about Lord Kenmore bar his name." Her expressive look eloquently conveyed to her papa that she meant that she had been unable to ascertain the extent of Lord Kenmore's fortune.

"I collect that Miss Hanbury is saying that she did not know if I could keep her in the manner to which she is accustomed," explained Francis, with great delicacy.

"And can you?" demanded Sir Joseph.

"I am confident that I shall be able to satisfy you on that score when we meet in private," replied Francis.

"And what of Lord Winchell?" barked Sir Joseph. "I have given him my word that Belinda shall marry him. The word of a gentleman cannot be broken, y'know."

This time Belinda was determined to speak for herself, for it was not necessary to invent what she wished to say. She went to stand before her father and looked up into his face. "Lord Winchell insulted me, Papa, last night at the theater. Had Lord Kenmore not come to my aid I—I don't know what would have happened.''

Sir Joseph looked down at his daughter's troubled countenance and awkwardly put his arm about her waist, drawing her to his side. ''Is this true?'' he demanded of Lord Kenmore in a gruff voice.

''It is. Your daughter was forced to employ violence to defend her virtue.''

''God damn the fellow! How could I have . . .''

Belinda could feel her father's trembling fury and guessed at the guilt he was feeling. She was extremely grateful to Lord Kenmore when he broke in to cover her father's embarrassment.

''In the circumstances, I think you will agree, Sir Joseph, that you would be fully justified in withdrawing permission for the marriage.''

''Most assuredly. And you intend to apply to me for my daughter's hand? Is that it?''

''I do.''

Sir Joseph looked down into his daughter's blue eyes. ''And *this* match is to your liking, puss?''

''Oh, yes, Papa.'' Belinda spoke the truth. How could she not be happy at the thought of marrying the most handsome and chivalrous man she had ever encountered? She refused to dwell for even one minute on the thought that this was to be a sham marriage of extremely short duration.

For the first time in a long while she saw her father smile, and was reminded of the affectionate, if undemonstrative, parent he had been before her mother's death.

''Then perhaps you should join us for dinner, Kenmore,'' he suggested. ''We keep country hours. Shall we say four o'clock, so that we may have our little discussion before we eat?''

''Four o'clock would be capital, sir,'' replied Francis. The thought of the expression on his long-suffering cousin's face when he announced that not only was he not going to London, but also that he had become contracted in marriage to Miss Hanbury, caused him a great deal of inner amusement.

Mind you, he was going to have the devil of a job persuading Ronald to keep his mouth shut.

Ten minutes later he had made his temporary farewells. It was a tremendous relief to escape the confined parlor, almost like escaping from imprisonment. But he had, at the same time, trapped himself in another sort of prison. Ah well, Francis, old fellow, you have done it now, he told himself as he made his way along the upper walkway of the Pantiles. No going back.

As her father's carriage lumbered along the narrow country lanes, Belinda's thoughts were in much the same vein. She gazed out the window, looking at the bare trees, their leaves still tight buds, many of them with cracked limbs from the burden of the snow that had weighed them down until the end of February. She was well aware of her father's surreptitious glances at her profile, but she wished to avoid any conversation with him. For one thing, she was afraid that he would ask her more questions about her previous meetings with Lord Kenmore; for another, she felt heavy with guilt at having to deceive Papa, particularly as this marriage would prove to be only a temporary solution to his financial problems.

So appalling was the contemplation of Papa's reaction when he learned this fact that she blotted the thought from her mind. She would have ample time to face that problem once she was married to Lord Kenmore.

As the carriage drew to a halt, he leaned forward to take her hand, so that she was forced to look at him. "You are sure that this marriage is to your liking, Lindy?"

"Yes, Papa. I love Lord Kenmore," she replied with feeling. It was amazing how necessity could make one almost believe one's own inventions.

"You realize that I—I cannot give my consent if—if . . ." He looked away, embarrassed at having to put it into words.

"If his fortune isn't up to scratch?" said Belinda, helping him out. "Yes, Papa. I know that. But I am convinced that it will be."

"I am in agreement with you. His dress alone proclaims

him a man of wealth.'' He drew his hand away and busied himself with taking a huge pinch of snuff, spilling half of it down his old-fashioned brocade waistcoat. ''I've not been much of a father to you these past few years,'' he said, his voice muffled by the handkerchief that covered the lower half of his face.

Belinda blinked back tears. ''Oh, Papa,'' was all she could say.

He blew his nose loudly and stuffed his handkerchief into his sleeve. ''Can't say how glad I am that this marriage'll make you happy, puss. Should never have forced Winchell on you.''

''Never mind, Papa. That is all over now,'' said Belinda briskly, embarrassed by her father's uncommon self-condemnation. ''Shall we go in? I must make the arrangements for dinner.''

''Lord, yes. Make sure you speak to Cook before Angelica gets to the kitchen.'' He heaved himself up and, with the assistance of his groom, descended from the carriage.

Within half an hour, Belinda had given orders to Cook for the preparation of dinner, set the servants to scouring and polishing every one of the public rooms, and warned them all that if they did not appear by four o'clock in crisply starched linen, with spanking-clean hands and faces, she would personally deal with them.

When Angelica came sailing in to demand what she meant by giving orders about the place without her authority she was succinctly advised by her stepdaughter to ''ask Papa.''

Once she was satisfied that everything was well under way belowstairs, Belinda sped upstairs to the little first-floor parlor, where she knew she would probably find Marianne.

It did not take long to give Marianne her amazing news, omitting, of course, the one salient point that this was to be a temporary marriage.

''Oh, Lindy.'' Marianne's beautiful eyes shone, and she clasped her hands to her breast in ecstasy. ''I have never in my entire life heard anything quite so romantic. It is superior to any novel I have read. Lord Kenmore sounds like one of those knights of the Round Table at the Court of King Arthur." She looked down at her lap, her chestnut hair waving about her face, and said, wistfully, "How I wish I could meet him."

"You *shall* meet him, you goose. At our wedding, if not before."

"No, no. I...I could not," protested Marianne in an anguished voice. "You *know* I could not, Lindy." Her fingers plucked at the tiny stitches she was setting in the new shirt she was making for Bertie.

"Do not fret yourself, dearest. We shall see when the time comes." Belinda hugged her sister to her breast. Although she was both smaller and younger than Marianne, she felt like a mother reassuring her precious child.

The one aspect about this "marriage" that deeply troubled her was the thought of having to leave her sister. If only she could take Marianne with her; but that was impossible, of course. A shiver ran through her at the thought of Marianne shut away at Denehurst, alone.

She had only just managed to turn Marianne's melancholy to laughter by giving her a graphic description of the awkwardness of the men in Petty's tiny, cluttered parlor when Bertie burst unceremoniously into the room.

"I say! You'll never guess who's coming to dinner tonight!"

"Won't I just?" responded Belinda, with a laugh. "Could it possibly be Lord Francis Kenmore, I wonder?"

Bertie's mouth fell open. "So it is true. James told me, together with some taradiddle about Kenmore marrying you, Lindy. What a bouncer! My sister marrying one of the richest men in all England! He's fabulously wealthy, y'know. One of the *crème de la crème*. Why, with his looks and fortune he could have anyone he wished as a wife."

"I must say that you are giving me definite feelings of inferiority, Bertie," said Belinda. "Do you mean to tell me that you are acquainted with Lord Kenmore?"

"Lord, I wish I were! I'd be made for life. He's a top-drawer nonpareil, y'know. That's why I laughed at the idea of his marrying you, Lindy. It wasn't any reflection on you personally, don't you know," he added, attempting to be kind. "It's just that such a match wouldn't fudge at all."

"Yes, I can see that," said Belinda reflectively. A large stone seemed to have settled in the pit of her stomach at Bertie's words.

"But Belinda *is* going to marry Lord Kenmore," protested Marianne. "She told me so herself."

Bertie turned on his younger sister. "You can't be serious, Lindy. Why on earth would the Bad Baron marry you? You haven't a fortune, nor—"

"Why do you call him that?"

"What? Oh, the Bad Baron? That's just a name he's been given because of his notorious reputation."

"Notorious for what?" Belinda's eyes narrowed, a signal to her brother that she was getting into one of those moods when it was exceedingly dangerous to cross her.

"I say, Lindy," he stammered, ignoring her question. "Don't tell me it's true that you're to marry him."

"Notorious for what?" repeated his sister, her eyes glittering.

Bertie drew himself up. "If you are to marry him, I should not be telling you," he said self-righteously.

"You'll be sorry if you don't tell me." Belinda advanced upon him, and he stepped back, only to find his way barred by a chair. "Tell me," she demanded. "As Lord Kenmore's future wife, I have a right to know."

"Oh, very well. But for heaven's sake, don't be telling Papa. Kenmore's famous as a connoisseur of the theater and drama in general. Apparently, he's an extremely talented actor himself. He's also, you might say, a connoisseur of actresses, both amateur and professional. There have been stories about . . . well, never mind that," he added hurriedly, meeting Belinda's eye. "And a year ago he killed his man."

"His man? In a duel, you mean?" gasped Marianne. "Oh, how splendid! Knowing how chivalrous Lord Kenmore is, you may be sure that he was defending the honor of a lady."

"Chivalrous? Kenmore? Ha!" Again, Bertie caught Belinda's eyes and decided it might be best to continue without any further personal comments. "Not a clue as to the reason for the duel, but apparently it wasn't all done according to the book. In any event, Kenmore took a boat for Jamaica directly afterward and didn't return to England until a year or so later. That would be about two or three months ago. No one knows why he stayed away so long, but he is said to have increased his fortune by investing in various plantations while he was there.''

''And you mean to tell me that these are the only reasons for his having been dubbed the Bad Baron!'' said Belinda disgustedly.

Her brother tugged at his intricately tied neckcloth, wishing profoundly that he had never begun this conversation. It was steering perilously close to murky waters. If this preposterous tale of Lord Kenmore being about to offer for his sister happened to be true, he was damned if he was going to tell Lindy the little he knew about Kenmore's numerous *affaires* and his notorious late-night theater parties.

''Probably mere rumors,'' he muttered. ''Society's rife with 'em. Besides, these stories about him were going the rounds before he left for Jamaica. More than a year ago.'' Bertie took out a blue-spotted handkerchief and wiped the palms of his hands with it. ''Enough about Kenmore's past,'' he said brightly. ''Tell me how you came to meet him.''

Belinda told him, again omitting the fact that the proposed marriage would be a temporary one.

Expecting him to be as enthusiastic about Lord Kenmore's kindness as Marianne had been, she was disappointed when she had completed her tale to see Bertie's frowning preoccupation. ''Strange, that,'' was his only comment.

''Strange,'' cried Marianne indignantly. ''Why is it so strange for a gentleman to rescue Lindy from that horrid man, Winchell, by marrying her? Besides, Lindy is a treasure beyond price. She deserves the most handsome, wealthiest, and kindest man on earth.''

Bertie flushed, recognizing a little too late that some of his remarks had been deuced unflattering to Belinda. Trouble was, that although he was in full agreement with Marianne on the subject of Lindy's merits, there was no escaping the fact that with her hoydenish ways, her lack of stature and, most of all, her lack of fortune, Miss Belinda Hanbury was no matrimonial catch.

"Of course she does," he agreed. "I said it was strange because it doesn't sound like the sort of thing a man like Kenmore would do, that's all. Mind you," he added hastily, "I'm not saying he wasn't motivated by the purest of reasons. In fact, must've been. There's no other possible explanation. But it's still decidedly odd."

"Oh, pooh! You are utterly without a vestige of romance, Bertie," cried Belinda. "Now please remember, both of you, that where Papa and everyone else is concerned Lord Kenmore and I have been secretly in love for several weeks, is that understood?"

She was sorely tempted to share with her brother and sister the secret that this was to be only a temporary marriage, but she knew that was impossible. She could trust Marianne implicitly, but knew that she would be unutterably shocked at such a plan. Bertie would not be shocked, but she could not trust him to keep it a secret.

"Oh, my goodness, look at the time," she said, glancing at the watch that hung from her waist. "I must fly. I have to dress and see if Ellen can do something with my hair. Then I must make sure that everything is working out in the kitchen before Lord Kenmore arrives." She grasped her sister's hand. "Come with me, Marianne, and help me decide what to wear. I vow I have nothing at all that would be suitable for such an occasion."

In a sudden rush of panic, which was inspired more by the knowledge that she was woefully inadequate for her role as the future bride of a nonpareil than anything else, she fled from the room and raced along the corridor to her bedroom.

chapter
6

The evening was, if not an unqualified success, a decidedly satisfactory one for all concerned. It had been a very long time since Cook had been given carte blanche to prepare a dinner befitting the status of Denehurst, but, alas, the event was a trifle marred by the necessity of having to do so in less than three hours.

It had also been a long time since the head of the Hanbury family had been seen in such good humor. Having been closeted with Lord Kenmore for almost an hour, Sir Joseph emerged to beam upon his family with such glowing bonhomie that it made everyone feel positively uneasy.

And Lady Hanbury was in her element, making her grand entrance into the drawing room dressed as if she were about to be presented at court, with a feathered headdress that must have been two feet tall, and presiding at the dinner table with a majestic grace, as if she were Queen Charlotte herself.

As for Bertie, he remained speechless most of the evening. Content to bask in the brilliance of one of society's leaders, he made mental notes of Lord Kenmore's elegant dress—particularly the new way he had tied his starched linen neckcloth—and every one of his dry witticisms, so that he might share them with his cronies.

Although Marianne did not venture downstairs, she received quiet enjoyment from both the tray of delicacies that had been sent up to her from the kitchen and her own eager anticipation of hearing a full resumé of the events of the evening later from her sister.

The chief participants enjoyed the evening for very different reasons.

Francis was highly amused at the delicious irony of the situation. Here he was being fêted, wined and dined, and fawned upon, when all he was doing was using them—in particular Belinda Hanbury—to win the wager with Rosaline and her husband.

He had to own that he was quite pleasantly surprised by the appearance of his future bride. Her dusky curls were brushed into an informal style and in them she wore a simple bow of lemon-yellow ribbon. Her dress was a lemon-yellow overdress with a white sarcenet slip. It was decorated with too many bows for his liking, but that was no doubt the influence of her stepmother.

As he would be forced not only to reside with her, but also to play the enamored husband until after the christening of Rosaline's child, it came as something of a relief to discover that Miss Hanbury could look positively pretty. To his eyes, however, she still looked no more than fifteen.

The object of his musings was glowing with happiness; indeed it was Belinda's vivacity that set the tone of the evening. And why not? She was free of Lord Winchell, free from the pressures of having to find a wealthy husband—for now, at least—and once more back in her father's good books. Moreover, for the next six months she would be Lady Kenmore, mistress of Luxton, Lord Kenmore's family seat in the Mendip Hills near Bath, and various other establishments. She had every intention of making the best of it while it lasted.

At Lord Kenmore's suggestion, it was agreed that the wedding would be a quiet affair, "... to avoid the gossip that might ensue from the rejection of Lord Winchell's suit and his speedy replacement by another bridegroom.''

Speedy it was, in truth. Belinda had but a few weeks in which to gather a trousseau together. Now that money was no longer an object, however, the local dressmakers and milliners and haberdashers were eager to rally to the cause, and it was not long before her wardrobe and the cedar-lined chest at the foot of her bed were filled with shawls and fur-trimmed mantelets, dresses of silk and sarcenet and satin, chipstraw bonnets trimmed with flowers and fruit and ribbons . . .

Alas, Belinda herself had little to say in the selection of fabric and trimmings or patterns for her various outfits, even for her wedding gown. Although she had taken little interest in clothes until now, she felt intuitively that the multi-flounced, belaced and beribboned ecru wedding gown that Angelica had chosen for her suited neither her slight figure nor her light brown complexion. She was determined, however, not to allow this to spoil her enjoyment. After all, this would not be her real wedding day. That would come later, with some other man: one she truly loved and who loved her.

As she stood at the back of the village church, she pushed aside the melancholy reflection that her second wedding would be, of necessity, a highly private affair.

Her doubts about her wedding gown were echoed in Francis's mind as he turned to observe his bride advance down the aisle on her father's arm. For a brief moment he closed his eyes. Good God, he thought, she looks like a china marionette in all those frills and flounces.

He fervently wished now that he had not accepted Lord Fotheringham's invitation to spend the first few days of their honeymoon at Donnington House, which was nearby. He feared that Belinda might prove to be an acute embarrassment to him. One thing was certain: If this chit was to share his life for the next six months, he must take her completely in hand; order new clothes for her, have Monsieur Jacques cut and style her hair and work on that brown complexion.

Now she was beside him, her brilliant sapphire eyes—her

best feature—gazing shyly at him through the misty veil. He summoned up a reassuring smile, trying to ignore the pang in his heart. God! If only this were Rosaline beside him, her emerald eyes shimmering through the veil, her voluptuous body pressing against his side . . . then, oh, then would he have been able to make the time-honored vows with heart-felt enthusiasm: ''With my body thee I worship . . . In sickness and in health . . .''

For Belinda, the entire day held the semblance of a long dream which, as the time to leave drew nearer, had begun to take on the darker aspect of a nightmare.

Throughout the wedding breakfast she had taken her cues from Lord Kenmore, responding to his affectionate glances, and to the jesting comments of her relatives and friends, with warm good humor. But by the time she was leaving Denehurst the strain of playing in this masquerade had begun to tell, and she felt weary beyond belief.

''Tired, little one?'' asked Francis, as his well-sprung traveling chaise set off on the short journey to Donnington.

She nodded silently, the lump in her throat preventing her from replying. The parting from her family, and from Denehurst itself, had been extremely painful. She had never before spent even one night away from home. Now the reality of being alone with an utter stranger pressed upon her like a dark cloud.

She turned her head away, ashamed to let him see the tears welling in her eyes.

''This is your first time away from your home and family?'' he asked.

Again she nodded.

He leaned across to take her gloved hand in his. ''Do not forget that it will not be long. In less than half a year you will be home again.''

Belinda gave him a faint, rueful smile. ''I doubt that, my lord. You are forgetting that I shall need to find another husband.''

''It is fortunate that our servants are traveling in the other carriage,'' he said with a smile. ''No sooner wed than you're talking of seeking another husband! Dear me.'' His dark eyebrows rose in mock surprise.

Blinking back her tears, she returned his smile. Her hand was given a reassuring squeeze and then relinquished.

''Never mind, my dear Belinda—I may call you that, may I not?''

''Why, of course.''

''And you must call me Francis.''

''Oh, no, I could not possibly do so,'' Belinda protested. ''Not in the circumstances.''

''Nonsense! In public you may call me 'Kenmore' or 'my lord' if you wish, but in private it is to be 'Francis'.''

She gave him a damp smile. ''Very well . . . Francis.'' She looked directly at him, frankly perusing his handsome face with its angular cheekbones, the dark, almost black, eyes with their ever-changing and usually unfathomable expressions. ''You have been so unutterably kind and generous to me that I cannot find words with which to thank you,'' she said shyly.

''Then do not try,'' he said abruptly.

She was startled by the strange flare of anger that lit his eyes. Then his expression changed, and she wondered what the new, twisted smile might signify.

Seeing that she was watching him, he raised his eyebrows at her. ''We shall deal very well together, my dear Belinda, you will see.''

Although used to living in a mansion of handsome proportions, Belinda was utterly overwhelmed by the magnificence of Donnington. Built of gleaming white stone, it towered three stories high above her, its many wings spreading to the left and right of its imposing, pillared entrance. This isn't a house, it's a palace, thought Belinda; and, as she very soon discovered, a miserably cold and austere palace at that.

The frigid atmosphere was reinforced by her cool reception from Lord and Lady Fotheringham and their guests. How Belinda wished they could have spent the first night of their honeymoon at Denehurst! But, she supposed, that would not have been at all correct.

All she knew was that if she had to listen to one more minute of the excruciatingly boring conversation, which constantly revolved around power and politics during the long, drawn-out dinner and afterwards, when the gentlemen rejoined the ladies, she would either run screaming from the room or deliberately shock the entire assembly by reciting one of Bertie's rudest bawdy poems.

It was with a tremendous sense of relief, therefore, that she received Lord Kenmore's whispered suggestion. "If you go to your room now, I shall follow shortly."

Blushing a little, she bade her host and his guests goodnight and followed Lady Fotheringham from the room, her blushes increasing at the rather ribald comments about wedding nights that she heard just before the doors closed.

The entire evening had been a frightful strain. She knew that everyone considered her a highly unsuitable bride for Lord Kenmore, which indeed she was: twelve years younger than he, with little knowledge of the world of high society and none at all of the world of theater and drama, which, she had soon discovered, was his ruling passion.

If only they could have stayed at some comfortable coaching inn, where she could have relaxed and been herself, instead of a tongue-tied ninnyhammer with a churning stomach, embarrassing her "bridegroom" by her evident lack of knowledge on just about every subject that had been discussed.

She was led up the broad staircase, down a long, cold corridor and into a vast, high-ceilinged chamber with a set of double doors at each end. In the center stood a huge four-poster bed on a dais. It was hung with faded curtains of magenta velvet, and its canopy was topped with the royal coat of arms.

"As you can see, we have given you the royal bedchamber," said Lady Fotheringham, her voice as cool and haughty as her manner. "I am sure that it will please Francis to be sleeping in the bed that once held King Charles the First.

Your husband is, as you doubtless know, a keen student of history.''

Belinda did not know, nor, at this point, did she care. She stifled a giggle, wishing she could share the joke with someone. How utterly ridiculous to think that a bridegroom would be excited by the history of the bed he and his bride were sharing on the first night of their honeymoon!

Once she had donned the bridal nightgown—more frothy lace and ribbons—Belinda climbed into the bed, trying not to sneeze from the dust in the folds of the bed-curtains. Feeling decidedly embarrassed at being watched as she lay in bed by her haughty-faced hostess, Belinda smiled sweetly at her, curbing an impulse to poke out her tongue.

Shivering, she pulled the bedclothes up to her neck. She sought the isolated patches of warmth on the icy sheets where the two warming pans had been and rubbed her feet against them in a vain attempt to warm them. Lady Fotheringham might be the mistress of one of the great houses in England, but to the practical Belinda, one of the prime duties of a good hostess was to ensure that her guests were warm. Perhaps the servants at Donnington thought that the bridal couple would supply their own warmth!

This interesting conjecture prompted Belinda to ponder the question of where Lord Kenmore would be sleeping.

"I should imagine that Lord Fotheringham will be bringing Francis up very soon now," said Lady Fotheringham, by now not even trying to hide her boredom. She looked down her horsey nose at Belinda and smiled, displaying large, protruding teeth. "Have you hung Lady Kenmore's wedding gown up yet?" she demanded of her abigail, who was hovering at the other end of the room.

The elderly abigail shook her head.

"Then do so at once," snapped Lady Fotheringham.

Belinda summoned up another honey-sweet smile. "I have already given my maid orders to look after my clothes in the dressing room, I thank you, Lady Fotheringham." If Lord Kenmore didn't arrive soon, she would leap from the bed and shout down for him to come up this instant and rescue her.

To her relief, she heard male voices outside the doors. She waited while Lord Kenmore was escorted to his dressing room by his host. He then entered the bedchamber, strode across the floor to thank Lady Fotheringham for her kind hospitality, and proceeded to bow her out of the room with such alacrity that he gave every impression of being an impatient bridegroom, eager to bed his new wife.

If that had indeed been Lady Fotheringham's impression, she might well have been a trifle surprised by the first words he spoke to his bride when the doors were closed.

"Devil take it! I never imagined they'd put us in this great mausoleum."

"Lady Fotheringham thought you would enjoy it as you are such a keen student of history," ventured Belinda, her lips trembling.

"Did she indeed!" he said incredulously. His eyes met hers, and she immediately dissolved into a fit of giggles. He burst out laughing. "I am pleased to see that our worthy hostess has her priorities in the proper order."

She grinned at him, delighted to find that he shared her sense of the ridiculous. How very attractive he is when he laughs, she thought.

"But, in all seriousness," he continued, striding across the vast room to warm himself by the fire, "I thought they would give us the guest suite which, if I remember aright, has two bedchambers. There's not even a couch here, only this." He indicated the large, needlepoint ottoman before the fire. "Hardly suitable for a bed. And there's nothing in my dressing room that would do, either. Anything suitable in yours?"

"N-no. Only two chairs with ladder b-backs." At present, Belinda was too preoccupied with trying to stop shivering from the cold to dwell on the question of where he was to sleep.

He advanced to stand beside the bed. "You look lost in there. Are you warm enough?"

"N-no, I am frozen."

"Why didn't you say so before?" He smiled and held out

his hand. "Come, get up and sit by the fire. Where are your slippers?"

"Somewhere at the side there." She threw back the bedclothes and slid out of the bed, crossing her arms in front of herself. It felt very strange to be standing before him in her nightgown, particularly as it was of a diaphanous material. Having discovered her slippers, he held them out for her to slide her feet into, and then her dressing gown which, thank heavens, was lined with rabbit fur. As she felt its warmth enfold her, she sighed with relief.

"You should have kept this on when you got into bed," he said, as he tied the sash around her waist, sounding like a father gently chiding his young daughter.

She looked up at him, her breathing a little ragged when she realized how very close he was to her. "I don't suppose it is usual for a bride to wrap herself up in fur-lined robes, do you?" she asked, with an impish grin.

"Infinitely preferable, I should have thought, to having the bride turn into a block of ice on her wedding night." He nodded toward the fire. "Sit down and warm yourself. Will you take a glass of champagne, or are you still too cold?"

"Oh, no, I should love some," replied Belinda, as she knelt before the fire.

"There's meat and cheese and fruit as well, enough to sustain us through the night."

Belinda drew the ottoman closer to the fire and sat down on it. She turned to observe Lord Kenmore as he went to the mahogany cabinet to pour the champagne. He looked particularly attractive tonight, his crimson-and-gold brocade dressing gown setting off his dark good looks to splendid advantage.

But as he handed her the crystal goblet filled with champagne, she saw that his eyes were glittering and there was a slight flush along his angular cheekbones. She had seen these signs before in the past few weeks. They warned her to tread warily with him, for she had soon discovered that his was an uneasy temperament. Although he had never actually lost his temper with her, he had on occasion come perilously close to doing so.

He sat down in the fireside chair, stretching his legs

across the hearth. Now it was his turn to observe her over the rim of his glass, his glittering eyes hidden behind half-closed lids. He stared at her for so long that she began to grow nervous beneath his scrutiny.

"It went well, don't you think?" she ventured at last, when she could no longer bear the silence.

"What?"

"The day in general. The ceremony, the breakfast and . . ." Her attempt at informal conversation ground to a halt.

"Oh, that. Yes, indeed. Very well."

More silence.

Eventually Belinda tried again. "What are you thinking about?" she asked, addressing his brooding profile.

"Actually, I was still wondering where I was going to sleep tonight," he replied, still gazing into the fire. He swilled the last sip of champagne around in his glass.

"Oh."

Silence again.

The tension in the room gradually increased. The ticking of the clock on the mantelshelf seemed to grow louder and louder; the heavy furniture loomed larger; the painted ceiling grew higher, so that Belinda felt as if she were imprisoned in a vast, echoing cavern. As she watched the dark, brooding visage of the man with whom she must share the next six months of her life, every nerve in her body felt as if it were twanging, like harp strings plucked by ghostly fingers.

A fit of violent shivering overtook her, so that she was forced to set down her glass before she spilled the liquid in it.

Now the shivering was audible; try as she might, she could not hide the sounds of her shuddering breath.

He looked up, his eyes glazed as if he were coming out of a long, deep sleep. Then, even as she watched, they cleared and she saw that the dangerous glitter, too, had disappeared.

"Is something the matter?" he asked.

Her lower lip trembled as she shook her head. How she wished she had remained in bed. Being frozen was infinitely better than behaving like a ninnyhammer before him. She tried to think of happier things: Papa's warm embrace before she climbed into the carriage; Marianne waving from the upstairs window... But these thoughts only served to accentuate her longing for home.

Tears filled her eyes and began to course down her cheeks.

He rose from his seat and knelt before her, taking her chin in his hand, so that she was forced to look up at him. "What is it, my little one?"

She had been prepared to flare up at him if he had mocked her, but this warm, caring voice was her undoing.

"Oh, my lord, I—I am so lonely," she wailed. "I never thought I'd miss everyone so much: Papa and Marianne and Bertie and, yes, even Angelica; and I keep thinking of how lonely Marianne will be without me."

Somehow, she wasn't at all sure how, she found herself scooped up and settled on his lap, her damp face buried in his warm neck, his strong arms holding her, his voice comforting her. "It is only natural that you should feel thus, little one. Particularly so in the strange circumstances of our marriage."

His hand continued to stroke her cheek, pushing her tousled hair from her face, as she sobbed against his breast. He spoke soothing words in a gentle voice and, as he did so, strange new feelings began to steal over her. Her sobbing eased and she relaxed against him, luxuriating in the pleasurable sensations his touch evoked.

"Better?" he asked eventually.

She nodded. Coming to her senses, she drew away from him, returning to her seat on the ottoman. "Pray forgive me," she said, drawing in a long breath. "I am not usually such a watering pot."

Smiling, he handed her his fine linen handkerchief and she mopped her face with it, thinking as she did so what a sight she must look. During the brief time of their engagement, she had often considered that Lord Kenmore could have had his choice of any woman in Europe as his bride, as Bertie had so tactlessly pointed out. This knowledge did not help to bolster her confidence in herself. Quite the reverse. It was odd that she, who had run Denehurst with the greatest efficiency, despite her lack of funds and her step-mother's continual interference, should be made to feel so inadequate by this man.

Perhaps it was a good thing for her self-esteem that she was not to remain wedded to him!

"Come, we have a long night ahead of us," said Lord Kenmore. "I vote that we make the best of it."

Miraculously, her outburst appeared to have swept away his melancholy.

"Do you play backgammon?" he asked.

"Of course."

"Good. There is a board here. I shall bring it and the tray of food over to the fireside, and we shall indulge in a veritable orgy!"

Two hours later, when Belinda could no longer keep her eyes open, Francis dragged the bedclothes off the bed and made up two makeshift beds before the fire, bundling the sleepy girl into one of them.

He hesitated for a moment, and then bent to press a brotherly kiss on her soft brown cheek. "Goodnight, little wife."

She smiled, murmured a muffled goodnight, and was asleep.

For a long time Francis sat before the fire, no longer brooding, indeed not moved by any emotion at all, thinking about the weeks to come.

One thing he had discovered from this strange wedding night was that he had one major hurdle behind him. From the innocent, intuitive response of Belinda's body to his consoling embrace, he conjectured that his task of convincing everyone—particularly Rosaline—that his bride truly loved him, that this was indeed a love match, was not going to be difficult. All he had to do in the next few weeks was encourage those feelings of affection in his "little wife" until they blossomed into love, and the wager would be won.

What might prove more difficult, however, was the task of maintaining his wife's emotions at simmering point until the christening, without having her boil over!

chapter

7

Belinda awoke the following morning to the strange sensation of being lifted and carried. She murmured something unintelligible in a sleepy voice as she found herself being deposited in the chilly bed once more.

"I thought it best to make it appear as if we did spend part of the night, at least, in bed," Francis said in an undertone as he pulled the bedclothes over her.

She looked up into his face, smiling a little when she saw that he was in need of a shave and that his usually impeccably groomed hair was tousled like a gypsy's.

"What are you smiling at, imp?" he demanded, leaning his hands on the bed to look down at her.

"You. Your hair is rumpled and your cheeks are all stubbly." She grinned sleepily at him, no longer quite so much in awe of him since she had spent a night pressed against his back in front of the fire.

"Are they, indeed." He rubbed a hand over his cheeks and chin. "You are the very soul of tact, my child-bride. You are, however, also correct. I am in need of a shave." He did not move away, but continued to gaze down at her with a slight frown.

"What are you thinking about?" she asked in a small

voice, wondering if she had vexed him. She must learn to curb her wayward tongue. It would not do to anger the man whose kindness and gallantry had rescued her and her family.

"I was considering two things: One, that you look infinitely more attractive than I in the morning; and two, whether or not we could flee this place today without offering insult to our hosts."

Belinda's face lit up. "Oh, my lord—I mean Francis, could we?"

"You like that idea?"

She sat up, clasping her knees. "Oh, yes. I feel so—so out of place here. I'm afraid I know very little about politics or theater or art. You see, Papa's guests come only to shoot or hunt or play cards, so their conversation rarely goes any farther than horse or hound breeding. I believe my poor mother used to be bored to distraction when she was alive."

"Poor Belinda. And here you are, also bored to distraction. I should not have brought you here, but I wished to postpone the journey to Luxton for a few more days, until the roads had improved." He gave her a rueful smile. "I must own that power and politics are not my favorite topics of conversation, either. Although I suppose I shall have to bone up a little if I intend to take my seat in the House of Lords."

"Will you do so?" Belinda found it hard to imagine him debating the latest corn prices or Catholic emancipation.

"Perhaps. I promised—that is, I vowed that one day I would settle down and become an exemplary peer of the realm."

Belinda wondered to whom he had made this promise; probably his mother or father, both of whom had died when he was only seventeen.

"Do you think it would be possible to leave Donnington today?" she asked, returning to the original subject. "I've been dreading the thought of spending another few days here, but knowing that Lord and Lady Fotheringham were your friends I didn't like to say so."

"Hardly my friends. They are acquainted with my uncle,

Ronald Gillridge's father. The prospect of staying here for even one more day is a decidedly daunting one, I agree.''

He sat unceremoniously on the side of the bed, as Bertie so often did at home. Belinda watched his profile, with its aquiline nose and long black eyelashes. He appeared to be making mental calculations. She waited, trying to curb her impatience, as she was now wide awake and hungry for breakfast. She was used to rising early and going for a gallop across Denehurst's paddocks when the dew was still on the grass. Not that there had been much dew so far this year, only snow and frost—bad riding weather.

Francis turned to look at her. ''What would you say to a week in London, little one?''

''London!'' she squealed. ''Oh, Francis.'' Quite without thinking, she flung her arms about his neck and pressed her lips to his cheek as if he were Bertie.

His arms instinctively drew her to him in response, but as he did so her body stiffened and she pulled away from him.

''Forgive me. I was thinking—that is, I forgot myself.'' Feeling extremely foolish, she gave an embarrassed giggle.

''My dear Belinda, you may forget yourself as often as you please,'' he said lightly. ''After all, if we are to play the newlywed couple who have been secretly enamored for months, we shall have to pretend a little, shall we not? Have you ever performed in amateur theatricals?''

''Quite often, when Mama was alive. I can remember the first time. We set up a makeshift theater in the drawing room one Christmas and put on a pantomime. *Puss in Boots*. I was a mouse.''

Francis smiled. ''I can see why, if you were smaller than you are now, as I imagine you would have been.''

''Do you find me too small?'' demanded Belinda, with a defiant lift of her chin.

''Not at all. I find you adorable.'' Unable to resist the rosy, pouting lips, Francis kissed her swiftly on her soft mouth before she had time to move away.

Her blue eyes darkened and she gazed at him warily, wondering what he would do next. His response was to stand up and stretch his arms above his head, as if the kiss had been merely a reflex action. She wasn't sure if she felt sorry or glad.

"I'll ring for Carter and order some breakfast to be sent up," he said. "Then we shall bathe and dress, and I shall seek out our hosts and make our apologies."

"What will you tell them?"

He turned to look back at her, raising one eyebrow in the mocking expression she so disliked. "Why, that we wish to be alone together. Not quite the thing for a married couple to admit, of course," he drawled, "but then I am certain that that will not surprise them. It is general knowledge that I rarely hunt with the pack."

He strolled across the room to pull the bellrope by the mantelpiece.

Belinda sat on the bed, tingling with excitement. London! She swung her legs over the side of the bed and pulled on her dressing gown. "I have never been to London, you know," she told Francis, as she tied her sash. She joined him before the fire, which he was poking to expose a few embers.

"Never?" He looked genuinely amazed. "Good God, you really have led a sheltered life, haven't you?" He contemplated her face. "I must own that I had at first thought that we should avoid exposing ourselves to the public eye. It occurred to me that the less we were seen, the less notice would be taken of our eventual separation."

A chill ran over Belinda, and her gaze shifted from him to the faint sparks in the fire.

"But on second thought, we might as well enjoy our few months together."

He did not, of course, give her his true reason for his change of plan: that if he hid his bride away Rosaline and her husband might suspect a ruse.

"Perhaps I might even be able to take you to Paris, if it falls to the allied army before the end of our time together. From the latest despatches from France it appears that might be a distinct possibility."

"Paris!" breathed Belinda, overawed at the thought of

being able to visit the country that had been at war with England for so many years.

"Meanwhile, I shall undertake to show you the sights of London—that is, those that are suitable for the eyes of a demure young bride," he added, a wicked glint in his eyes.

"Oh, how disappointing," she responded with a mischievous grin.

As Carter shaved him in the chilly, dark dressing room, Francis wondered if he were not insane to be proposing to take Belinda to London. Her gaucherie could very well make him the laughingstock of the town. Not that he cared one jot for public opinion, but he did prefer at all times to be in control of any given situation, and he knew, from the Winchell episode, that Belinda's conduct could prove volatile, to say the least.

His pulses quickened at the *frisson* of danger this thought evoked. Perhaps, after all, this temporary marriage might add some excitement to a life that had been confoundedly dull since his return to England. The lips of his mirrored image quirked at him as Carter completed his toilette with a dash of aromatic hair lotion.

While Carter assisted him into his exquisitely cut coat of blue superfine, Francis reflected that however disastrous this sojourn in London might prove to be, it would last only two weeks. Then they would go directly to Luxton to await the birth and christening of Rosaline's child.

A shiver ran over him. Although he was not given to prayer, he made a mental plea to the Almighty that Rosaline would come through her coming ordeal safely. He knew of too many women who had perished in childbirth or from childbed fever not to feel acute anxiety about Rosaline's approaching confinement. Courtenay had promised that he would send him notice of her safe delivery by express, and Courtenay was a man of his word, but this did little to relieve his present anxiety. Perhaps it was a good thing he would have Belinda to distract him during the next few weeks!

"Thank you, Carter. You may pack now, and tell Mary to pack for Lady Kenmore."

"Very well, my lord." Although he had been given to understand that his master and his bride were to remain at Donnington for a few days, the valet's countenance remained impassive. After twelve years of serving Lord Kenmore, he had learned to expect anything and everything from his volatile master. Until a few weeks ago, there was little his lordship could do that surprised him, but this latest escapade—marriage to an unknown little rustic whose family hadn't a feather to fly with—took the cake. Apart from the Countess of Beresford, his lordship had never come within a thousand miles of getting leg-shackled; and even with the Countess the thought of marriage hadn't entered his lordship's mind till it was too late. He'd never been quite the same carefree person after that. Now, all of a sudden, he'd wedded this little dab of a female, in a ceremony with nobody on his side but his cousin. A right havey-cavey business, and no mistake. His lordship was up to some mischief all right, but God alone knew what.

"Might I enquire as to where your lordship is moving on to?" he asked, his face a disinterested mask.

His lordship's eyes glinted with amusement. "You may. You may also remove that bland expression from your face. We're off to London, Carter. What do you say to that?"

The valet's smooth face broke into a grin. "Why, nothing, my lord, except that I'd best be sending word ahead, as all the servants is down at Luxton, awaitin' the coming of yourself and her ladyship."

"Lord, yes. I'd forgotten that. I'll write a letter to Perrin in London immediately. See to it that he gets it as soon as possible. We'll stay at the King's Arms in Westerham tonight. That should give Perrin enough time to open up Kenmore House and hire the necessary servants."

"Shall I send to Luxton for Besley and Mrs. Griswold?"

"No. I intend to remain in London for only two weeks. Much as I detest temporary servants, we'll have to make do with whatever Perrin comes up with. I shall rely upon you, Carter, to ensure that everything runs as smoothly as possible."

"Yes, m'lord."

The valet's face registered not one hint of the dismay he felt at the thought of breaking in a houseful of new servants to his master's exacting standards for a two-week stay. It was a good thing he was paid a handsome wage. Not that he'd ever dream of leaving his lordship. He'd grown used to the excitement of never knowing what to expect next. After all the escapades he'd been through with Lord Kenmore, the normal life of a valet would bore him stupid.

Within two hours all was settled: letters written and sent post-haste to London and Westerham; their bags packed; and before noon they had taken their leave of Lord and Lady Fotheringham.

"Did they not mind that we left so unexpectedly?" Belinda asked Francis, as the carriage moved off down the long avenue lined with poplar trees.

"Good lord, no. Why should they? Oh, I am forgetting that you have never traveled. It is quite a common thing to use the homes of others for an overnight rest on a journey. My only reason for any hesitation about changing our plans was that I had told Lord Fotheringham last night that we would be staying for three nights. Surely you have had friends or acquaintances apply to you for accommodation on their journey?"

"Yes, of course. Many times. But never having traveled myself, I suppose it didn't occur to me that we could come and go as we pleased."

Belinda was becoming increasingly aware that the extent of her lack of knowledge regarding the ways of society was enormous.

The night they spent at the comfortable coaching inn in the little town of Westerham was a marked contrast to the night at Donnington. Belinda shared a delicious dinner with Francis, who regaled her with slightly risqué stories about famous people. After a most amicable evening she retired to her warm bedchamber in the suite of rooms Carter had miraculously procured.

Next morning, refreshed by an undisturbed sleep, Belinda

climbed into the carriage once again, a thrill of excitement running through her as she realized that in a few hours she would be seeing London.

As they drew nearer to the great metropolis, however, her initial excitement turned to trepidation at the thought of appearing in public as the bride of Lord Kenmore. She wondered if his manner would change once he was moving in society circles again. Perhaps he would become cold and distant. She knew that, despite his remarkable generosity in having married her, he was not perfect. Indeed, there were times when he grew impatient with her lack of knowledge of the world and its ways; and she herself found it hard to control her own quick temper and unruly tongue when she saw that glint of mockery in his eyes. But, ever mindful of the sacrifice he had made for her and her family, she had exerted tremendous self-discipline. At times she felt like a pot of boiling water with the lid clamped on.

"What is the matter?" asked Francis.

Belinda started, for she had thought he was asleep. "Why, nothing," she replied, giving him a nervous little smile.

"Then why are you pulling tufts of fur from your muff? At this rate it will be bald by the time we reach Grosvenor Square. Come, out with it. What is troubling you?"

The impatience was there again, troubling her further. "I'm afraid that I shall fail dismally at behaving as the wife of Lord Kenmore should behave," she told him directly. "I know almost nothing about the ways of society, apart from the balls and card parties at Tunbridge Wells." She gave him a proud little smile. "I have no desire to make either myself or you appear foolish. I don't think we should have come to London."

It was too late now, however, for they were almost at the point where the Kent Road entered the southeast end of the city.

Francis leaned forward, his dark eyes fixed upon hers. "If you undertake to submit to my tutelage, I give you my word that you shall not fail," he said, in a tone of conviction that belied his own very real doubts about this decision to come to London. "Despite your occasionally gauche manner, you have a natural charm and vivacity."

Belinda's cheeks flamed. How dare he call her gauche! She was about to take him to task for doing so, but, upon reflection, decided against it. He was right. She was gauche at times. It would be rather pleasant not to be considered a hoyden, and to feel a serene confidence upon entering a roomful of strangers. She smiled at him. "I shall try very hard to do as you tell me," she said meekly.

He gave her his rare boyish grin, which was so much more attractive than his mocking smile. "I realize that won't be easy for you, my sprite. But it will be only for a week or so, you know. One week to prepare you for your entrée, and then one week of balls and routs and your presentation to the Prince Regent. After that, we shall abandon the giddy whirl of London society and escape to Luxton."

"I shall manage very well," she told him, her confidence restored, "so long as you don't desert me."

"I shan't desert you—yet," was his reply. She felt again that chill of foreboding at the thought of the inevitable conclusion of their marriage.

She turned her gaze to the sights of London that were sweeping by her: the buildings, both mean and majestic, crammed in together without much semblance of order; the cobbled streets crowded with all manner of carts, drawn by horses or pushed by men, who yelled out the merits of their particular wares in raucous cockney voices: "Brahn eggs, fresh from the country!" "Pots and pans, last yer a lifetime!"; most of all, the people that thronged the streets and flagways.

Belinda felt hemmed in by noise and people, and being used only to fresh country air, the close, dusty atmosphere threatened to choke her.

After battling through the busy streets at a snail's pace, the carriage reached the spacious avenues and crescents and squares, which were lined with elegant town houses. Eventually it drew up before a tall, porticoed house. The square in which it stood surrounded a large, iron-fenced garden filled with horse-chestnut and lime trees, which promised a delightfully cool oasis of green once the warmth of spring opened their tight buds.

"Kenmore House," announced Francis. "Welcome to your London home, my little bride." As he spoke, his mouth twisted into his wry smile. Before she had time to reply, he had descended from the carriage and turned to hand her down.

The entrance hall of Kenmore House was as dramatic as its owner. The floor was black-and-white marble set in bold, diagonal stripes. The straight staircase leading upward was covered in a vivid crimson carpet. At the head of the flight of stairs stood an exquisite bronze statue of a female nude, less than two feet high, on a gilt pedestal.

The scent of beeswax and fresh potpourri pervaded the entire house, evidence that the newly recruited regiment of servants had been at work.

As Belinda surveyed the place that would be her home for the next two weeks, she felt both apprehension and regret. Apprehension, because the supreme elegance of the house only served to emphasize Lord Kenmore's position in society; regret that she would never be able to think of this beautiful house as hers.

When they had finished dinner, Belinda rose to leave the dining room.

Francis held up his hand. "No need," he said brusquely. "Not when we're dining alone, as we are tonight."

His tone brooked no argument. Having ordered the butler to carry in the decanter of pale cognac, from which he had been liberally helping himself for the past half hour, he led the way into the library.

It struck Belinda, as she surveyed Francis across the hearth, that he was in a strange mood tonight. His dark eyes glittered and there was a stiffness about his jawline. A dull flush had crept into his cheeks, whether from the drink or from feverish excitement she did not know. All she knew was that she was seeing a new side of Francis Kenmore tonight, and she was not certain that she liked it.

He looked up, to find her watching him. "Come here," he barked.

Startled, she stared at him defiantly, making no move to obey his peremptory command.

"Did you hear what I said?"

"I did," she replied coldly, "but as I am not used to being spoken to in such a manner I chose to ignore it."

He set his glass down on the rosewood side table and slowly got to his feet. Inwardly she flinched, suddenly fearful of this stranger before her. He made her a mocking bow and, when he lifted his head, she saw the derisive smile she was growing to detest.

"Pray forgive me, my lady wife. Would you be so kind as to draw nearer so that I may assess what must be done to turn you into a lady of fashion?"

She rose and marched right up to him. Her eyes lifted to his in a direct, unwavering gaze.

"By God, Belinda," he said, after a seemingly interminable pause, "I like your spirit. You must pardon me, my dear," he added in a harsh tone. "I am a trifle cast away tonight."

"You need not concern yourself about that," she informed him calmly. "I am used to seeing Bertie foxed."

"Are you, indeed? Well, you shouldn't be. He's far too young to be drinking deep. Something needs to be done about that young pup, methinks. But first to you, my Ariel."

He took her chin in his hand, tilting her face to the light, turning it this way and that. "Excellent bone structure. Good coloring. You need only a subtle touch of face paint to highlight your best features. A dash of midnight-blue eye shadow to emphasize those magnificent eyes."

As he spoke the touch of his fingers on her face sent little darts of pleasure through her, despite her indignation at being assessed as if she were a filly at a horse market.

"Your two main problems are your hair and your height, or the lack of it. The hair we can do something about, of course. Monsieur Jacques, the most exclusive dresser of hair in London, shall be brought here to cut and style it into something less resembling a rat's nest.''

"And my height?'' she demanded. "I suppose you intend to set me up on a pair of stilts to mitigate that problem!''

He laughed. "Bravo, my Ariel. Well said.''

"Why on earth do you keep calling me that?''

"What? You mean 'Ariel'? Why, because you remind me of Prospero's faithful sprite in Shakespeare's *Tempest*, of course.''

"Oh,'' was all she said, not wishing to admit her ignorance.

"Don't tell me you have never read *The Tempest*!'' he said, profoundly shocked.

"No, I have not,'' she countered, her eyes flashing. "Nor would you have done so if you'd been left motherless at thirteen and had to manage a household practically by yourself since then. I would remind you, sir, in case you have forgotten, that my education as a young lady ceased when my mother died. I had little time for books and theatricals and such flummery.'' Her face was hot with indignation.

He appeared utterly taken aback by her fury, but his eyes held a glimmer of admiration. "Lord, I have opened a Pandora's box, have I not?'' He smiled his most brilliant smile at her. "A thousand pardons, my dear Belinda. I have a toplofty way of expecting everyone to be as deeply engrossed as I am in the world of theater. I have the distinct feeling, though, that given time you might come to enjoy theatricals almost as much as I, my little one.''

Given time, she might, but time was what they did not have. A few months at the most. She gazed up at him, unaware that her feelings were exposed to him as clearly as if she had actually voiced them.

He turned away to break the spell, aware that if he did not do so, matters might progress faster than was his intention. He was surprised to find himself imbued with a desire to gather this game little creature into his arms, and to coach her slowly and tenderly in the art and pleasures of lovemaking.

Shaken by this strange emotion, he deliberately set a distance between them by striding across the room. Good

God, he thought. This period of enforced celibacy is definitely not agreeing with me. He must somehow contrive to pay his current *chère-amie* a visit as soon as possible.

He turned to survey the shelves that housed his extensive collection of books about theatrical costumes.

"It is not difficult to suggest height. It can be achieved with feathers, tall headdresses, what have you," he informed her, across the room. "It is my intention, however, to make your smallness an advantage, not a detriment."

He returned to stand before her. "We shall toss out all those frills and laces and flounces your stepmama chose for you and begin anew, with an emphasis on elegant simplicity."

Again he took her small face in his hand, his smile now warm, his manner enthusiastic. "In one week I intend to make you *un grand succèss*, and then, alas, I shall whisk you away to obscurity."

He bent his head. For a moment Belinda held her breath, thinking, *hoping* that he would kiss her. But then, having drawn a casual finger down her cheek, he released her.

"One week only, but so great a success will you prove that, once our marriage is dissolved, men of rank and fortune will be standing in line to offer you proposals of marriage."

chapter

<u>8</u>

One week of preparation for her debut had seemed a reasonable time to Belinda at the outset. But after several days of either standing for hours at a time, having fabrics pinned on her, or being slathered with creams and lotions, and lemon juice to bleach her complexion, while she sat, eyes smarting, she was heartily weary of all the fuss attendant upon her entry into society.

Nevertheless, when she looked into her full-length mirror on the evening of her presentation to the Prince Regent at Carlton House, she had to admit that Francis and his minions had wrought a miraculous change in her.

Gone was the childlike hoyden with rough-skinned elbows and unruly hair. In her place stood an exquisitely dressed young woman, her dark hair cut in the new Roman style. Her gown was of white satin embroidered with crystal beads. Apart from the small, curved train the style was simplicity itself, enhancing her slight figure.

"It needs but one or two pieces of jewelry to complete her ladyship's toilette," said Denton, Belinda's new and extremely efficient dresser. The middle-aged woman's shrewd eyes assessed her mistress, before reaching toward the jewel chest. But before she could open it, Lord Kenmore waved her away, ordering her and the maids to wait at the other end of the room.

He stood before Belinda, surveying her through his gold-handled quizzing glass, one hand behind him. Then he let his glass fall, so that it hung on its crimson ribbon, a bold splash of color against the severe black of his swallow-tailed coat and the white expanse of his neckcloth and watered-silk waistcoat.

He moved one pace nearer and drew from behind his back an oblong box covered in blue velvet.

Belinda paled. "Oh, no," she breathed. "You must not."

"Open it."

She lifted the hinged lid with trembling fingers. Inside, nestled on a bed of white silk, was a necklace of filigree silver with three small, perfect sapphires alternating with delicate spheres of crystal. Two sapphire eardrops flanked the necklace. Speechless, Belinda stared down at the jewels.

"Well, do you like them or not?" demanded Francis.

She searched his face, trying to determine the meaning of this gift from his expression. "Of course I like them. They are the most beautiful things I've ever seen, but I cannot possibly accept such a gift," she said in a loud whisper. "Not under the circumstances."

His dark brows drew together, and he almost snatched the box from her. "Let me hear no more from you about it. It appears I shall have to teach you how to accept a gift graciously. Bend your head forward."

She did as she was told, biting back the retort that it was he who was in the wrong for giving her such a valuable gift when their marriage was only a temporary one. He drew the necklace around the base of her throat, the touch of his fingers sending little *frissons* of pleasure darting downward to her breasts.

"I shall return them to you—afterwards," she whispered, hoping that neither her maid nor her dresser, both of whom stood at the other end of the room observing them with studied disinterest, could hear.

"They are a gift from me to you, a permanent gift," he told her as he fastened the clasp of the necklace and helped her to put on the eardrops. It occurred to Belinda that he was not new to this. She could not imagine Bertie or Papa dressing a woman with jewels with such expertise.

"There now. Look in the mirror," was his command.

She sat down on the gilt-legged stool to survey herself in the mirror. The jewels were perfect. She marveled at the exquisite delicacy of the workmanship and could not help noticing how the glowing color of the sapphires accentuated the blue of her eyes.

He leaned down, cupping her shoulders with his hands, to observe her in the mirror. "I vow my little jewels are quite outshone by the brilliance of your eyes."

She met his suddenly intense gaze in the glass and, recognizing his intention, closed her eyes as his warm lips pressed against the nape of her neck. She leaned back against him, overcome by a sweet languor, as he trailed little kisses from her neck to her right shoulder.

When she could bear it no longer, she turned with a little gasp and flung her arms about his neck to press her eager mouth to his. Drawing her up from the stool, he pulled her body close to his, and she knew the sweet ecstasy of their first true kiss. His lips were firm but gentle and, in response, her mouth opened like a newly blossomed flower beneath their searching pressure.

To her great disappointment, he drew away. "I do not think we should continue," he said with a quirky smile, tilting his head in the direction of the servants. Seeing that their interest had been observed, the servants suddenly became very much involved in folding clothes and putting them away in the wardrobe.

"Oh, heavens," exclaimed Belinda, with a nervous giggle. "I had quite forgotten them." Her cheeks aflame, she looked into his dark eyes, wondering what sort of game it was that he was playing with her. Had this demonstration of affection merely been part of the plan to convince the servants that they were happily married? At times, it was extremely difficult to anticipate or counter his various moves.

She looked again into the mirror. "I cannot believe it. Is it truly me?"

"It is truly you, my sprite," he responded, "and a devilish attractive you, too."

She turned to gaze in wonderment at herself again. "How I wish Marianne and Bertie could see me now."

"Are you missing them, little one?"

She turned to look up at him. "You must understand that it's not that you are not a good companion. Indeed, you are exceedingly generous and good to me," she hastened to assure him. "But I should love to be able to share all this, all my good fortune, with them."

It struck Francis that if Gilbert Hanbury were to come to London it would not only please his wife, but her brother might also serve to take Belinda off his hands for a few excursions, freeing Francis for the more exotic entertainments he occasionally craved.

"Why don't we invite your brother to come up to London immediately so that he may stay here with us for a few days before we leave for Luxton?"

He omitted mention of Marianne Hanbury, knowing that a girl who had slipped into the back pew of the church for her sister's wedding, and who had not even attended the wedding breakfast, would scarcely be capable of visiting London.

"Oh, Francis, could we?" Belinda's eyes glowed. "How very kind of you! I should like that above all things."

"Then we shall send him an invitation first thing tomorrow."

The thought of seeing Bertie again made Belinda's happiness almost complete. It needed only Marianne's presence to complete it, she thought half an hour later, when she settled into the landau's comfortable seat, but, alas, that could not be. She chose to ignore the knowledge that her happiness was fleeting, temporary. She must live for the present and forget the future. A shiver ran across her shoulders, despite the warmth of her ermine-edged mantle.

"Nervous?" asked Francis.

"A little. You will stay near me tonight, won't you? If I make a faux pas you won't need to say anything. I shall be able to tell from your expression."

He studied her face for a moment in the light of the carriage lamp. "Am I such an ogre, Belinda?"

"No, no. Of course not. Indeed, I think you are extremely patient with me." She regarded him, her head tilted to one side. "There are times, though, when I wonder if the Lord Kenmore I see is the real person. Do you know what Bertie called you?"

In the flickering light she saw his jaw tighten and she cursed her wayward tongue.

"No. What did Bertie call me?" His voice was as cool as his expression.

She wished with all her heart that she could have changed the subject. "It was something silly: the . . . the Wicked Baron. No, the Bad Baron, that was it. Isn't that stupid?" She gave a nervous little laugh. "I told him that if you had been called the Bad Baron, your character must have completely changed since your sojourn in the West Indies, for you could not possibly be called that now. Bertie agreed that it must be so."

"Your faith in me is infinitely touching," said Francis in an acid tone. He settled into a corner of the carriage, turning his face to the window, the action effectively blocking her out.

She leaned forward to touch his gloved hand. "I cannot blame you for being vexed with me, Francis. It was extremely tactless in me to repeat such stupid gossip when it is so patently untrue. You are the most generous, the most kind-hearted man in the world, as I and my family can attest."

"Enough." She shrank from the hard glitter in his eyes. "If you once again allude to the settlement I have made upon your family, I shall get down immediately from this carriage and our entire arrangement shall be at an end. Is that understood?"

"It is. But I cannot consider it fair that I am forbidden to voice my gratitude to you," she protested hotly.

"You have already done so, *ad nauseam*. Let us speak no more on the subject."

The ensuing constraint between them threatened to put a

damper on her anticipation of the evening. But as the carriage turned through the iron gates of Carlton House, he leaned forward to take her hand in his. "Forgive me, little one. I should not have flared up at you. It is just that I am rather sensitive on the subject."

Her heart swelled at this further evidence of his noble spirit, and she gave him a beaming smile. "I do understand. And I give you my word that I shall do my utmost not to mention it again, difficult as that might be."

Their reconciliation, together with the thought of seeing Bertie again and being able to share all the excitement of London with him, gave an added radiance to Belinda's lively countenance. Thus it was that when the new Lady Kenmore entered the crimson drawing room in Carlton House, a murmur of both surprise and approval rose from the assembled crowd.

The gossipmongers who avidly read all the notices in the papers were able to confirm that this was indeed Kenmore's bride, although those who knew the Baron's taste in women had been expecting her to be some tall, voluptuous beauty in the grand theatrical style he was known to favor. They were stunned, therefore, by the revelation of the tiny, dazzling creature on his arm. She moved with an air of confidence, her head held high, her large sapphire eyes reflecting the brilliance of the light from the countless crystal chandeliers. Lady Kenmore's serene expression betrayed not one hint of the terror she was feeling inside.

Francis pressed her hand against his heart. "A magnificent performance," he whispered.

Coming from a connoisseur of the theater, this was praise indeed! His approval and support buoyed her up, so that the air of confidence she had assumed upon her entry into Carlton House swiftly became reality.

"How can this possibly be called a house," she whispered to Francis, as they moved forward. "It is a palace."

"Of course it is," he whispered back. "But Prinny chooses to call it a house to placate the populace. He is unpopular enough as it is because of all his extravagances, to the point where he is booed whenever he goes out in his carriage. He certainly doesn't wish to own to having built an incredibly expensive palace in London.''

Incredibly expensive it must have been. His chandler's bill for candles along would surely have paid for all the servants' wages at Denehurst. Belinda had never seen so much dazzling light. The carpeting beneath her feet was like velvet, and when she studied it more closely, she saw that it was patterned with the insignia of the Garter. Everywhere she went, marble columns and huge paintings and golden ornaments filled her eye.

She was presented to so many people that it was impossible to recall their names and faces, but of one thing she was absolutely convinced: not one of the gentlemen she met was half as handsome or as elegant as Francis. It was the first time she had seen him dressed in the court dress of black coat and black silk knee breeches. Apart from the crimson ribbon of his eyeglass, the only other touch of color was the sapphire pin in his neckcloth. ''Worn in your honor,'' he had told her, his eyes dancing. His one other touch of theatrical flamboyance was the ornate gold watch chain across his waistcoat.

Moving with great expertise through the crowd, bestowing a smile here, a touch on the elbow there, he led her into the throne room, which dazzled the eye even more if that were possible: gold, gold, everywhere gold. Belinda was beginning to find the ornate magnificence of the Regent's palace rather overpowering, a feeling that was exacerbated by the intense heat.

''Is it always so warm here?'' she whispered to Francis.

''Yes. Prinny likes everything overheated. Appalling, isn't it?''

She knew that he was not referring merely to the heat. His own taste in decor could not in any way be termed austere. He, too, loved crimson and gold, as she had seen at Kenmore House, but, thank heavens, his taste did not extend to gilded griffins and larger-than-life-size marble statues.

Before she had time to grow nervous again, she found herself before the Prince Regent, the man who had reigned over England for more than three years, while his mad, blind father, King George III, was shut away in Windsor Castle.

The Prince was extremely fat, his corpulent belly tightly corseted. Belinda was aware of a vast amount of neckcloth and a gold satin coat with the brilliant blue sash of the diamond-studded garter across it. All this finery was surmounted by a rather attractive, fleshy face with surprisingly kind slate-blue eyes.

"Charming, Kenmore. Utterly charming," was the Prince's pronouncement as Belinda rose from her deep curtsey. She found her hand pressed between the plump royal fingers, and then she retreated one step as the Prince and Francis exchanged pleasantries.

Feeling more than a little awkward, she smiled as if she were including herself in the conversation. In fact, she was praying that Francis would be able soon to extricate himself from the Prince. Her head was swimming from the intense heat and the accumulated strain of this, her first public appearance. She longed to be able to escape the noise and heat and the crush of people, if only for a few minutes.

As she waited for Francis, her eyes moved idly along the assembly that flanked the Prince of Wales, to encounter suddenly the intense and unmistakably malevolent gaze of Lord Winchell.

chapter
9

To Belinda's relief, Francis had not seen Lord Winchell. She wished to avoid what might prove to be an ugly confrontation between the two men. As soon as Francis rejoined her, she clutched his arm, determined to remove him from Lord Winchell's vicinity as soon as possible.

"I am feeling a trifle faint. Could we go somewhere else?" she pleaded. "Somewhere cool and quiet."

He looked down at her, concern in his eyes. "Of course. But I am not certain that it will be possible to find a cool place inside the house. I shall take you to the conservatory, and if that is still too warm for you, we can go out into the garden."

Despite her swimming head and the shock she had received upon seeing Lord Winchell again, Belinda could not repress a chuckle when they entered the conservatory.

"I thought it might please you," said Francis, his eyes glinting with amusement.

She again experienced a warm glow at this acknowledgment of their shared sense of the ridiculous.

The so-called conservatory was the most ostentatious place imaginable. It was for all the world like a cathedral in the grand gothic manner, together with a most extraordinary mixture of baroque and Turkish styles: marble pillars and gilded cornices, oriental arches and stained-glass windows. Exotic plants in golden tubs and some ornately carved benches were the sole indication that this was meant to be a conservatory.

"I have never seen anything quite so incredible," Belinda whispered.

"I had an idea you might enjoy it. It makes one shudder to think what the new palace at Brighton will be like when it is completed!"

He led her to a cushioned bench near the garden door, which was slightly ajar, so that a soft breeze wafted in. "Is this better?" he asked.

She nodded, but continued to fan herself with her delicately carved ivory fan, one of the many little gifts with which Francis had presented her during the past few days.

"Wait here," he told her, "and I shall fetch you a glass of lemonade."

Before she could tell him not to trouble himself, he was striding down the center aisle of the conservatory. She was left alone to enjoy the coolness and comparative quiet. Several others had come here to escape the crowds and the heat of the public rooms, so that when a masculine figure halted nearby, she was not concerned. When she realized that he was not moving on but had advanced to stand before her, she looked up to discover, to her dismay, that it was Lord Winchell.

"Good evening, Lady Kenmore." His greeting was accompanied by one of his unctuous bows.

"Good evening, Lord Winchell," she responded coolly. Thank heavens her voice was steady, not betraying the increased beating of her heart.

His eyes ran over her seated figure, lingering on the exposed curve of breast above the bodice of her modish gown, and he smiled. "Charming. Lord Kenmore has excellent taste. I must remember to congratulate him on having captured your heart and hand in such a phenomenally short time."

She made no response to this, but snapped open her fan

again and began to wield it vigorously, employing it as a barrier between them.

"Your family, Sir Joseph and Lady Hanbury and your brother and sister, all are well, I trust?" he asked, undeterred by her silence.

Belinda wished with all her heart that Francis would return. Although she knew she was fully capable of dealing with Lord Winchell, she was also aware that she was forced to remain in this spot until Francis returned, or they would never find each other in the crush. "All are well, I thank you," she replied crisply.

So unnerved was she by the way he continued to survey her with those seawater eyes of his that she hurriedly added, "My brother will be coming to London for a brief visit."

"Will he, indeed? How very pleasant that will be for you. And your sister, Marianne? Will she be accompanying your brother on this visit?" he added in his most oily tone.

Belinda's eyes narrowed. "No, she will not. My sister prefers not to travel."

"Ah, yes, of course. If I recollect aright, she has never been seen in public: I certainly never had the pleasure of meeting her. I believe it was one of your own servants who told me that Miss Hanbury rarely ventures downstairs even in her own home."

Belinda darted a venomous look at him. So the gloves were off! What mischief was this toad up to now?

"Very sad," he continued. "But then I suppose every family has its secrets, does it not? Of course, one naturally prefers that they remain secret if one has aspirations of getting on in society."

Her hands clenched into fists, but she knew that although she might have been able to get away with striking him with a champagne bottle as Miss Hanbury, as Lady Kenmore she must behave with more decorum. Therefore, she gave him the sweetest smile she could muster. "I have no secrets to keep, sir. Besides, being a success in London society is of no importance to me. As the wife of Lord Kenmore, my place in society is already assured."

He moved closer, thrusting his face forward. She recoiled from the smell of wine and snuff that emanated from him.

"Ah, there we have it in a nutshell, do we not, my little fortune hunter?" he said. "I'd give a hundred guineas to discover how you managed to entrap Kenmore in your net. I was quite good enough for you until a younger and richer man came along."

"You!" Belinda struggled to contain her fury. "You were never good enough for me, sir! I always found you utterly repulsive. I would never have married you."

"Not even to rescue your family from penury and disgrace?"

"No. Not even for that. Oh, I own that I was seriously considering it, for the sake of my family, but your disgusting conduct at the theater put an end to any further consideration of marriage between us."

She threw a desperate look down the length of the conservatory, but Francis was still nowhere in sight.

"Would you think it cynical of me to suggest that your change of heart would not have been so sudden had Lord Kenmore not happened upon the scene?"

He drew his gold snuffbox from the pocket of his garishly striped waistcoat and, having taken a large pinch of snuff from it, sniffed it inelegantly, part of the brown snuff spilling from his nostrils down his cravat and frilled shirtfront. The sight made Belinda feel positively nauseous.

"What a romantic meeting that must have been," he continued relentlessly. "I believe there had been a long-standing but secret attachment between you." There was no mistaking his sneering innuendo. "An attachment that no one else had even guessed at. It was natural, therefore, that the gallant baron should come to the rescue of the maiden he loved."

Snapping her fan shut, Belinda stood up. "May I suggest that you rejoin your companions, Lord Winchell, as my husband should be returning at any moment now? I am sure you will agree with me when I say that this conversation is going nowhere."

"Oh, but it is, dear lady, it certainly is." His curiously opaque eyes grew hard. "Surely you cannot imagine that I would believe all this tomfoolery about a long-standing attachment between you and Lord Kenmore, madam? This marriage is a farce, but, alas, it was *I* who was made to look ridiculous. It was most unwise to make an enemy of me, my dear lady, as you will discover. Oh, I own that your husband has gone to a great deal of trouble to make you appear presentable, but the question I keep asking myself is: Why? It is a commonly known fact that Francis Kenmore has never in his life done anything for anyone that does not directly benefit himself.''

He gripped her wrist and bent his head towards her. For a horrid moment she thought he would attempt to kiss her, and her fingers curled into talons ready to defend herself, but his move was made to bring his mouth closer to her ear.

''It is likely that in snaring Lord Kenmore you have set a trap for yourself, fair Belinda. When you are lying in your husband's arms tonight, whisper these two names in his ear: Denise Bouchard and Rosaline; and watch closely to see what his reaction is. Can you remember those names? Denise and Rosaline.''

She could feel and smell his sour breath on her cheek. Lifting both hands, she pushed him away so that he staggered and would have fallen had he not grasped at a marble column to save himself. ''Don't come near me again, you evil toad,'' she spat at him. ''And you may keep your insinuations and threats to yourself, for they make no impression upon me, I assure you.''

To Belinda's overwhelming relief, before Lord Winchell could respond, Francis at last appeared. He paused, holding her glass of lemonade in one hand and lifting his quizzing glass to survey her tormentor with the other. ''Up to your old tricks again, Winchell?'' he drawled. ''Here you are, my dear,'' he said, handing her the glass, before turning to loom over Winchell. ''Been annoying you, has he, my love?'' he asked Belinda, as he surveyed the other man.

''I am quite capable of dealing with him.'' Belinda shuddered. ''For heaven's sake, Francis, let him go.''

''Happy to. My desire, also. But I must warn you,

Winchell: If I find you pestering my wife once again, you shall be sorry for it.''

"What will you do, Kenmore?" blustered Winchell. "Shoot me down in cold blood, as you did Prescott? I'm not certain you'd get away so easily a second time."

A tiny nerve jumped in Francis's lean cheek. "Remove yourself, Winchell," he said in a soft voice that held far more menace than a shout could have done. "If you value your friendship with Prinny, you had best keep away from Lady Kenmore. I doubt that even Fat George would condone the attempted rape of an innocent young gentlewoman in a theater box." He made a threatening move toward Winchell, who hastily retreated beyond the marble column.

"Don't concern yourself, Kenmore. I'm going. But I give you fair warning I shall repay you both for having made a fool of me."

"My dear Winchell," drawled Francis. "You cannot lay the blame for that at our door, when it was a fait accompli long before we met. Now, are you leaving, or must I demean myself by throwing you out into Prinny's exotic garden?"

Beads of moisture stood on the older man's forehead. So heavy was his breathing that Belinda was concerned that he might be in danger of collapsing, but he rallied sufficiently to make her one of his creaking bows. "Your servant, Lady Kenmore. I trust you have committed those names to memory."

He disappeared into the shadows before she had time to respond.

"Damn the man. I should never have left you alone." Francis turned to give her a frowning look. "What was the meaning of that last remark of his?"

"Which one was that?" she asked, feigning ignorance.

"Something about names."

"Oh, that," she replied vaguely. "He was asking after two neighbors of my father, that was all." Her eyes avoided his.

"I can always tell when you are lying to me, you know." His voice held a note of menace that did not augur well for the remainder of the evening. "I insist that you tell me the true meaning of his remark."

She threw up her head to give him a scalding look. "I do not like to be badgered, my lord, particularly not after having had a most unpleasant encounter with that detestable man."

Their eyes clashed, and she saw in his the blaze of anger she had seen before on a very few occasions. Usually it disappeared as fast as it came. This time it remained.

"And I would remind you that I do not like to be toyed with," he said. "Tell me, if you please, what names these were that you were to remember."

She glared at him openly now, her breath coming fast. "I refuse to be bullied like this, sir," she flung at him.

She shrank back as he towered above her, his face grim. "Tell me now," he demanded. He grasped her wrist so tightly that the silver bangle she wore dug into her skin.

"You are hurting me," she informed him in a cool, clear voice.

He glanced down, his expression suggesting that he had been unaware of his actions, and instantly released her. "Forgive me. I had no intention of hurting you." His voice was cold and formal, like that of a stranger.

He turned abruptly and strode to the arched doorway, remaining there for a moment to stare out into the garden, the breeze ruffling his hair.

When he returned, the only visible sign of his anger was the two bright spots of color on his cheekbones. "I recognize that you would prefer to be taken home immediately," he said in a low voice. "Our early departure would be noticed, however, and might give rise to the gossip we are both anxious to avoid. I suggest, therefore, that we cry pax for now and make an endeavor to maintain this charade for another hour or so. There is no reason why we should not be able to take our leave then."

He swung his eyeglass on its crimson ribbon, fixing his gaze at some point above her head. His jaw was rigid from the control he was exerting upon his temper.

She drew in a deep breath, determined to emulate him,

and nodded her head briskly. "Yes. I think that would be for the best. Although, of course, I should infinitely prefer to go home immediately." She swallowed, forcing back the tears that lay behind her eyes. Not only was this their first real quarrel, but she had been particularly hurt by his reminder that this evening, which had begun so well, was indeed a charade, as, for that matter, was their entire marriage.

Proffering his arm, Francis took her back into the crowded ballroom where he introduced her to several people, all of whose names she forgot as soon as she heard them. The sparkle had gone from the evening. Her head ached and her feet were sore, and she wished with all her heart that they could go home. Even when he led her into a lively quadrille, Francis was aloof, unbending. He was behaving so much like a spoiled, sulky child that she felt like slapping him.

As he was leading her back to her seat, he spied yet another acquaintance nearby. "Ah, now here is an old friend you must meet," he told her.

Belinda emitted an exaggerated sigh, which drew yet another crushing look from him, but she submitted to being led up to an elderly woman of indeterminate age, whose dark eyes twinkled in a heavily rouged face.

"Ah, Kenmore," she cried, rapping him on the arm with her fan. "I wondered if you'd ever get around to presenting your bride to me."

Francis was all charm. "My dear Dorothea, I did not realize you were here until I saw you just a moment ago. Since when were you a regular attender at Prinny's hothouse crushes?"

"Ha! It so happens that my niece is presenting her daughter and enlisted my support. I was a fool to come. Getting far too old for all this flummery." As she spoke, her penetrating eyes were raking Belinda from head to toe. "I'm waiting," she informed Francis sharply.

"Forgive me." He made the formidable old lady a mock bow, his eyes twinkling in response to hers. "May I have the honor of presenting my wife, Belinda? Belinda, this is a dear friend of mine, Lady Calvin.''

Belinda made a deep curtsey and found her hand taken by dry fingers.

''Might I leave Belinda in your very capable hands for a while, Dorothea?'' asked Francis.

Vexed at being disposed of without a ''by your leave,'' Belinda turned away to study the dancing.

''Of course you may. Making your escape to the card room, eh? Don't stay away too long, for I've a notion to take a few hands myself before the night's out.''

She motioned him away peremptorily and patted the seat beside her. ''Sit down, my dear.''

Belinda did as she was told.

''So you're Maria Hanbury's daughter.''

''Oh, did you know my mother?'' Belinda's face brightened.

''I did, indeed. Her mother was a friend of mine. A beautiful girl, your mother was. You're not at all like her.''

Belinda grinned, not one whit put out by this forthright statement. ''I regret not. Marianne, my sister, is the one who favored Mama.''

''Not that you haven't a great deal of style, mind, despite your lack of inches. That's a perfect gown for you. No doubt Francis chose it.''

Belinda's chin went up. ''Yes, he did,'' she admitted.

''No need to put your nose in the air with me! When it comes to women's clothes, Francis Kenmore has exquisite taste. But you need not always let him have his own way about things, you know. As you have no doubt discovered, he has been thoroughly spoiled, which makes a man hard to live with. I could see you'd had a falling-out this evening.''

Belinda flushed and opened and shut her fan.

''Don't tell me what about, for I've no interest in lovers' quarrels.''

''Did you know him as a boy?'' Belinda asked eagerly. Lady Calvin nodded. ''Tell me what he was like.''

Lady Calvin smiled. ''Much the same as he is now. Charming, spoiled, pampered. He was the only child of parents who had given up all hope of ever producing an heir. Had they lived, he might have matured slowly under their guidance, but, as it was, he was left alone at the age of seventeen, extraordinarily handsome, heir to a considerable fortune and with an abundance of personal charm. The result was that, having been kept close and cosseted for so many years, he was suddenly let loose on the world and fell in with the wrong set. A common story. Too much money and not enough to do. Only, unlike many others, Francis had the devil's own luck: far from losing his fortune, Francis increased it. Everything he wanted was his. Not good for a young man, that. He grew to think that everything in this world was his for the taking.''

Belinda met the wise old eyes. She was bewildered by this description of Francis. It certainly did not fit the kind and generous man who had sacrificed himself to help her out of a predicament. Yet, after only a few weeks she had already discovered that Francis Kenmore was an extremely complex person. ''Francis has been very kind to both me and my family,'' she told Lady Calvin.

''Kind? Generous, perhaps, but 'kind' was never a word I would have applied to Francis. Still, I gather marriage must have changed him, and I rejoice to hear it. I always said there was good stuff in Francis Kenmore. It just needed the right woman to bring it out.'' She examined Belinda's countenance once again, without in any way trying to hide the fact that she was doing so.

''You're thinking that I am not his sort of female, are you not?'' said Belinda, jutting out her chin again.

''You certainly are not. He always went for tall, full-breasted females, the kind who would play Lady Macbeth on the stage.''

Belinda blushed. ''And I am small and definitely not full-breasted.''

''You'll do,'' said Lady Calvin. ''You've mettle enough to deal with him. Take my advice: stand up to him when you can, and charm him out of his ill temper when you can't. I opine that you've a good measure of both charm and spunk in you. Use them in equal portions and you'll have him schooled in no time. Men are like horses, y'know. They need firmness and gentleness in equal measure.''

What was the use of all this sage advice, thought Belinda, when in a few months she would probably never see Francis Kenmore again? She swallowed, forcing back the large lump that appeared to have settled in her throat.

''Now,'' continued the loquacious Lady Calvin, ''tell me all about your family. I have heard precious little about any of you since the time of your mother's tragic death. You were how old then?''

''Thirteen.'' Belinda gave her a faint smile and twisted her diamond and sapphire engagement ring around her finger.

''Thirteen. Poor child. Such a great tragedy to strike a promising family. And your poor sister, Marianne, how is she now?''

Belinda met the kindly old eyes and felt relief at being able to speak freely on a subject that was generally prohibited. ''Much the same, I fear. She keeps to her room most of the time. Occasionally she walks about the grounds. That, and her reading, is her life. She reads voraciously: novels, poetry, plays, newspapers—she knows far more about politics than does any other member of our family.''

''No doubt she misses you now that you are no longer at Denehurst; and you miss her.''

Belinda blinked back tears. ''Yes,'' was her succinct reply.

''Well now,'' said Lady Calvin briskly. ''No point in getting maudlin. Tell me about your father and brother, and Denehurst. Most of all I wish to hear how you first met Kenmore and came to marry him.''

Belinda told her almost everything: about her stepmother, and her father's and Bertie's gaming debts, and the mortgaging of Denehurst . . . She omitted nothing but the important fact that her marriage to Francis was merely an amicable arrangement. *That*, no one—particularly this newfound friend—could know.

She had little time to consider that she had been, in effect, deserted by Francis, despite his assurance that he would remain nearby during the entire evening. Lady Calvin was a veritable guidebook to the ton. After one hour spent in Lady Calvin's company she knew just about all there was to know about the cream of London society.

Armed with this knowledge, she danced and held conversation with those of whom Lady Calvin approved. Indeed, Belinda was singularly proud of her achievements this evening. She might not have found a suitable candidate for her second husband, but she had discovered that she was perfectly capable of managing to move in society circles without her present husband hovering protectively at her side.

chapter
<u>10</u>

Belinda was engaged in dancing with an effete young dandy whose pale hair was brushed up into a peak on the top of his head, making him look rather like a pineapple, when she saw that Francis had returned to the ballroom.

She was so happy to see him that she was tempted to rush across the room, until she saw that he was deep in conversation with a striking, fair-haired beauty whose voluptuous figure appeared to be in danger of spilling out of the bodice of her low-cut dress.

A sharp stab of jealousy caught her breath. Then she sharply reminded herself that it was ludicrous to be feeling jealous when this mock marriage would come to an end before the year was out. _Beware_, said an inner voice, and she determined to heed its warning.

A few moments later, Francis came to the sofa where she and Lady Calvin were seated, both engrossed in sharing delicious snippets of gossip.

"I most humbly beg your pardon for interrupting such a cosy tête-à-tête, Dorothea, but I regret that I must tear my wife away. We are expecting her brother Bertie tomorrow, and she particularly requested that I remind her not to stay too late."

They made their farewells to Lady Calvin, with promises on both sides of a visitation before the Kenmores left for Somerset.

"I am glad you came," Belinda whispered to Francis, as they made their way through the throng. "I was delighted to meet Lady Calvin, but I was bored to tears by my dancing partners, all of whom spoke of nothing but the war."

In fact, the main topic of conversation at Carlton House that evening had been the likely capitulation of the French army in Paris, and Napoleon's possible abdication and the restoration of the French monarchy.

"Wouldn't it be wonderful if we could go to Paris?" continued Belinda, when they set off on their short journey back to Grosvenor Square. She was determined to restore their usual rapport and cursed Lord Winchell for having been the cause of this first rift between them, which, no doubt, had been his exact intention.

Francis leaned his head against the cushions, his eyes closed. He opened them to respond. "It is a decided possibility," he replied, in a languid tone. "Many of those I met tonight were already making plans to cross the channel as soon as they received confirmation that Paris had indeed fallen."

She sat on the edge of her seat, staring out the window at the gas-lit streets. It had started to rain, and everything she saw was distorted by the streaks of moisture on the glass. Tears welled in her eyes, induced no doubt by the dismal sight of the rain. She blinked several times, trying to hold them back, but to her dismay found that she could not. What a ninny she was, to be weeping when, in fact, her debut had been quite a success.

The more she held herself rigid, the more the tears flowed. She scrabbled in her crystal-beaded reticule for her handkerchief—to find Francis seated beside her, his arm about her, his handkerchief mopping her tears.

"Oh, Francis," she wailed. She turned her face against his chest, weeping more from relief now than anything else.

"I have been a monster tonight," he told her. "I cannot believe that even I could behave so badly! To berate you after you had had to contend with Winchell by yourself, and then to abandon you on your first outing in society. Monstrous!''

She gazed up at him through wet eyes, smiling a watery smile. "In actuality, I believe it was good for me to be left alone. I must own that I felt rather scared at first, but then I began to enjoy myself. Besides, I wasn't alone, for I had Lady Calvin with me. Did you know that the Prince danced with me?''

"I did. I observed you from afar. To own the truth, although I was sulking like a schoolboy, I did endeavor to ensure that you were managing very well without me. What did you and Prinny talk about when you danced?''

"The war, what else? You would think that the Prince had won it himself, single-handedly, to hear him talk! The war, or the end of it, was what everyone was talking about. I suppose, in a way, that that was fortuitous. It meant that I did not have to invent conversations myself, and I knew enough from having had to listen to Bertie on the subject of the battles in the Peninsula to be able to respond with a smattering of knowledge.''

"Don't tell me your brother is pining for a pair of colors? If so, I regret to tell you he will be unlucky, for we are about to be swamped with discharged officers, I fear.''

"No. The problem with Bertie is that he doesn't really know what he wants to do, apart perhaps from traveling around the world. He is constantly restless. And Papa doesn't even attempt to teach him how to manage the estates, which is too bad of him, considering that one day he will fall heir to Denehurst, if there's anything left of it! Poor Bertie. He was never very good at his books, but he used to spend hours in the library poring over the globe and our large atlas. I sometimes think he would have been happier living in the days of Queen Elizabeth; then he could have sailed with men like Raleigh.''

"He certainly should be permitted to sow a few wild oats before he is forced to settle down.''

"As you did, my lord?'' Belinda smiled up at him, her head tilted mischievously.

"As I did, my sprite; except that, alas, mine was a veritable acreage of wild oats! Speaking of Bertie, you may have noticed that I used him as an excuse for our speedy departure from Carlton House, but I have not forgotten our conversation earlier this evening. If you are not too fatigued to write him a note this evening, I could arrange to have it delivered to him first thing tomorrow morning."

"Are you sure, Francis?" She turned within the comforting weight of his arm to peer up at him.

"Yes, I am, my little one. Despite my reprehensible conduct tonight, it is ever my wish to please you, you know."

"I am well aware of that," she said warmly. "It is just that I do not like to be bullied. It makes me dreadfully stubborn. You can understand that, I am sure," she said in a coaxing tone.

"I can, and shall endeavor not to bully you again. Come, here we are, almost home. Let's kiss and be friends, shall we." He took her face in his hands and tilted it up to his. His lips brushed hers in an achingly brief kiss and then pressed against her forehead.

Resisting the strong desire to fling her arms about his neck, she drew away from him as the carriage halted before Kenmore House.

As she descended the carriage steps, Belinda reflected that the next few months might prove to be, in a paradoxical way, both the shortest and the longest in her life.

The following morning, after a rather restless sleep, she awoke to the unaccustomed clamor of church bells and raised voices from outside. What on earth was happening? It wasn't Sunday and, besides, she knew from the previous weekend that even on Sunday the bells of London churches did not all ring at precisely the same time.

Dragging on her swansdown-trimmed dressing gown, she rushed to the window, kneeling on the velvet-cushioned window seat to peer through the sashed window. To her amazement, a throng of people was flocking into the square, laughing and singing and bearing flags.

She turned as her bedroom door opened and Francis appeared, already dressed in his dark blue morning coat, buff breeches and top boots. He was followed by the chambermaid, who bore a breakfast tray.

"What in the name of goodness is going on?" demanded Belinda, as the maid set down the tray on the oval table, bobbed a curtsey, and departed.

Francis came to stand beside her at the window. "Paris has surrendered to the allied forces. It is now only a matter of time before Napoleon will be forced to accept defeat."

"Oh, what wonderful news!" cried Belinda, clapping her hands. "Peace at last, after all these years!"

"London has gone mad with joy. If you think it is noisy here, Carter tells me that the City itself is in an uproar, with people dancing in the streets and fireworks exploding everywhere."

"How marvelous! Oh, Francis, what a pity Bertie isn't here to see it all."

"Well, that's my other exciting news, my little one." Francis drew a folded sheet from the inside pocket of his coat. "Knowing that we have only a very little time left in London, I sent your message to Bertie by express last night. Here is his reply, received by return this morning."

Belinda took the paper from him, but did not open it. "How very good you are to me." Her eyes searched his. "How can I ever hope to repay you for all you have done for me, for us?"

"You may pour me some coffee for a start," he said lightly, moving away to sit at the table. "Then I must leave you for a while. I must see Perrin about my investments. It will be interesting to see how this news has affected the market."

Belinda bit her bottom lip. How he hated being thanked! She must try to remember that it vexed him.

She poured his coffee, adding a very little cream and two teaspoonfuls of the brown sugar crystals from his own plantation in Jamaica.

He smiled as she handed it to him. "How very comfortable it is to have my coffee prepared just as I like it," he said. He crossed one leg over the other and leaned back in his chair. "Read your letter from Bertie."

She did so, perusing the hastily scrawled lines in a few seconds, and then lifted a glowing countenance to Francis. "He will be here this very afternoon, he says. As the weather is so much improved, he intends to ride. He thinks he should be here before five, just in time for dinner." She laughed. "I fear that demonstrates what rustics we Hanburys are. He has forgotten that dinner in London is served a good deal later than five o'clock."

Francis made no reply. He appeared to be lost in thought, his forehead creased. "Perhaps we should dine early tonight. You may recollect that I was planning to take you to Astley's Amphitheatre for the spectacle there this evening. Come to think of it, they may even put together a special piece on the Fall of Paris. Why don't you take Bertie as your escort?"

"Won't you come with us?" Despite her longing to see her brother, Belinda relished every precious moment she spent with Francis, and had particularly hoped to spend tonight in his company, after the debacle of the previous evening.

"The spectacle at Astley's is not high on my list of preferred entertainment," he said with a cynical lift of his eyebrows. "No, no, you two young people go and enjoy yourselves."

Setting down his cup, he pushed back his chair. "Besides, I shall be escorting you to Almack's tomorrow. I doubt your brother will wish to spend an evening there. He will be hoping for other more masculine pursuits, I should imagine."

Belinda experienced a sinking feeling beneath her heart. "Oh, no, Francis. You surely cannot mean gaming houses?"

Francis bent to run his fingers across the frown on her forehead. "Do not worry your little head, my Ariel. I shall do my level best to arrange that he be steered clear of the less reputable clubs. I intend to place him in the hands of a trustworthy friend tomorrow night. But I would remind you that your brother is of age, little worrier. You cannot be forever trying to keep him locked up. He must learn by himself to curb this tendency to play beyond his means.''

''I know that. But he is so easily led. I fear—''

He bent to press a small kiss on her forehead. ''Do not fear anything. I shall arrange for a watch to be kept on him tomorrow, and shall keep him under my own surveillance for the remainder of the week. But he must find his own way in life, you know, as I had to do.''

''Yes, yes. You are right, of course. It is only that I have always had to take care of him and Marianne.''

''Well, for now, at least, you will allow me to take the burden of responsibility for Bertie from your shoulders.''

As he tooled his curricle down Piccadilly a short while later, it occurred to Francis that acting as nursemaid to a headstrong youth of twenty-one would be a new experience for him.

This entire escapade was proving to carry far greater responsibilities than he had dreamed of. Although Belinda was a surprisingly delightful companion, he found her frequent displays of gratitude confoundedly embarrassing, and her hero-worship of him constrained him to keep a tight check on his temper. There had been several times in the past weeks that he had felt as if he would burst if he could not escape and be himself.

Thank God tonight, at least, he would be able to visit Denise. He would also have to make arrangements to set her up in an establishment in Bath, so that he could visit her there once they moved to Luxton.

No word from Courtenay yet about Rosaline. Of course the child was not due for another week or so. He must remember to send word to Beresford Castle to inform them that he was removing to Luxton at the end of the week.

His hands tightened on the reins, so that his matched grays checked for a moment. Recollecting where he was, Francis slackened his grip a little and concentrated his mind fully on guiding the curricle through the crowded west end streets.

* * *

Bertie Hanbury's estimation of his arrival had not taken into account the impossibilities of being able to move at a regular pace through London when the entire city was celebrating, so that it was nearer six o'clock when he plied the knocker on the imposing front door of Kenmore House.

Belinda had been on fire with impatience and concern since long before five, quite certain that he had been set upon and robbed. She ran down the hall and, not even giving him time to remove his fashionable curly-brimmed beaver, flung her arms about her brother's neck.

"Oh, Bertie. I was convinced that you had had an accident or been robbed."

"An accident?" he repeated scornfully. "Not I! I have never seen anything like it in my life. Wreaths of laurel on every door; dancing in the streets; barrels outside the inns, dispensing free ale to all comers!"

Bertie stepped back, holding Belinda at arm's length, overcome with embarrassment to be caught kissing his sister before Kenmore and all the servants. "Damme, Lindy, you look as fine as ninepence. That's a dashed attractive rig-out you're wearing."

Lord Kenmore moved forward and held out his hand. "Welcome to London, Gilbert."

Bertie gripped his hand, his face reddening. "Bertie, sir. *Bertie*, if you don't mind. Can't abide 'Gilbert'." He drew his hand away, the flush darkening. "Deuced good of you to invite me, sir," he murmured, with a tentative smile.

Lord Kenmore responded with the mocking half-smile that Bertie remembered well. It had the ability to make him feel like a grubby schoolboy. "It was your sister's invitation," said Francis, as he led the way into the library, "but sent with my full approval, of course."

"You are forgetting that it was your idea, Francis," Belinda reminded him.

Lord Kenmore smiled. "I stand corrected, my love. A glass of something to refresh you after your long journey, Bertie?"

"Thank you, sir. But I don't like to sit down here in all my dirt."

"Then stand if you must. A glass of madeira and then I shall show you to your room so that you may change."

"You cannot take too long, Bertie," Belinda informed her brother. "We are having a light dinner, as you are to escort me to Astley's Amphitheatre for the spectacle there."

A beaming smile lit Bertie's handsome face. "Oh, I say. Capital! I have always wished to go to Astley's. I say, sir, that is most kind of you."

The boy's enthusiasm prompted Francis to wonder whether he would have been quite so excited, at the age of twenty-one, at the thought of spending a roisterous evening watching a noisy spectacle that held not one redeeming feature of dramatic artistry or good taste. Perhaps. But the difference was that his excitement would have been hidden beneath the veneer of worldly wisdom he had assumed at an early age, and which consequent experience had made habitual.

This recollection of himself as a youth prompted Francis to bestow an indulgent smile upon Belinda and her brother, so that Bertie was ready to proclaim his brother-in-law, of whom he was very much in awe and more than a little afraid, a capital fellow after all.

It was a memorable evening. The huge amphitheater was packed with people waving union jacks and singing patriotic songs. When the curtains that surrounded the circular center stage were swept back to reveal the skyline of Paris, with the church of Notre Dame towering above it, the crowd went wild. And if the soldiers who fought their way through Montmartre to the heart of Paris wore British uniforms, rather than those of the Prussian and Russian allies, no one was about to register a complaint. For wasn't it Wellington himself who was the brilliant commander of all the allied forces? And weren't the British troops still fighting in southern France to end this long, bloody war for good and all?

So the audience roared its approval, and Belinda, seated in a box high above the swaying, singing crowd in the pit, roared with them, her ears ringing from the boom of cannon and fusillades of shot, her eyes almost blinded by the flashing lights and smarting from the billowing plumes of smoke that issued from the stage.

The evening ended with a stirring rendition of *Rule, Britannia*, which was bellowed rather than sung by everyone there. By the time she and Bertie had battled their way back to the carriage, Belinda was so hoarse she could barely speak.

"Oh, Bertie, what an absolutely marvelous time I have had," she said, once they were safely seated and moving off to cross London Bridge. "I don't think I've ever enjoyed anything quite so much." She flung her arms about her brother's neck and kissed him.

As they were alone in the carriage, he was happy to accept and even return her embrace. "You're happy with Kenmore, aren't you, Lindy?"

"Oh, yes." Her eyes glowed. "He is the kindest and best of husbands."

"Glad to hear it. Must say I'm still surprised, though."

"Oh, you mean because he was once called the Bad Baron? I can't imagine how he could possibly have earned that title. Oh, I know he was a little wild when he was young. And I must own that, even now, he's not perfect, but then I should find it hard to live with a saint, as you well know, Bertie. As it is, I sometimes find it exceedingly difficult always to be holding my temper in check, for you know how easily I can lose it."

"I certainly do," agreed Bertie. "I have the scars to prove it!"

She punched him on the arm. "You have not, you wretch," she cried, laughing out loud. "Anyway, enough about me. You've already told me how Marianne and Papa and Angelica are; now to yourself. What have you been doing since I left Denehurst?"

"Doing? What is there to do at Denehurst? It's a dead bore."

"Are you going to apply to be reinstated at Oxford?"

"What the devil's the point? I'm a dunce when it comes to studying, and I only get into even more trouble when I'm there. If I get sent down once more that's the end of it, so I might as well quit now.''

He turned to her, his face wearing the old sullen expression she knew so well. ''I can't tell you what it's like to be cooped up at Denehurst with nothing to do. I've begged and begged Papa to let me learn something about the management of the estate, but he tells me I'm a blockhead and would only cause trouble. God, I'd do anything to escape the boredom, to see the world. But now that the war is almost at an end, I can't even become an officer.'' His voice was fraught with bitterness. ''I'm an only son, so I can't emigrate to the colonies, and, even with Europe soon to be open to us again, I can't go there either, without money.''

He flung himself back against the cushions like a spoiled child.

Belinda was tempted to slap him and hug him at one and the same time. She kept her hands to herself, clenching them together beneath the soft rug that was wrapped about their knees. ''Oh, Bertie,'' she said with a sigh, ''what in heaven's name are we to do with you?''

She eyed the sulky face beneath the chestnut curls. Since he had been a youth of fifteen her brother had been a constant source of concern. What he needed most was the guidance of an older, more experienced man. Unfortunately Papa was not a suitable guide for anyone, particularly a restless, undisciplined colt like Bertie. ''I sometimes dread to think what will become of Denehurst when you inherit it from Papa.''

''I couldn't be any worse than Papa,'' he shot back at her. ''Never mind all that. What's on the cards for tomorrow?''

''Francis plans to drive us to Richmond Park.''

The project did not appear to excite her brother.

''Perhaps he'll let you take the ribbons for a spell,'' coaxed Belinda.

Bertie's face brightened. ''Lord. Now you're talking. I'd give anything to have the handling of those grays of his.''

''Then, in the evening, we are engaged to go to Almack's, but Francis has arranged for a friend of his to take you to Watier's.''

"I say!" Bertie's good humor was now fully restored. "Your husband is a regular out and outer, Lindy."

Belinda was always eager to agree with any praise of her husband's merits, but by the time Francis returned home, at two o'clock in the morning, her patience had been sorely tried. Determined to share her evening's experiences with him, she had been fighting sleep for the past two hours, for they had made a habit of sharing the last hour or so together, whatever the hour.

She had almost succumbed to sleep, when she heard his soft footsteps mount the stairs and enter his room. She waited for him to knock on the communicating door, but he did not do so. Eventually she dragged herself reluctantly from her warm bed and, pulling on her dressing gown, went to knock on the door.

She had knocked four or five times, growing all the time more exasperated, before it was flung open.

"Good God, never tell me you are still awake!" was his unexpectedly brusque greeting.

He made no move to invite her in, but stood in the doorway, his face marred by a dark, brooding expression. Belinda was forcibly reminded of Lord Byron, to whom she had been introduced that very afternoon when Francis had taken her to view the Elgin Marbles.

"I wish to tell you all about the spectacle at Astley's. You were right, Francis; they did perform the Fall of Paris. I wish you had been there to see it!"

"Better I hadn't." His voice was as icy cold as a day in January. "I should have been so bored that I should have quite spoiled it for you both."

Her eyes widened, but she was determined not to lose her temper with him. "Did you not enjoy your evening?" she asked him in a coaxing tone. She came a step closer, running her hand down the lapel of his coat . . . and inhaled the potent aroma of scent that emanated from him.

She felt as if a cold, hard rock had settled in the pit of her stomach. "Aha," she said lightly, adopting his own mocking smile. "So tonight was an amorous rendezvous."

"What the devil do you mean?" he demanded.

"You reek of scent." All at once Belinda was blazingly angry. "Could you not have waited until the end of our marriage, or at the very least until Bertie went home, before visiting another woman? After all, you have only a few more months to wait until you will be rid of me!"

"Go to bed!"

He was actually shutting the door in her face! She pushed herself forward, bodily preventing him from closing the door. "Which one was it?" she demanded, her breath coming fast. "Denise or Rosaline?"

His reaction terrified her. A look of raw hatred flared in his eyes. He gripped her by the elbows, hauling her against him. "By Christ, you'll explain that remark."

Her eyes shifted from his wild glare to fix their watery gaze on his pearl waistcoat buttons.

His hands slid to her upper arms and tightened, as if he intended to shake a response from her. "Answer me, madam. What made you use those particular names?"

"They were the two names Lord Winchell gave me: Denise Bouchard and Rosaline." She was trembling now. She was also very much afraid that she might break down and weep before him, and she had no intention of giving him that satisfaction. Why, oh why, had she not remained in her warm bed?

She looked up at him, blinking back her tears, to find that the fury had died from his eyes. She wasn't sure that she didn't prefer his anger to the cold, uncaring expression that had replaced it.

"Winchell? Ah, yes, now I understand. You are correct, my lady wife," he said in a harsh voice. "I was with a woman tonight: my mistress, Denise Bouchard. And if you were not a little country hoyden without even the least vestige of good manners, you would have accepted that fact with good grace, as a well-bred wife should, and not railed at me like a fishwife from Billingsgate."

He released her arms and stepped back a pace from her. "I would remind you that you hold no rights whatsoever over me, madam. Even if you did, however, I still would not consider myself answerable to you for my actions. Now, if you will excuse me, I am going to my dressing room to prepare for bed. I expect you to be gone from my room by the time I return.''

He turned away from her, and she retreated silently into her own room. It was only as she was shutting her door that she realized that, although she had learned, to her cost, who Denise Bouchard was, ''Rosaline'' was still an enigma.

chapter

11

The mood of warm companionship that had marked the first week of their marriage was at an end. Indeed, Belinda marveled at her ability to have lasted even two days with such an ill-tempered husband. Lying in bed, she rubbed her eyes dry with a corner of the sheet, and then took great pleasure in pummeling her feather pillow while imagining it to be the arrogant face of Lord Francis Kenmore. Now she knew why he had been dubbed "The Bad Baron"!

She slept very little; another disturbed night. Consequently, when she stared gloomily into the mirror the next morning she saw a small, pale face, made even smaller and paler by the dark smudges beneath her eyes.

"I shall take breakfast in my room," she informed Mary, when her maid carried in a steaming jug of chocolate and some almond honey biscuits. "What is the time?"

"Ten minutes after eleven, my lady."

"Heavens! I must get dressed. My braided green carriage dress and pelisse, I think, for driving to Richmond." That is, if we are still going to Richmond, she murmured to herself. "Tell Denton, if you please, Mary."

"Yes, m'lady." The fresh-faced girl hovered by the door. "Pardon me, m'lady, but his lordship said as how he trusted you would do him the honor of joining him for breakfast downstairs.'' Mary anxiously seesawed from one foot to the other.

"Did he indeed?" snapped Belinda. She was about to issue a scathing comment on the extreme unlikelihood of her joining Lord Kenmore in the breakfast room, but decided against it. Having been accused of behaving like a fishwife from Billingsgate last night, she recognized that it would not be seemly to make unflattering comments about one's spouse to the servants, however great the provocation. "Bring me my robe, the one with the sapphire ribbons, Mary. Then you may advise his lordship that I shall be with him in fifteen minutes."

As Mary scurried away, Belinda applied her silver-backed brush to her hair, trying to bring some semblance of order to her tousled curls. She applied a hint of rouge to her pale cheeks and just a touch of color to her lips. Perfume? she wondered, looking at the beautiful *cloisonné* enamel scent-bottle set with pearls. Definitely not! She had had her fill of perfume last night. His mistress must be a common doxy to apply scent so lavishly that its aroma remained about him. Of course, Frenchwomen were shameless. It was more than likely that she sprayed perfume all over her body, so that when they . . .

She must not think of it, she told herself, springing from the dressing table stool. Although the thought of Francis lying with another woman had seared her mind most of the night, she now was determined to pretend their quarrel had never happened. Otherwise, the next few months would be purgatory for her.

Exactly fifteen minutes later, she slowly descended the main staircase, wondering what she was about to face. The thought of Francis's coldness last night set her shivering.

The breakfast room door being closed, she motioned to the footman not to open it until she gave him the signal. She drew in several deep breaths to compose her nerves and, to her surprise, breathed in a delicate, sensuous fragrance. Heavens, now she was even imagining perfume where there was none!

Nodding to the footman, she braced herself as the door was opened. She stepped across the threshold . . . to find herself in a bower of roses: white and gold and cream and ivory and the palest of yellows. Roses in golden vases; roses in vases of burnished copper; roses in gleaming crystal bowls. Roses on the dining table, the buffet, the occasional tables; on the mantelshelf and the sofa table. Roses, roses, everywhere roses, emitting their heady fragrance.

Francis stood by his chair at the head of the table, his dark eyes watching her reaction. He nodded brusquely to the footman, who hastily retreated, closing the door behind him.

Belinda gazed at her husband. Despite the hundreds of roses massed about the room, she now saw nothing but Francis, registering the new, rather tentative smile that hovered about his mouth. "Oh, Francis," she whispered, her own mouth quivering.

She flew across the room, to fling her arms about his neck, and found herself crushed against him so that she could barely breathe.

"I was certain that you would never speak to me again," she said indistinctly, her face pressed against his striped waistcoat.

"Not speak to you?" He gently put her from him to search her eyes, and then took her face between his hands, forcing her to look up at him. "I thought it would be you who would never speak to me, my little bird." His fingers entwined in her hair. "Can you ever forgive me?" he asked, his voice rough with emotion.

"Oh, my darling Francis, of course I can."

As his face drew nearer, her eyes closed as if they were weighted with lead. She felt his mouth upon hers, but this time it was not one of his brief, chaste kisses. Sweetly, maddeningly slowly, he moved his mouth upon hers, then gently pried it open with his tongue. As her mouth opened to his, his arms drew her even closer. One hand stroked up and down her spine, sending little shivers of delight through-out her body, while the fingers of his other hand brushed her neck, then feathered down her throat, to slip inside the bodice of her robe. His touch was as gentle as gossamer against her breasts.

Belinda moaned deep in her throat as his lips followed the path his fingers had taken.

"My God, how lovely you are, my darling little wife," he murmured against her.

His voice broke the spell.

It was Belinda who pushed against his restraining embrace; Belinda who stepped back, now shivering with the cold, when she had been fiery hot a moment before. "You are forgetting," she whispered. "We must not."

A strange expression entered his eyes, and she knew that for one ecstatic moment he had indeed forgotten. She wished with all her heart that she had not stopped him.

But, no. To permit him to continue would have been foolish beyond belief. To entrap him, so that he would be forced to remain married to her, would only cause him to despise her.

He stood for a moment, bewildered, and then he smiled wryly. "You should not have stopped me," he said, watching her through half-closed lids as she adjusted the bodice of her robe.

She did not trust herself to make an answer to this. "I'm not very hungry," she said. "Shall I pour you some coffee? Then we could sit down and discuss our plans for the day."

"Before we do, there is one matter I must touch upon briefly."

She shook her head vigorously. "Not last night, Francis, I beg you."

"Yes, last night." He took both her hands in his, but did not draw her to him this time. "Shall I tell you why I was so ill-tempered when I came home?"

She shook her head, having no desire to hear any more about Denise Bouchard.

"Look at me, Belinda." He ran one finger down her cheek and twirled one of her curls around it. "I must tell you now, quite frankly, that celibacy does not agree with me. But last night was an utter disaster. Whenever I tried to make love to my ravishingly beautiful mistress, the elfin face of my Ariel interposed itself between us."

Belinda pulled away from him. "Don't make fun of me."

"I am not making fun of you. I am telling you the truth. You quite spoiled my evening."

This time she grinned mischievously at him. "Would you be vexed if I were to say I'm glad?"

"Wretched sprite! First you tantalize me, then you deny me satisfaction, and then gloat at my frustration." Belinda was relieved to hear him chuckle. "Come, little one, now that we are friends once more let us be seated and make our plans for the day like a staid old married couple."

It was a full day that they planned: the drive to Richmond Park, luncheon at the Star and Garter Hotel, then an early supper at home before going to Almack's. Bertie would accompany them until the evening. Then Sir Gregory Follett would call for him, and the two men would set off on their tour of the town.

"I must own that I should feel far less uneasy about Bertie being let loose in London if you were with him," Belinda told Francis.

"He won't be let loose. I have given Follett strict instructions to keep Bertie on a tight rein and not to let him out of his sight at any time."

Belinda sighed resignedly. "Very well, but I shall feel very much relieved once he is in your company."

Although the day in Richmond was a huge success, by the time the evening came Belinda's uneasiness had returned in full measure. Her love for her brother did not in any way blind her to his faults. Bertie's face was flushed with excitement, his eyes unnaturally bright. She knew all the danger signals of old and was forced to clench her teeth to withhold an admonition to him to take care.

"Have a good evening, Bertie." She squeezed his hand, knowing he would be mortified if she were to kiss him.

Her only source of reassurance, as she watched his slender figure leave the room, was that Francis had advanced him only two hundred guineas; that should keep him away from any of the tables where the play was deep.

The rigid formality of Almack's, which kept her continually on her mettle, and the happy knowledge that Francis was by her side, served to banish Belinda's concern about Bertie. She was also aware that she was the object of envy to many of the women there. The gown of silver lace over rose-colored satin was, she knew, especially becoming to her coloring, but she also knew that it was for her husband, not her gown, that they envied her.

The warm look in his eyes whenever they rested upon her was all the approval Belinda needed, but, in fact, although she did not realize it, within one hour she had been judged—and approved—by the all-powerful patronesses who ruled Almack's and, therefore, London society.

"A pretty-spoken girl with an unassuming manner," pronounced the Countess Lieven.

"But with a definite *élan*, don't you think?" added Lady Jersey. "Her smile is charming, and she has none of that rustic awkwardness or mock bashfulness that I do so detest in a young girl."

"Oh, most certainly," concurred the Princess Esterhazy. "And such refreshing enthusiasm. One grows so weary of a pretense at boredom. I think she may well prove a highly suitable wife for Francis Kenmore."

"I agree," said the Countess. "Although I must own to some amazement at his choice of bride. She is not at all what I should have expected."

"But he himself appears to be much taken with her," remarked Lady Jersey, subjecting Lord Kenmore and his bride to further scrutiny. "A definite love match, I think you will agree. It will be most pleasant to have Francis amongst us again."

Thus it was that Lord Kenmore, who had been on Almack's blacklist for more than two years (most regrettably, for the Baron was well liked by the ladies) was restored to favor once more by this unanimous approval of his marriage.

Belinda basked in this heady mixture of approval and envy, but she did not let it go to her head. She had already gathered that success in society could be a fleeting thing, and was therefore determined not to take any of it too seriously.

She was still glowing when they returned home.

"You look positively radiant, my little one," Francis told her. "This debut will be the making of you." He gave her a strange, quirky look.

She tilted her head in a silent question, as the footman helped her out of her cloak.

Francis bent to whisper in her ear. "Never tell me that you have forgotten that you are on the lookout for a new husband."

His reminder was like a dark cloud suddenly covering the sun. She shivered as she met his eyes. They were gleaming with mockery, but there was also some other expression hidden in their depths, which she was far too weary to fathom at present.

"If you will forgive me, I think I shall go to bed directly. I had not realized how tired I am until we came inside the house."

Determined to end the evening on an amicable note, she leaned forward to give him a sisterly hug, and then ran up the stairs before he could say any more.

She had barely entered her room when she heard a rustling sound and saw a movement in a dark corner by the window. She stifled a scream as a figure rose from the shadows cast by the branch of candles that stood on the oval table.

She now saw that it was Bertie. As he advanced into the light, her heart lurched as she smelled the liquor on his breath and saw the hangdog expression she had grown to dread.

"What is it, Bertie? What has happened?" Tossing her reticule onto a chair she went to him.

"Curse it, Lindy!" he blurted out, his face as white as chalk. "I never meant to do it."

Mary had followed Belinda into the bedroom. She stood just inside the doorway, darting glances at them both.

"Come back when I ring for you," Belinda told her. Without waiting for the maid to reply, she bustled her from the room, locked both doors, and then turned to confront Bertie.

"In the name of heaven tell me what has happened, or I vow I shall scream the place down." She grasped her brother's arm and forced him down into a chair.

"Oh, God, Lindy, what am I to do?" He hid his face in his hands.

Stifling a strong desire to shake him, Belinda fell on her knees and gently drew his hands away. "Tell me what has happened. I am certain there is a way out of whatever trouble it is you have become embroiled in, if you will only *tell* me."

"I doubt it." His eyes were wide with terror. "This time I'm truly done for."

She gripped his hands between hers. "Look at me, Bertie," she commanded, "and tell me this instant what has happened or I shall order you from this room, and that will be an end of it."

His eyes met hers briefly and then fixed their gaze on some point above her head. "I lost two thousand guineas tonight."

Belinda's heartbeat seemed to stop. "Nonsense, Bertie," she heard herself say. "You could not have done so. You did not have two thousand guineas to lose."

Bertie closed his eyes in anguish. "He accepted my vouchers. I used Denehurst as collateral."

"You did what?" Belinda yelled, scrambling to her feet. "By God, Gilbert Hanbury, if this is the truth, you really are done for! And this time, remember, there's no out. We can no longer plead the old excuse that you are a minor. To whom did you lose this money, or was there more than one sharp taking advantage of your inexperience and arrant stupidity?"

Bertie hung his head. "Only one."

"Who was it? And by the bye, where was Sir Gregory

when all this was happening? Francis gave me his word that Sir Gregory would keep a watchful eye on you. How did you escape him?''

''He was watching me like a hawk all the time,'' muttered Bertie, ''but I slipped out the back entrance of Watier's.'' His face flushed bright red as he met his sister's wrathful eyes.

''So you went somewhere else?''

''Private club.''

A chill of foreboding crept over her. ''With whom did you go? Who was it that enticed you away?''

Bertie struggled to his feet, to stand, swaying, behind the chair, using it as a protective barrier between them. ''No need for you to know who it was. I'm of age now. My business. I'll deal with it myself.''

This attempt at bravado did nothing to assuage his sister's fears; indeed, it only made her more furious.

''Oh, certainly you will,'' she said scathingly. ''All you need do is turn Denehurst over to this man and you will receive credit for several nights more of gaming! Let us have done with all this flimflammery, Bertie. Who is he?''

His eyes shifted away. ''Not going to like it.''

''I don't like it already. For God's sake tell me.''

He mumbled inaudibly.

''I beg your pardon.''

''I said: it is Winchell,'' he shouted.

''Winchell!'' The chill became a fire coursing through her, flaming into her face. ''By God, Bertie, I could kill you for this,'' she said through her teeth. ''How could you? When you knew what Winchell had done to me! To place me in that man's power once again!''

She had never come closer to hating her brother.

''Gammon! Nothing to do with you,'' he muttered.

''Oh, has it not, indeed?'' She grasped his lapels, forcing him to look down at her. ''You fool! He vowed he would have his revenge on me for having made him look ridiculous. He set his trap, and you fell right into it!''

Bertie's mouth trembled. ''Forgive me, Lindy. I never intended to let it go so far. Winchell gave me his word that the play would be for moderate stakes, and when I began winning, I thought my luck was in at last. I saw my chance of gaining a fortune. I could repay Lord Kenmore, so that he'd no longer think the Hanburys were mere spongers, and I'd restore Denehurst to its former glory. It wasn't for myself that I wanted the money, I swear.''

Tears of recrimination and self-pity swam in his eyes. He sank into the chair again, turning his face into its cushioned back.

Belinda made no move to console him, but stood still, her breast heaving, her mind filled with her hatred of Lord Winchell. She saw now how very easy it would be to commit murder. Her hands clutched together convulsively. ''I shall go to him first thing tomorrow,'' she announced.

Bertie started up. ''No you shall not. I'll not have my sister fighting my battles for me.''

''It wouldn't be the first time.''

''Perhaps Lord Kenmore might—''

She marched forward so purposefully that her brother involuntarily stepped back, fearing that she intended to strike him. ''If you dare to say anything to Francis about this,'' she hissed, ''I shall never, never forgive you. Lord Kenmore has done more than enough for all of us. It is high time that the Hanbury family stood up for itself, instead of forever battening off others.''

''Dammit, Lindy, you cannot expect me to agree to you seeing Winchell alone, surely? There's no saying what that man might do. Let me deal with him,'' pleaded Bertie.

''No, you have no aces up your sleeve. I do. There is one thing above all that Lord Winchell fears. Like his friend, the Prince Regent, he is terrified of public ridicule and will do anything to avoid being made to appear ridiculous in the eyes of society. I intend to employ that weapon against him.''

Bertie could not hide his relief, but he was also filled with apprehension. ''Take care, Lindy. He's a bad man to cross.''

''Too bad you did not think of that earlier,'' she said caustically.

"I know it. Can you ever forgive me?"

She gave him a wry smile and then put her arms about his waist and hugged him. As his arms crept around her, she could feel him trembling.

"Curse it, Lindy," he said, his voice breaking, "I can't think how I'd manage without you. I give you my word it won't ever happen again. Won't you at least let me go with you tomorrow?"

"No. I must do this alone."

Next morning, having bribed a reluctant Mary and the under-footman to keep quiet, she crept down the back stairs and out the servants' entrance to clamber into the hackney coach that stood waiting. Recoiling from the stale air inside it, she sank back against the cracked leather seat to consider the bleak future that lay before her.

Even if she did manage to extricate Bertie from this tangle—for which, in a way, she blamed herself—the thought of a lifetime of dragging Bertie out of scrapes, bailing out her father, running Denehurst with no funds, and keeping Marianne in touch with reality, was a sadly daunting one. Where in heaven's name would she find a husband who would be willing to take on a wife with such insurmountable difficulties?

"First things first," she muttered to herself, squaring her shoulders as the hackney turned down St. James's Street.

Her heart beat fast as she drew down the heavy veil to cover her face. "Wait here for me," she told the jarvey as he helped her down. She stood looking at the imposing house for a moment and then mounted its three steps. The swag of laurel above the door gave it an incongruously festive air, at odds with the heaviness that weighed upon her heart.

Her hand hovered over the bell-pull. She glanced about her, wondering if she were being watched. No doubt she was, for this was the male bastion of London society, home of gentlemen's clubs and lodgings. Still, even if she were being watched, it would be impossible for anyone to recognize her. She was not only heavily veiled, but also clad in an all-enveloping black cloak, which must have looked decidedly peculiar on a warm April morning.

Striving to control the urge to run back to the safe confines of the hackney, she took a deep breath and pulled the bell.

She could hear it pealing within the house; in her imagination, it was like a death knell. Footsteps sounded in the interior hall. For a moment panic swept over her, and she turned to flee down the steps. *You fool! Remember Bertie and Denehurst*, she reminded herself.

Straightening her shoulders, she turned back to wait for the door to be opened.

chapter
<u>12</u>

When Lord Winchell's footman opened the door, he thought at first that the small black-clad figure was a child dressed in adult's clothing and was about to shoo it away, but then the figure spoke in the melodious tones of a well-bred female, demanding to see Lord Winchell.

Although a trifle startled at this strange request at such an early hour, the servant decided that it might be best to refer the matter to his lordship's butler, who was more knowledgeable about the whims of their master, and so he bowed the lady in and showed her into his lordship's library.

It was an expensively decorated but rather cold room, with a blue wallpaper with ivory sprigs. There were several prints adorning the walls and as her eyes grew accustomed to the light in the room, Belinda saw that each print consisted of a male and female figure artistically entwined.

There was no time to examine the pictures more closely—which was, perhaps, for the best—for she could hear heavy footsteps in the tiled hallway, and then Lord Winchell himself appeared.

Belinda was dismayed to see that his portly figure was

swathed in a full-length dressing gown of green velvet. From the swaying of his figure, she gathered that he had not donned his usual corsets. Surely he could have taken a few more minutes to dress! But, of course not. She realized that his appearing before her *en deshabille* was a deliberate insult. This realization prompted her to lift her chin and stiffen her spine as she confronted him across the room.

"My dear Lady Kenmore, what a surprise," he said, his voice like slowly pouring oil. "A wholly delightful surprise, I must hasten to add."

He sauntered across the floor and, before she had time to stop him, possessed himself of her hand and pressed his moist lips to it. She felt as if a snail were slithering across her fingers.

She snatched her hand away, wiping it down the back of her cloak. "Forgive this early intrusion, Lord Winchell," she said in a brisk voice, "but I have some urgent business to discuss with you."

He smiled. "Ah, no. Never say it, dear lady. Pleasure, not business, is what I associate with beautiful members of the fair sex such as you."

Shivering, she took one step back from him, willing herself not to run from him.

"Are you cold?" he asked. "Come, move closer to the fire."

He took her arm. Feeling the hidden strength in his plump fingers, Belinda was reminded of her frantic struggle in the theater box at Tunbridge Wells. The thought made her almost light-headed with fear. As he led her nearer to the fire, she prayed that he might not sense that she was afraid of him.

"Pray be seated, my dear. Some sherry, perhaps, or ratafia?"

She shook her head. "Nothing, I thank you." Still standing, she faced him across the hearth. "I should prefer to get down to business immediately. You must be wondering why I should visit you here in your own home."

"Not at all, dear lady. It is what I anticipated, knowing,

as I do, how your brother always ran to his sister whenever he was in a scrape. Of course, it did occur to me that you might appeal to your husband, but then I realized that your pride would prevent you from asking him to bail your family out yet again.''

Shaking his head, he heaved an exaggerated sigh. ''I am certain that your husband would not consider this visit prudent, but then you always were a trifle headstrong, my dear. If I remember aright, even as a child, prudence was not your strongest suit, was it?''

Wishing to set some distance between them, she moved away from the fireplace to stand behind the sofa table.

''Are you certain that I cannot persuade you to sit down?'' he asked, indicating one of the heavy wing chairs by the fire.

''I prefer to remain standing.'' She was determined not to entrap herself in the confined area by the hearth, hedged in as it was by the two large chairs and the high-backed sofa. ''My brother lost two thousand guineas to you last night, Lord Winchell. Is that correct?''

''He did, fair lady. It is with the deepest regret that I must own that he did.''

''Oh, come sir.'' Belinda's eyes burned with scorn. ''Have done with these pretenses! It was your intention to ensnare my brother; do not deny it. When I so foolishly informed you that he was coming to London, you saw the perfect opportunity to have your revenge.''

She confronted him across the length of the sofa table, her hands tightly gripping the metal clasp of her reticule. ''I have every intention of repaying the money in full, but I cannot lay my hands on such a sum immediately.'' It was a flat statement, with no hint of regret or pleading. ''You will have to wait.''

He spread his plump hands. ''Ah, my dear Lady Kenmore, I regret that you do not comprehend the code of honor amongst gentlemen. I am not a usurer, to make loans to your brother, you know.'' He still smiled, but the unctuous tones now held a thin edge of steel. ''Unless I receive payment within forty-eight hours, I deeply regret that I shall be compelled to foreclose on Denehurst."

Belinda swallowed the large lump in her throat. "It will make a fine story," she told him, summoning up a sugary-sweet smile.

"Story?" he repeated, with a frown.

"Yes, my lord. *Story*. Not only do I intend to circulate this tale amongst Lord Kenmore's friends, but also to see that it is published in the papers. Can you not see it now? 'It is rumored that a certain Lord W., close companion of the Prince Regent, deliberately sought out Lady K.'s brother to fleece him, in revenge for her having jilted him.' I wonder what the Prince would think of that?"

Lord Winchell's face blanched. "You would not dare." His sea-green eyes darkened. "Despite his scandalous conduct in the past, Kenmore would not permit his wife to drag his name through the dirt. No, my dear, you are merely bluffing."

He stepped around the table, laughing softly as she instinctively recoiled from him.

"If you so much as touch me, I warn you my husband will carry out his threat to deal with you."

"Ah, what a flower of chivalry is Lord Kenmore," he sneered. "Always eager to fight for the ladies he loves! But do you seriously think he would again risk permanent exile by fighting another duel? I hear that he was bored to distraction during his sojourn in the West Indies, with only one third-rate theater to interest him. He was willing to make that sacrifice for his fair Rosaline, but would he do it for you, my dear? That is the question. I regret to say that I very much doubt it."

Rosaline. That name again! Belinda's heart jumped as he spoke it. She had come to loathe the very silken sound of it.

"You know, my dear Belinda, you would have been much better advised to have married me, rather than a man who was still obsessed with his love for another woman."

His arm slid around her waist, drawing her closer to him.

Her hand flew up to deal him a stinging blow across the face. "Oh, no you don't!" she cried, springing back from him.

Her eyes blazing, she faced him, ready to strike him again if necessary. "I am leaving now, sir. You shall have your money by the end of the month. I warn you, however, that if you make one move to touch either Bertie or Denehurst, I shall not hesitate to reveal the whole sordid tale of both this plot and of your attempted ravishment of me in a public place. I doubt that the Prince would be willing even to acknowledge you after that."

She turned on her heel and was about to make her way to the door, when she heard a commotion in the hallway. To her utter dismay, she could hear Francis's voice.

"By God, you shall not stop me! Stand aside, or I shall knock you down."

The next minute the library door flew open and Francis burst in, the frightened face of Lord Winchell's butler peering from behind him.

"By God, Winchell, this time you have gone too far." Francis strode forward with deadly purpose, his riding whip clenched in his hand.

Belinda darted across the room to bar his way. "No, Francis. Let him be. It is all settled."

Her husband's eyes blazed down at her. "What the devil do you mean, 'it is all settled'? Go out to the carriage. It should have arrived by now. You will return to Kenmore House immediately."

Seeing that she did not move, he grasped her arm. "*Now*, madam. Out!"

Belinda stamped her foot. "Oh, why did you have to come! I vow I shall *kill* Bertie when I see him. He gave me his word that he would not tell you."

"I had to damn well choke it out of him until he coughed it up." He glared down at her. "Good God, Belinda. Do you realize what a risk you took in coming here alone?"

"Nonsense!" she said lightly. "Lord Winchell and I had already come to an agreement before you arrived, had we not, sir?'' Her expression dared Lord Winchell to deny it.

He gave a sickly smile. ''Why, certainly we had, Lady Kenmore,'' he agreed, seizing the opportunity to escape a thrashing, or worse. Keeping a wary eye on Lord Kenmore, he sank into a chair like a deflated balloon.

Francis looked from one to the other, an expression of mingled fury and amazement crossing his countenance. Then he shook Belinda's restraining hand from his arm and strode across the room to confront Lord Winchell.

Drawing a sheet of folded paper from the inside coat of his pocket, he flung it at Winchell's feet. ''My draft for two thousand guineas. I'll have a receipt for it, if you please.'' He bent down to haul the heavier man to his feet and pushed him toward the desk in the corner of the room. ''And, by God, Winchell, this is my last warning. If you ever again have any sort of contact with my wife, or any member of her family, you will not live to see another dawn. Do I make myself clear?''

Eyes bulging, Winchell nodded. He opened the brass-handled drawer in the desk, drew out a sheet of paper and began to write, the scratching of the pen across the paper the only sound in the room. Then, without uttering one word, he handed it to Francis who swiftly perused it and then stuffed it into the pocket of his pale-gray doeskin breeches.

Before Belinda could say one word, she found herself propelled out into the hallway, down the steps and out to the carriage, into which she was unceremoniously thrust.

''I shall see you back at Kenmore House,'' Francis told her, his face grim. ''I am riding.''

The door was slammed shut and the carriage moved off, the horses' hooves clattering over the cobblestones. Belinda leaned her head back against the cushions, suddenly overcome with such exhaustion that she was trembling from it.

She was torn with a mixture of emotions: anger at Bertie, hatred of Lord Winchell, and apprehension at the thought of the coming confrontation with Francis. But all these paled in comparison with the one phrase that rang in her mind: *A man obsessed with his love for another woman*. That was how Winchell had described Francis.

And the woman's name was Rosaline.

Before this day was out, she was determined to discover who this Rosaline was, even though she knew that any further inquiry would mean she again ran the risk of incurring Francis's wrath.

_____ chapter _____
13

By the time the carriage reached Kenmore House, Francis had already gone inside. As Belinda entered the hallway, the fragrance of roses assailed her, a poignant reminder of their sweet reconciliation the previous morning. Roses had pitifully short lives. Soon their fragrance would turn stale and they would fade and die, even as her amicable arrangement with Francis was drawing swiftly to a close.

She handed her cloak and veiled bonnet to the footman, who forgot his place sufficiently to give her a fleeting sympathetic smile. " 'is lordship's in the library, m'lady," he informed her. Before she had time to find some excuse to delay the meeting she was dreading, he was leading the way upstairs and opening the library doors for her. It was evident that he had received orders to convey her ladyship there immediately upon her arrival.

Her entrance interrupted the tirade Francis was already directing at Bertie, who stood facing him across the Sheraton desk. Although his expression was that of an about-to-be-whipped puppy, Belinda was glad to see that her brother stood straight and tall, his chin raised in a brave but by no means defiant posture.

"Be seated, madam," said Francis. She had never before heard him sound so cold.

"I prefer to stand." She moved to Bertie's side and squeezed his arm, her anger at him dissipating at the sight of his extreme pallor.

"Very well." Francis leaned both hands on the desk and surveyed Belinda and Bertie with dark, glittering eyes. "I was about to place Lord Winchell's receipt for two thousand guineas in your brother's hands."

"You have not yet given me an opportunity to make you an explanation or to thank you, my lord," said Bertie stiffly.

"I have no intention of doing so. We are beyond such niceties, Hanbury."

Belinda thought she had seen Francis in all his variety of moods, but this was a totally different Francis. It was obvious that he was beside himself with rage. It was also obvious that he was fighting to hold his rage in check. His jaw was clenched so tightly that his angular cheekbones jutted out, as if his face were carved in stone.

"I have already conveyed to you my opinion of your abuse of my hospitality," continued Francis, "and of your shabby behavior toward a friend of mine who had given up his evening to escort you about town. What I still find utterly impossible to comprehend is how, having dragged your sister into this mess, you could have permitted her to visit Winchell, unescorted, on your behalf. Good God, sir, what kind of man are you to let your younger sister and, I would remind you, my wife, visit such a man by herself?"

Belinda felt Bertie's arm tremble against hers. "You must not blame Bertie entirely, Francis," she ventured. "I insisted on visiting Lord Winchell by myself. Bertie did not wish me to go."

Ignoring her as if she had not spoken, Francis raised his quizzing glass to his eye to address Bertie yet again. "Are you unable to answer for yourself, Hanbury? Is it not time that you ceased to hide behind your sister's skirts?"

Bertie drew away from Belinda, a tide of red flooding his face. "What more can I say, sir?" he muttered. "I have already tendered you my apologies. I have also given you my word that the money will be repaid as soon as possible. I . . . I deeply regret having involved Belinda in this. I suppose it . . . it is just that we have all grown so used to coming to her with our troubles. I . . . I forgot that—''

"That you are now of age and must henceforth fight your own battles? Exactly so. I advise you not to forget it again. Do I make myself clear?''

Francis came from behind the desk and put a casual hand on the younger man's shoulder. ''Next time you're in a fix, come to me.'' His face relaxed into a wry smile. ''Although this is probably not the time to be telling you this, I do not think that there is one sin you have committed that I myself have not committed thricefold. But there was one difference: I was not fortunate enough to have someone call a halt to my excesses.'' He shook Bertie's shoulder. ''Now, leave us. It is your sister's turn to face my wrath.''

Bertie's chastened expression changed to one of concern. ''You must not place the blame on her, my lord,'' he insisted. ''It is I who am wholly to blame.''

''Well said, young 'un, but she is very much at fault for risking not only her own, but also my good name in visiting Lord Winchell.''

''You cannot—''

''Go!''

Casting a despairing glance at Belinda, Bertie squeezed her hand.

''I shall be all right,'' whispered Belinda. ''Leave us now.''

She did not wait for the doors to close fully before turning to Francis. ''I imagine you will be wanting Bertie and me to leave London,'' she said, having decided that it would be best to anticipate his wishes.

''You imagine correctly.''

''I shall go and make the arrangements immediately.'' Not by one flinch of emotion did she betray her dismay at this abrupt ending to their marriage.

''The arrangements are already made. You have only to give your orders to your personal servants regarding the packing up of your clothing, et cetera.''

"I shall do so." She looked up into his impassive face, a small smile trembling on her lips. "I am only sorry that it had to end this way, Francis. You have been so exceedingly generous to our family, and see how we repay you!"

"Never mind that," he said curtly. "Can you be ready to leave first thing tomorrow morning, do you think? I should like to set off by nine o'clock, so that we may reach Reading long before nightfall."

"Reading? But . . . but I don't understand. Why are we going to Reading?"

"Why? Because we cannot possibly reach Luxton in one day, of course."

"Luxton?" she repeated, utterly bewildered.

"Yes. Luxton." His voice betrayed his impatience.

Belinda's face crumpled. "Oh, Francis, I thought you were sending me home to Denehurst," she whispered, vainly seeking in her reticule for her handkerchief.

"Remind me to go through that reticule of yours one day to find out just what it is you do carry in there," remarked Francis caustically. "It certainly seems to be lacking such mundane items as pins and handkerchiefs." He drew his immaculate handkerchief from his sleeve. "You silly goose," he said fondly, as he wiped the tears from the large blue eyes that were turned up to his. "Did you in all honesty think that I would send you packing because of your brother's folly?"

She nodded. "How could I blame you for doing so? I know it was wrong of me to go to Lord Winchell's house by myself, but you need not have known about it. By the time you arrived, I had him cornered."

He raised one eyebrow. "I see that when it comes to dealing with villains like Winchell my little wife has no need for a Sir Galahad." He took her chin in his hand, running his thumb over her mouth. "I should still prefer, however, that you come to me first."

"Next time I shall, but I've a feeling there won't be a next time. I think Bertie may have learned his lesson at last."

"Hm, I sincerely trust he has. Meanwhile, in the event

that he has not, I have informed him that he is to accompany us to Somerset. I shall also despatch a note to your father to inform him of our departure. I have plans for Bertie, but as they will take some time to formulate, I shall say no more on the subject at present.''

''Oh, Francis, how good you are.'' She took the hand that still rested against her cheek and drew it to her lips, pressing little kisses into his palm.

His eyes darkened. ''Belinda, you are utterly adorable,'' he whispered. His fingers slid through her hair to the nape of her neck. He bent to kiss her, his lips brushing hers in a series of little butterfly kisses that kindled in her an unbearable longing to press closer to him. Unable to resist, she slipped her arms around to his back and pulled him close, at the same time opening her mouth to his.

He seemed surprised, but his response was entirely acceptable to Belinda. ''My little enchantress,'' he said in a husky voice. His arms tightened about her, his mouth seeking hers with a hunger she had never known in him before. His hands were upon her body now, touching, stroking, igniting little fires of pleasure wherever they went. She arched against his lean body, longing more than anything else in the world to become one with him.

In one giddy moment, she found herself swung off her feet and deposited on the chaise longue, with Francis half kneeling upon it, half lying upon her, his hands now at the bodice of her dress.

Now he will be mine forever, she thought exultantly. This time she would not stop him.

He began to slide her skirts up, and she raised the lower half of her body to assist him, thinking to herself, with amusement, how adept at sofa seduction he appeared to be, when, all at once, the library door opened.

''Devil take it!'' Francis sprang to his feet. ''Get out!''

''Pardon me, m'lord,'' murmured the abashed footman. He backed out, hurriedly pulling the door to behind him. But his retreat came too late, for the moment between them was lost.

Belinda sat up, awkwardly pulling her skirts down. She felt both embarrassed and frustrated by the interruption.

Francis paced across the room to stand at the long, sashed window that overlooked the rear garden. *Fool!* he admonished himself. What the devil was the matter with him, anyway, to be so far forgetting himself as to be almost taking the one woman in this world he must *not* lie with! One slip was all it needed for him to be leg-shackled to this sprite-woman for a lifetime. An Ariel indeed, for she must have cast some sort of spell upon him to make him forget what making love to her would mean.

He turned to look at her across the room. She sat watching him with those enormous sapphire eyes. At times the burden of her infinite trust in him was almost too much to bear. He strolled across to her and flicked her cheek with a careless finger. "You almost had me there," he said, smiling his twisted smile. "You really must try not to be so demmed bewitching, my Belinda."

He knew she was hurt by his flippancy. She did not respond to his casual smile, but continued to sit, hands tightly clasped in her lap, gazing up at him.

"Francis."

"My dear?"

She took a deep breath. "Before I go to prepare for our move to Luxton, I wish to ask you one question. But first you must give me your word that you will not flare up at me when I ask it."

"Aha! So now you are beginning to recognize that I have an exceedingly short temper, that I am not quite the perfect knight, after all. That is good." He smiled, but the smile did not quite reach his eyes, which remained wary. "Ask on, O Ariel."

Her hands gripped together so tightly that her nails dug into her palms.

"Who is Rosaline?"

He did not actually move, but she sensed that his entire body had tensed at the sound of the name she had come to dread.

"Why do you ask?"

"Lord Winchell has told me at least twice that I . . . I should ask you about someone named Rosaline."

"Winchell!" He gave her a stiff little smile. "And you are so eaten up with curiosity that, like Pandora, you would open up this one secret box, is that it?"

She nodded, now fervently wishing she could retract the question.

He smiled his ironic, one-sided smile. "I regret, my dear, that you will find the answer a trifle too prosaic for your romantic imaginings," he drawled. He stationed himself like an actor upon the stage, leaning his shoulders against the mantelpiece, his arms folded. "Who is Rosaline, you ask? Rosaline is the Countess of Beresford, wife of Richard Courtenay, a member of His Majesty's House of Commons." He raised his eyebrows at her. "What more do you wish to know?"

Stop there! cried her inner voice, but, certain that there must be more, she ignored it. "What is the Countess of Beresford to you?"

"To me? My dear Belinda, I am shocked! The Countess is a happily married woman." His eyes were full of mockery, but behind his expression was a warning that she was treading on dangerous ground.

"Then what *was* she to you? Lord Winchell said that you had fought a duel over her."

The curtain fell away, and she met the full brunt of the menace in his eyes. "It was not such a tale of romance as you make it appear." His voice was frost-cold. "Rosaline's cousin, Prescott, had attempted to murder her. He was her heir. To avoid a scandal, I forced a duel upon him."

"And killed him?"

"And killed him."

"Why did you fight him? Why not her husband, Richard . . . ?"

"Courtenay. Richard Courtenay. He was not her husband at the time. As a matter of fact, he was my private secretary."

"Oh, I see," she said, understanding nothing.

"As Courtenay intended to embark upon a career in

politics, he could not afford to become embroiled in a scandal by killing his affianced wife's heir. So I did it for him, for them.''

"Oh, Francis.'' Belinda gazed wide-eyed up at him. "You mean to say that you fought this duel on your friend's behalf, and endured exile, to save him and his future wife from becoming involved in a dreadful scandal?''

Francis studied her glowing countenance. "Something like that,'' he drawled.

She sprang up to fling her arms about his neck. "You really are the most gallant and heroic person ever! To do all that: to fight a duel, to leave England and live in exile, all for your friend!'' Tears rushed to her eyes. She drew his head down and pressed her damp cheek to his. Then, coming to her senses, she gave an embarrassed little laugh and stepped back from him, but her eyes still shone with admiration of his heroic self-sacrifice.

He cleared his throat. "I must add, as you have raised the subject of the Countess, that it is not only because of Bertie's escapade that I wish to leave for Luxton immediately. The Countess is about to be brought to bed of her first child, and I have been asked to stand as one of the child's godfathers.''

"You?'' Belinda's voice rose in astonishment.

"Yes. I. Is that so very strange?'' he demanded.

"No, not at all, in the circumstances,'' she hastened to reply, anxious not to hurt his feelings. "It was only that . . . that I did not think you were religiously inclined. Godparents have to make solemn vows to undertake the spiritual guidance of the child, do they not?''

He studied his signet ring. "Not quite in my line, you think?'' he asked grimly.

"Of course it is,'' she replied. "You are such a good and kind person that you will make a perfect godfather.''

Fearing that she might continue to say the wrong thing if she stayed, she got up and walked to the door. "I must get on with the packing.'' She turned when she reached the doorway. "I am so anxious to become acquainted with your friends, Francis. Here I was, thinking that Rosaline must be part of some dark secret of yours, and instead I discover that she and her husband are your good friends. How glad I am now that I asked you about her!''

She closed the door, leaving Francis bemused. He walked to his pedestal desk, aimlessly picking things up and putting them down. Devil take the girl! Glad that she had asked him, indeed! If only she knew what pain she had caused him with this conversation. Still, at least he had been able to talk about Rosaline without giving his true feelings away. But their discussion had brought up one aspect of the matter that he had not considered before: his worthiness to act as godfather to Rosaline's child.

Now he began to understand Rosaline's hesitation when he had suggested that he be her child's godfather, and her insistence that he prove to her that he was a changed man before she would agree to it.

Changed? Upon reflection, he decided, much to his own amazement, that, yes, the past weeks had, of necessity, wrought a change in him. Since the time of his engagement to Belinda, he had learned to curb his quick temper and to tolerate another person's annoying foibles. But, alas, he suspected that these were hardly the momentous inner changes Rosaline had meant when they had first agreed on the wager.

For the first time since this entire insane entanglement had begun, Francis seriously considered the option of admitting defeat and immediately quitting England.

Almost as soon as the thought came into his mind, however, it was rejected. He now had responsibilities beyond his own selfish gratification. Before this sham marriage came to its inevitable conclusion, he was determined to free Belinda of the burdens that for so long had weighed upon her tiny shoulders. He owed her that, at the very least!

No, this charade must continue for a while longer; not so much for his own sake now, but for Belinda's.

chapter
<u>14</u>

Belinda fell in love with Luxton House the moment she caught sight of it, set like a jewel in its beautifully landscaped setting, the sunlight glinting on its windows. Replete with such romantic extravagances as battlements and soaring arches, the two-storied mansion would have delighted Marianne, and any other avid reader of gothic novels. In fact, as Francis had already informed her, the house had been built less than a decade ago to the design of John Nash, the great architect, with much assistance from Francis himself.

"Oh, Francis, how beautiful it is," breathed Belinda. The carriage circumvented the fountain with a life-sized statue of Venus at its center, and drew up before the short flight of wide steps leading to the terraced entrance.

"Ah, but you have yet to see the interior," Francis said, visibly pleased by her appreciation of this, his chief residence.

As Belinda was ushered into the spacious entrance hall, she had only a moment to take in the elegance of the gracefully curving staircase and the fluted pillars of purbeck marble, before turning to meet the row of servants that lined the length of the hall, waiting to greet the new mistress of Luxton.

A spasm of guilt caught her. How happy this meeting would have made her had she truly been the new Lady Kenmore. As it was, she felt like a usurper.

One by one, the servants were presented to her: Besley, the stately, gray-haired butler; Mrs. Griswold, the house-keeper, a most important person to have as an ally had Belinda been a permanent incumbent at Luxton; Carter, Francis's valet, and Berry, his head groom, she already knew; the head cook, who in turn presented to her his kitchen staff . . .

To her utter surprise she was suddenly confronted by two black faces, their teeth gleaming white in broad smiles.

"Oh," Belinda gasped, and turned, open-mouthed, to Francis.

He smiled. "I brought Anna and William back from Jamaica with me. When you taste some of their exotic dishes, you will understand why. And this is their son, Billy. How day, Billy?"

A boy of about nine, dressed in the full regalia of a page—blue satin breeches, gold-braided coat and lace cravat—darted forward to give his master several bobs of his curly head. "I's fine, massa," he replied. He made a deep bow to Belinda. "Welcome to Massa Kenmore's house, m'lady," he said, and then stepped back into the line, his solemn face splitting into a wide grin.

Belinda smiled back. "Thank you, Billy." She had seen a few blackamoor pages in London, but never before had she seen an entire family of black people.

"Are they slaves?" she whispered to Francis, as he led her and Bertie down the hallway.

"Yes."

"But I thought slavery had been abolished."

"No. Only the slave trade itself, and that only in Britain, not in the rest of Europe."

"Oh." She looked doubtful. "So you actually own them?"

"I assure you my slaves are treated no differently than are any of the servants on my estates in England. In other words, better by far than are most indentured servants."

"Yes, but can it be right to *own* human beings, Francis?"

"What do you know about such things?" he demanded, turning upon her.

Vexed at his disparaging tone, she lifted her chin. "My sister and I are great admirers of Mr. Wilberforce and read all the reports about him in the newspapers."

His jaw tightened. "I hardly think this is the time or place to be lecturing me on the emancipation of slaves, Belinda."

"Quite right, sir," said Bertie from behind them. "Stow it, Lindy! I say, sir, what a stunning room!"

"This is the yellow saloon."

Belinda stepped inside and looked about her. She was immediately reminded of the roomful of roses she had left behind at Kenmore House. The yellow saloon was dazzling. Everything—the gilded furniture, the gold and ivory paintwork, the yellow damask draperies—seemed to reflect the glowing warmth of the sunlight that shone in its full-length windows.

"Bertie is right, Francis. It is stunning," said Belinda. "I adore Luxton already."

"You have much to see yet: the picture gallery, the crimson drawing-room, and, most particularly, my theater." His good humor was completely restored by her approval of his home. "Some refreshments first, I think, then I shall show you to your respective rooms. Later, I shall take you on a tour of the house." He turned as the door opened. "Yes, Besley?"

The butler approached him, bearing a golden salver upon which lay a sealed note on cream-colored paper. It appeared to Belinda that the elderly butler was displaying signs of apprehension, although his austere face betrayed no emotion. It was the twitching of the white-gloved hand at his side that gave him away.

Francis picked up the letter. As he turned it over, the blood drained from his face when he saw the crest. "Oh, God," he whispered.

Alarmed, Belinda went to him. "What is it?"

He looked beyond her, as if he were blind. "It is from Courtenay, from Beresford Castle."

"Beresford Cas— Oh!" She gazed at him. "It will be news about the Countess. Open it, Francis."

His dark eyes fixed upon hers as if he were trying to fathom her words and could not. Then he took the letter-knife Besley was proffering and, with one sharp movement, broke the seal. He ran his eyes down the lines. Then, as if he had not comprehended them on the first reading, he perused them again more slowly.

"She has been brought to bed of a son," he informed no one in particular. "A son." He ran a shaking hand across his forehead. "Pardon me. I must speak with the servant who brought this." He almost ran from the room, closely followed by Besley.

"Deuced odd behavior, Lindy," said Bertie. "What's amiss, do you know?"

"Oh, nothing. Nothing at all," she said distractedly. Her fingers itched to pick up the letter, which lay on the desk where Francis had dropped it. All her previous suspicions and Lord Winchell's words flooded back. Bertie was right; to behave in such a frenzied manner because a friend's wife had borne a child *was* deuced odd!

"The Countess of Beresford and her husband are close friends of Francis's," explained Belinda. "This was their first child, so naturally he was rather anxious."

A few minutes later, the door flew open again and Francis reentered. This time he was smiling. He went straight to Belinda and gripped her hands in his. She could see that his black eyelashes were damp. "Forgive me, my dear. I wished to make sure for myself that she . . . that they . . . that both she and the child were well. The messenger says they are thriving. As the child was born five days ago, the danger should now be past."

"I am so glad," she said very quietly, and stood on tiptoe to kiss his cheek.

He blinked. Then his eyes narrowed as if he were trying to focus upon a new scene. "Thank you, little one," he said in an undertone. He gave her a faint smile and then swung around. "Now, Besley, where the devil's that champagne I ordered?"

"I have it here, my lord, having already anticipated your orders." The butler hurried toward the footman, who was already busily involved in pouring the pale gold liquid from a magnum of champagne into the fluted glasses.

Once his glass had been filled, Francis held it up. "My lady wife and my dear brother-in-law, I bid you welcome to Luxton, and then I must ask that you join me in a toast: To the future Earl of Beresford!"

"The future Earl," murmured Belinda, bemused by his almost hysterical excitement.

Two spots of color brushed his cheekbones. "Again!" he barked at the footman, who hastened to refill their glasses, although Belinda had barely touched hers. Francis raised his glass once more. "Another toast, if you please: To the parents of the new Earl, Rosaline, Countess of Beresford and her husband, Richard Courtenay!"

"The parents," repeated Belinda and Bertie. As she sipped the cool, effervescent liquid, Belinda was assailed by a mixture of emotions. Surely, only a man who was still deeply in love would behave so strangely, she told herself.

"Champagne all round for the entire household, Besley," said Francis, dismissing the servants with a wave of his hand.

"Might I read the letter?" asked Belinda, rather tentatively.

"Certainly." He picked it up from the desk and handed it to her. "The child arrived a week early," he told Bertie, attempting to explain his behavior. "The news took me by surprise."

The note was written in a beautiful copperplate hand. Belinda read it to herself. Then she looked up. "What does this part mean?" She read it out loud. " 'We reiterate our invitation to you to stand as godfather to our beloved son at his christening, provided, of course, that you are able to meet the requisite criteria agreed upon when we met earlier this year.' What does Mr. Courtenay mean by that?"

Francis snatched the note from her fingers, the color on his cheekbones deepening. "Lady Rosaline was a trifle leery of having a man of my past reputation as godfather to her child." He gave a self-conscious laugh. "No doubt she and her husband wish to ensure that my reformation is complete."

"And what exactly were these requisite criteria?" asked Belinda.

As if he had not heard her, Francis turned to speak to Bertie. "Come, Hanbury, I'll take you to your room. Mrs. Griswold will show you to yours, Belinda."

Without even a backward glance at her, Francis marched Bertie from the room, leaving Belinda even more convinced that she had not yet learned the truth about his involvement with the Countess of Beresford.

Still, at least she had another few weeks before she had to come face to face with the enigmatic Countess. Besides, she reminded herself, what does it matter to you? In a few more months she would be gone from his life forever. This bleak reminder helped to place her concern about Lady Rosaline in perspective, and she vowed to fret no more about Francis's past but to enjoy each day she was able to spend with him.

"Francis," she said one morning a week or so later, as she was taking breakfast with him.

"Yes, my little one," came the reply from behind *The Bath Herald*.

"When I was out for my ride this morning, I caught sight of one wing of a large old house. Whose is it?"

"Which direction?"

"To the west of us. I saw it from the rise just beyond the west wood. The house was at least three stories high, with great bay windows."

"Ah, you must mean Charnwood. It is a beautiful old house, built in the days of Queen Elizabeth."

"Who is its owner?"

"The young Earl of Ainsworth. His estate marches with mine." Francis bit into a crisp piece of toast and fastidiously brushed the crumbs from his buff waistcoat.

"I should love to see inside the house. Would it be possible to visit there, do you think?"

"I regret not."

Francis retired behind his newspaper again, but Belinda, sensing a mystery, was not so easily put off. "Why? Is the Earl of Ainsworth not resident at Charnwood?"

"He is permanently resident there." Sighing heavily, Francis set down his paper. "Tell me, O sprite: is it your intention to continue this delightful inquisition?"

"What in the world can you mean? I was merely making conversation."

"Precisely. Were you never told that most men prefer to be silent over their breakfast?"

"Oh, I see." She grinned at him down the length of the table. "Just tell me why we cannot pay the Earl a visit, when he is, after all, your neighbor; then I shall be good and not pester you anymore."

"How can I resist such a promise? Very well, my dear. We cannot pay the Earl of Ainsworth a visit because he is a recluse."

"But you said he was young."

"So he is. Twenty-five, twenty-six . . . thereabouts."

"Then why on earth is he a recluse?" Her eyes widened. "Is he crippled . . . or insane?"

"He is neither crippled nor insane." Francis shot a glance at Belinda and then returned to his ragout of lambs' kidneys and tomatoes. "I have met him only a few times, most of them by accident. He is handsome enough: fair-haired, medium height, slender build. But he has a speech impediment, an excruciating stammer, that makes him so painfully shy that he shuns all social intercourse."

"Oh, how sad! That sounds exactly like Marianne."

Francis laid his knife and fork on his plate. He leaned back in his chair, the fingers on his right hand toying with the gold fob on his watch-chain. "Belinda, what exactly is the matter with Marianne? You have never told me. For a long time I wondered if she might be, well, not quite . . ."

"Sane? That's what most people think. It makes me so angry! Marianne's one of the sanest and cleverest people I know!"

"I'm relieved to hear it. But you cannot blame people for thinking the worst when your family never offers any explanation, can you? Your sister hid herself away whenever I was at Denehurst. She refused even to come to our wedding breakfast. You must own that that is not exactly normal behavior. Would you be so good as to satisfy my intense curiosity and tell me what is wrong with her?''

Belinda hesitated, separating the shreds of orange marmalade on her side-plate. "She hates me to tell anyone, but I suppose she would understand if I were to tell you."

Francis patiently waited, his tomatoes and kidneys growing cold. The footman indicated that he would warm them up again, only to find himself ordered from the room. "And tell Besley that we are not to be disturbed," added Francis as the door was closing.

Belinda looked down at her plate of steamed haddock topped with poached eggs, and then pushed it aside, no longer hungry. She sat upright and looked directly at Francis.

"As you know, my mother died when I was thirteen. What I have never told you is that she died from the smallpox. Marianne insisted that no one but herself should nurse Mama. 'I am the eldest,' she said. 'It is only right that I should do so.'" Belinda drew the fringe of her linen napkin back and forth through the prongs of her fork. "She would not permit me even to enter the sickroom. Two days after Mama died, Marianne fell sick."

Francis had to strain to hear her now, so low had her voice become.

"We thought she would die, but our old housekeeper came to nurse her, and eventually she recovered."

The napkin was now being drawn so frantically through the fork that Francis expected soon to see it shredded to pieces.

"Marianne was the most beautiful girl you have ever seen: Thick hair the color of ripe chestnuts; brilliant blue eyes; a perfectly proportioned figure—she is taller than I am now by about five inches. She was the epitome of perfection in every way imaginable." Belinda's voice grew hoarse. "Her . . . her complexion was as delicate as the finest porcelain, all palest pink and white."

She hesitated. Even from a distance, Francis could see that her eyes were awash with tears. Although he longed to go to her, he remained perfectly still.

"Such beauty," she whispered, shaking her head. "Such

perfect beauty." She began to rock back and forth in her chair, quietly sobbing.

Francis started up. When he reached her, he knelt down to gather her into his arms as if she were a small child, his hand smoothing her cheek, her hair.

"Don't you see?" she sobbed against him. "It should have been me, not Marianne. I was the plain one, the untidy one, the tiresome one. It should have been *me*."

"My poor little darling." He cradled her in his arms as she blurted out all her pent-up guilt and remorse. Most of what she said was incomprehensible, but that did not matter. What did matter was that she was at last able to share the almost unbearable guilt she had felt for so many years.

Eventually he lifted her and carried her to the chaise longue by the window. She was shivering convulsively. He put his arm around her, drawing her head onto his shoulder.

After a while, she sat up. "What a ninnyhammer you must be thinking me," she said, sniffing loudly.

"Not at all. I am glad that you told me. It must have been extremely difficult for you to bear all these burdens without a mother to advise you. But if your mother had lived, do you know what she would have said about Marianne's self-sacrifice?"

He tilted her chin up and peered into her tear-drenched eyes. She shook her head, half smiling at his earnestness.

"She would have informed her youngest child that it was not only natural but right that her eldest daughter should nurse her. Being the firstborn brings not only privileges, but also responsibilities, as I am sure Marianne herself has told you."

"She has, a thousand times. She becomes exceedingly vexed with me when I argue with her about it."

"And so she might. What is the point of endlessly mulling over what is past and irreversible?"

"It is just that . . . her life is utterly blighted. Oh, Francis, if you were able to see her face you would understand." She turned from him to stare out the window at the tubs that stood on the terrace, filled with scarlet geraniums.

"I *shall* see her face," was his eventual reply.

"When? What on earth can you mean?"

His lips slid into a secretive little smile. "I have an idea. You are sadly missing your sister, are you not?"

"You *know* I am."

"Very well. You will write your sister a letter this very morning, telling her how much you miss her and begging her to come to Luxton. She will be promised absolute privacy and need not even meet me if she does not wish to."

Belinda's eyes grew enormous. "She will never come."

"I shall assist you in writing the letter. Perhaps we should tell her that I beat you."

"Oh, Francis," gurgled Belinda. "Do be serious."

"No?" He tilted his head, his eyes dancing at her. "Perhaps that is too extreme. Never mind. If you make your appeal sufficiently heart-rending I doubt that your sister, with her strong sense of duty, will be able to resist it."

"And then?"

"And then, once we return from Beresford Castle, Marianne will pay you a long visit. You will then have both your brother and sister by your side, so that you will cease to worry about them."

"And that is all?" she asked, sensing the air of excitement he was trying to conceal.

Francis drew away from her and stood up, to strike a dramatic pose by the window, eyebrows—and quizzing glass—raised. "Not quite," he drawled. "I also intend to entice the reclusive but eminently eligible Earl of Ainsworth from his lair."

Belinda sat bolt upright, her tears forgotten, to gaze at him with open-mouthed astonishment. "You mean . . . Marianne and the Earl?" she asked incredulously.

"Exactly so," replied Francis, and he stepped forward and executed his most flourishing, theatrical bow to his audience of one.

chapter
<u>15</u>

Having completed their meager breakfast, Belinda and Francis swiftly repaired to the library to write the letter to Marianne. The library was one of Belinda's favorite rooms. The predominant colors at Luxton, crimson and gold, were repeated in the wallpaper and carpeting, with a contrasting ceiling of ornately decorated plasterwork, its panels painted a delicate *eau-de-nil* green, the ornamental work picked out in gold.

Francis went to sit behind the mahogany pedestal desk, which was topped with red moroccan leather inlaid with gold. Setting several sheets of paper before him, he took up the pen, dipped it in the marble inkwell, and began to write, frowning in his concentration.

Belinda paced about the room, agitatedly picking up books and setting them down. She was both excited at the prospect of seeing her sister and fearful of the disappointment she might suffer if Marianne refused their invitation. "She will never come," she declared. "Nothing could persuade her to leave Denehurst."

"Would you kindly sit at peace or leave the room!" said Francis. "I am attempting to write a first draft so that you can then adapt it to your own style of writing. But I cannot

150

concentrate with you darting about the place like a distracted hen!''

Grimacing, Belinda meekly chose a book from the shelves and sat in the chair beside the desk.

The book being a dry tome about ancient Rome, she soon set it aside, content to sit and observe Francis as he worked. His head was bowed over the desk, so that all she could see was his dark, wavy hair and classic profile. One long-fingered hand moved the quill pen quickly over the sheet of paper while the other held it in place. He wore two rings, a heavy gold signet ring on his left hand and a large, square-cut ruby in an ornate gold setting on his right.

Could this man achieve the seemingly impossible: persuade Marianne to leave her refuge at Denehurst? Belinda's heart stirred with a sudden feeling of hope, which Francis's own exuberant enthusiasm had instilled in her.

Her eyes dwelt lovingly on his bowed head. How dear he had become to her in the past weeks! He was far more human than the knight in golden armor she had at first envisaged, of course; more human—and, alas, infinitely more dear. It had taken her jealousy of both his mistress and Rosaline to open her eyes to her own heart. As each day passed, she was reminded that she had one day less to spend with the man she had grown to love.

''What do you think of this?''

She blinked, startled by his voice.

''Wake up, little one. Where were you?''

Her smile was fleeting. ''I was merely thinking that we have been married more than three weeks.''

''So we have.'' His fingers ran up and down the feathers of the pen. ''It has all gone rather well, has it not?''

She nodded, not trusting herself to make an unemotional response.

As their eyes met, his breathing quickened. ''Belinda,'' he began, setting the pen back in the inkwell. Then he hesitated.

She looked questioningly at him, her head tilted to one side. For a moment he surveyed her face, as if he were seeing it clearly for the first time, then he leaned forward to ruffle her curls. "Come, imp of my heart. To work. Read this and see if it will do."

Wondering what it was he had been about to say, she read the letter he had drafted. So filled was it with poignant allusions to her loneliness and her longing for home, and to have her beloved sister beside her, that it might just work. Had it been addressed to her, she certainly would have been unable to resist it!

"This is excellent," she told Francis. "You should take up writing."

"My dear child, I have written and privately produced four plays. Were you not aware of that?"

How she hated it when he assumed his haughty, superior expression. "How should I?" she snapped. "I am continually being told by your friends how great an actor you are; how marvelous were your theatrical productions at Luxton! You seem to forget that I have never seen any of this for myself."

"You have that pleasure to come."

She bit back a suitable rejoinder. Whenever he spoke of the theater, she felt left out. Had she truly been his wife, she would have asked him to teach her all about plays and acting, so that she could be part of his world, but . . .

He leaned across the desk to run his finger down her cheek. His hand smelled of almond oil. "Before our time together comes to an end, Belinda, I mean to put on *The Tempest*, with you in the role of Ariel. I swear it."

She laughed uncertainly. "I doubt you would be pleased with my performance."

"I am always pleased with you, my sweet. And your Ariel would please me greatly, I am convinced of it. The only problem would be the costume. I am not sure that I wish an audience, even one consisting of friends, to see my wife's delightful figure revealed in the brief costume Ariel should wear."

She was tempted to remind him caustically that by the time his dream of putting on *The Tempest* came to pass, she probably would no longer be his wife. Instead she took up the pen. "I must get on with the letter."

She began to write, forcing her mind to concentrate only on Marianne.

The long-awaited reply did not arrive until two days before their planned departure for Beresford Castle.

By then, deeply disappointed and greatly concerned that Marianne might be unwell, Belinda had given up hope of even receiving a reply to the letter. "You see," she had told Francis. "I knew she would not come. But I cannot comprehend why she has not written in reply. I am convinced that she is either extremely vexed with me for having invited her, or else she is not well."

It was Francis himself who came looking for her when the letter arrived. He found her in the archery yard, standing with Bertie before the butts, her bow poised in her hand.

"The bow's as tall as you are," he said as he approached them. Belinda looked extremely fetching in a plain, round Indian-cotton dress and short spencer, which admirably suited her diminutive stature and slight curves.

Not wishing to break her concentration, Belinda made no reply to Francis's comment. She released her arrow and it whistled across the green to land less than an inch from the edge of the bull's-eye.

"Very well done," cried Francis, surprised. "Bertie has taught you well."

Bertie laughed. "Lord, she surpassed my teaching years ago. Lindy's been shooting arrows with me since she was eight."

Francis raised his slanted eyebrows in recognition of his wife's prowess at the butts. "Forgive me for interrupting you, but I have here a letter for Belinda, which I imagine she might wish to read."

She flung her bow to the ground. "Is it from Marianne?" she cried, dragging off her leather gloves. "Oh, why didn't you say so before?"

"Because I am not absolutely certain that it is from your sister. I didn't wish to disappoint you." He handed her the letter. "As you can see, it bears your father's crest."

She ran her thumb under the seal and ripped open the

letter. "It is from Marianne," she told them, her voice shaking with excitement.

She walked away to the white cast-iron bench beneath the large horse chestnut tree and sat down. Only then did she begin reading the letter.

> *My dearest sister,* Marianne had written in
> her neat hand. *Your letter must have been
> heaven-inspired!! I have been missing you so very
> much and now, without even Bertie to jolly me
> along, I find myself in a melancholy mood far
> too frequently for my good. I was desolate to
> learn that you have been so exceedingly un-
> happy.*

Belinda felt a pang of guilt at this. Perhaps they had overemphasized her unhappiness in the letter to Marianne.

> *It is far worse for you, situated as you are
> far from your home and the scenes of your
> childhood.*

She had never realized before quite how much Marianne was growing to sound like the novels she read!

> *Your invitation to come to Somerset tore me
> asunder. In part I was determined to leave for
> Luxton the very next morning after I received your
> letter; yet I shrank from such a journey, from
> the thought of having to encounter strangers, in
> particular your dear husband, Lord Kenmore.
> Even now I am still convinced that he would be
> appalled to find that you have such a hideously
> disfigured sister, and perhaps revile you for not
> having disclosed my dark secret to him before
> your marriage.*

"Oh, lord," groaned Belinda to herself. "Now she'll be thinking I'm married to a tyrant."

But was Marianne coming or not? She hurriedly scanned the rest of the letter, straining to read the close-written lines that crossed the pages and ran around their borders.

> *... and so, my beloved sister, with terror and yet not a little excitement at the thought of what lies ahead, I have at last come to the decision to venture forth from this house, my haven for my entire life until now, to journey to Luxton to bear you company and, I hope, cure your melancholy. The thought of your unhappiness is insupportable; you, who have been my dearest companion and consolation all these years, to be permitted to remain unhappy? Never! It is but a small sacrifice that I must make to ensure the well-being of my darling girl.*
>
> *All I beg is that you send Bertie back, so that he may accompany me on my journey. I do not think I could undergo it alone, with only a servant to bear me company. If it is possible, please beg him to come very soon, before I lose my courage.*
>
> *And so, my dearest Lindy, I say au revoir. Until we meet again—which will be in a very short while, I promise you—I remain your loving and ever-grateful sister, Marianne.*

Belinda sprang from the bench. "She's coming," she shrieked. She raced across the green. "We did it!" she cried, flinging herself against Francis, hugging both him and the bow he was holding at one and the same time.

"I can't believe it!" said Bertie.

"You must. There!" Belinda stuffed the letter into his hands. "Read it!"

She was so beside herself with excitement that she jumped up and down, clapping her hands together like a small child, so that her chipstraw bonnet slid off and hung askew.

Smiling down upon her like an indulgent parent, Francis

straightened the bonnet and retied the apple-green ribbon at a jaunty angle beneath her chin.

"How can I ever thank you enough?" she said, catching his hand and holding it to her cheek.

"Now, none of that," he admonished her.

"No, Francis. Do be serious for once. You do not seem to realize what you have achieved. No one has been able to coax Marianne from Denehurst. She hasn't been farther than the village church since her illness. I can never thank you enough."

Bertie looked up from the letter. "I must echo that, sir," he said, smiling his attractive, boyish smile.

Francis appeared embarrassed. "I did it solely to make Belinda happy," he told Bertie shortly.

"And you have," said Belinda. "I have never been happier than I've been in these past few weeks, and now my happiness is complete. Indeed," she added with a giggle, "Marianne is going to think it exceedingly strange that I appear so content at Luxton, when I wrote to her with such a harrowing description of my unhappiness!"

She took Francis's arm and walked back to the trees with him, not wishing Bertie to overhear what she wished to say. "Even if the other thing—you know, with the Earl of Ainsworth—doesn't come to anything, and I doubt it will, I am so happy to know that Marianne will be here with me and that she will see Luxton—Oh, Francis, how she will love Luxton!—and will meet the most wonderful man in this world, my husband." Her hand tightened on his arm, and she gazed up at him adoringly.

There was no mistaking her feelings. They were revealed to Francis as clearly as if she had shouted out her love for him at the top of her voice. This was not mere hero-worship that shone from the brilliance of her eyes. He had known too many women intimately not to recognize the unmistakable signs of a woman deeply and irrevocably in love.

Christ in heaven, how had he permitted it to go this far? Yes, he had wished it to appear that this was a love match, but he had never stopped to consider how deeply Belinda might be hurt in the process.

He gripped her hands tightly in his. "Belinda," he said urgently. "I must speak with you in private. I—"

"Pardon me, sir." Bertie appeared behind Belinda.

Curse the boy! Francis released Belinda's hands. "Yes?"

"You haven't yet had the chance to read Marianne's letter. She wishes me to go to Denehurst to fetch her as soon as possible, but I am not certain . . ." His voice trailed off, as he realized that he was interrupting a private conversation between man and wife.

For a moment Francis hesitated, as if he were trying to gather his thoughts. Then he gently set Belinda aside.

"A capital idea, Bertie. You shall set off early this afternoon in the smaller traveling chaise, with the under-coachman, and take Berry with you. You may trust him to make the arrangements along the way, but mind you take note of all he does, so that you may learn the traveling ropes for yourself. A gentleman must be prepared for all contingencies, even the unthinkable one of journeying without any servants to see to his needs!"

Placing his arm about Bertie's shoulders, Francis marched him off to make the preparations for his journey, leaving Belinda to wonder, once again, what it was that Francis had been about to say to her.

chapter
<u>16</u>

Two days later Lord and Lady Kenmore set off for Beresford Castle to attend the christening of the future Earl of Beresford. The castle, which lay just within the border of north Devon, was a day's travel away from Luxton, and they were hoping to reach their destination before nightfall.

As far as Belinda was concerned, she would have been perfectly content if they never were to reach it. As soon as Bertie had left Luxton, she had begun to make preparations for their visit to Beresford Castle, but Francis had shut himself away, spending most of his time in his study, so that she was unable to approach him. This strangely reclusive behavior caused all her old apprehensions about the Countess to sweep over her once again. She had been positively looking forward to meeting Lady Rosaline and her husband until that day when Francis had received the news of their child's birth. Now she was dreading it.

The change in the scenery about them did nothing to allay her fears. For one who was used to the gentle rustic lanes and green rolling downs of Kent, the last stage of their journey was like venturing into a terrifyingly alien world. The treeless moor stretched as far as she could see, bare but for a few sheep cropping at the rock-strewn grass. The moor was not flat, however, but mountainous, sloping down to incredible ravines. The hills were so steep that twice Francis and Belinda were forced to descend from the carriage and climb the almost vertical slopes on foot.

Her apprehension was in no way mitigated by Francis, who sat grim-faced, rarely addressing more than a few words at a time to her.

Eventually she turned to him from her contemplation of the dizzying drop to the white-capped sea hundreds of feet below. "Are we almost there?" she asked in a small voice.

Francis turned. His face was pale and tense. "I should imagine it will not be much more than half an hour." He was about to turn his eyes back to the landscape when something in her expression must have caught his attention. "Is something the matter?"

She shook her head, giving him a valiant attempt at a smile.

Frowning, he moved across to sit opposite her, his knees pressed comfortingly against hers. "I haven't been much of a companion to you on the journey, have I?" He took her hand in his. "Forgive me. But then I don't believe I have ever known you to be so quiet, either. Usually you are as chirpy as a canary in a cage."

"I am not used to all this." She waved her gloved hand at the vast expanse of moor and craggy rocks. "No doubt Mr. Wordsworth might find it romantic, but to me it is utterly terrifying."

"Exmoor terrifying?" He looked surprised. "Well, yes, I suppose in a way it might be to one who is not used to its wild terrain. But having been raised nearby and having hunted here since I was a youth, it holds no terrors for me."

"And Lady Rosaline? Has she always lived here?"

He gave an almost imperceptible start. "As far as I am aware, she has. But she, too, loves Exmoor, although I believe she was not overenamored of the castle itself. I am not surprised. I remember it as a bleak and drafty place with massive stone walls."

Belinda shivered. "Then it is not like Luxton?"

"Lord, no. Luxton's a sham castle, whereas Beresford's an ancient pile more than five hundred years old."

Although Belinda was not usually of a timid disposition, by the time the carriage climbed the hill to the castle gate, she was feeling quite sick with apprehension. She leaned forward to peer at the turreted towers and the forbidding walls built of huge blocks of stone.

Now they were drawing up before the massive oak door, whose iron bars and nails would have withstood any attempt at invasion. With her heart thumping against her ribs, Belinda took the liveried footman's white-gloved hand to descend from the carriage. Francis proffered his arm; she slipped her hand into it, and they were led inside.

She found herself in a vast, echoing great hall with a soaring hammer beam roof, its wainscoted walls hung with ancient tapestries. About to remark to Francis how much Marianne would love this place, Belinda felt the muscles beneath her hand tense. She knew even before he had disengaged himself from her that the woman entering the hall must be Rosaline, the Countess of Beresford.

"Francis, Lady Kenmore," she cried in a rich, vibrant voice as she hurried across the hall to greet them, hands outstretched.

Belinda's heart plummeted. Lady Rosaline was the most strikingly beautiful woman she had ever seen. Almost as tall as Francis, she had a voluptuous figure. This was enhanced by her gown of dark green velvet with its unusual crossover bodice, whose folds clung to her body. The gown, and her rich auburn hair that lay on the nape of her long neck in a heavy coil, made her appear like a woman from another century, as if she had stepped down from a painting by Titian.

Francis clasped both the outstretched hands. "My God, Rosaline, you look positively radiant," he exclaimed reverently. His eyes shone as he bent to kiss her hands.

She laughed: a deep, rich sound. "Certainly I do. Motherhood agrees with me immensely, does it not, Richard?"

She turned to address her husband, who had followed her

into the hall, and who now came forward. "It does indeed, my love," he replied.

Richard Courtenay was a very large man, a good few inches taller than Francis, with massive shoulders. To Belinda's surprise, she saw that he wore gold-rimmed spectacles. Despite the spectacles, it was still hard to imagine this man as Francis's private secretary.

"Welcome to Beresford, Lady Kenmore," he said, smiling. He had one of the warmest smiles Belinda had ever encountered, and the large hand that clasped hers was also warm and welcoming.

"Oh, what a rattlepate you will be thinking me, Lady Kenmore!" exclaimed the Countess. "To be greeting Francis before you! I echo my husband's welcome—a trifle belatedly, I regret to say." Her dazzling smile was as warm and friendly as her husband's had been, but Belinda was also aware that she was being keenly assessed by the beautiful emerald eyes.

Francis appeared to be slowly coming out of his trance. "Mine is the blame for not having presented Belinda to you first." He made one of his exaggerated, almost mocking, bows to the Countess and her husband. "May I present my wife, Belinda: Belinda, may I present my dear friends Lady Rosaline, the Countess of Beresford, and her husband, Mr. Richard Courtenay." His mouth tilted into a smile. "There, now we have satisfied convention."

"Thank you for your welcome, Lady Rosaline, Mr. Courtenay," said Belinda. She lifted her chin proudly, determined not to let herself be intimidated. "May I offer my sincerest good wishes on the birth of your son."

"You may indeed," said Lady Rosaline with a laugh. "You may also submit yourself to being persuaded to come and see young Robert—Robin, we call him—even before I permit you to go to your rooms!"

"Perhaps we should offer Lord and Lady Kenmore some refreshment before the obligatory viewing of our son and heir?" suggested Mr. Courtenay.

His speech was slow and measured, with a hint of a

country burr, but behind his spectacles his brown eyes twinkled at his wife.

The bond of love between this man and woman was almost tangible. Belinda had come to Beresford prepared to detest the Countess and her husband; but she knew already that, were it not for her suspicions about Francis, she and they could soon become fast friends.

"What am I thinking of!" cried Lady Rosaline. "The excitement of seeing Francis again and of meeting his bride must have quite turned my brain. Will you not come into the drawing room to meet our other guests?"

Francis turned to Belinda with a questioning look. "What do you think, my dear? I, for one, must own that I should prefer to wash off some of this dust before I do anything else."

Belinda was delighted to have a chance to catch her breath. "Yes," she agreed, looking down at her dust-smeared pelisse and gloves. "If you would not mind, Lady Rosaline, I think that I also would prefer that."

"Then I shall have you shown to your rooms immediately, and order hot water and refreshments to be conveyed to you there. We keep country hours at Beresford, Lady Kenmore, so we shall be dining at seven. No formalities, if you please. Rest until then, if you wish. Our greatest desire is to have you feel at home in our home."

A servant appeared at her elbow and, within minutes, Belinda was ensconced in a magnificent suite of rooms in the west wing of the castle. The bedchamber would have proved a sad disappointment to Marianne, hung as it was with watered silk, with a pattern of pastel-colored stripes, to cover the gothic stone walls. The furniture was not sturdy oak, but light mahogany with gold inlay. The bed, although large, had tented hangings in the same blue and shell-pink silk as on the walls. The entire decor was a delightful contrast to the stone-mullioned window that overlooked the moor and the cliffs beyond it.

When they had both completed their toilette, Francis came to join Belinda in her room. He nodded a dismissal to

Denton and Mary, who left immediately and closed the door behind them.

"This is not at all what I had expected from your description of the castle," said Belinda, looking about the bedchamber. "I could hardly believe it when I saw it!"

Francis poured himself a glass of madeira and sat down, crossing one long leg over the other. "Now I come to think of it, when we last met in January, Rosaline did say something about having made the castle a comfortable place to live in, as had been done with Warwick Castle."

He got up to walk about the room, peering at the Watteau paintings, lifting and examining the various objets d'art on the dressing table and mantelshelf. Then he swiveled around to face her. "What do you think of . . . of them, Belinda?" he asked, his manner uncommonly tentative.

"Of Lady Rosaline and Mr. Courtenay?" she asked slowly, trying to give herself time to formulate a suitable reply.

"Naturally," he said impatiently.

It occurred to Belinda that Francis had never appeared more handsome, or more dear, than he did now, clad in his wine-colored dressing gown. How eminently suited to each other he and the Countess would have been: two beautiful people.

"It is difficult to say, when I have only just met them." She looked down at the silver-backed buffer she had been using to polish her nails. "Mr. Courtenay seems a very kindly man, extremely shrewd as well, I should imagine. Someone whom you could trust implicitly. And Lady Rosaline? She is, without exception, the most beautiful woman I have ever seen."

A line of dull red appeared over his cheekbones. "Yes, she is, is she not," he said, almost feverishly. "Yet without the conceit that normally accompanies such beauty." He came forward, his expression anxious. "You do not mind me admiring her, do you, my little one?"

Belinda's heart beat furiously. "Mind? Certainly not. No one could hope to compete with such beauty." She met his troubled eyes without flinching.

"My God, Belinda, you are a woman in a million!"

She found herself crushed against him, his arms holding her so tightly that she could barely breathe. She felt his lips on her hair, and then her face was lifted up to his. His mouth bore down on hers in a kiss so raw and passionate that his teeth bruised her lip.

She did not resist him, but, with a little sob, flung her arms about his neck and responded without any restraint, allowing all her pent-up tension to go into this release.

His hands explored her body, cupping her breasts and kissing them above the bodice of her shift, running over her hips, molding her to him . . . so that she became so frantic with longing that she felt impelled to tear off her clothes, and his.

"Belinda," he groaned against her mouth. "My darling little wife." He swept her up and carried her to the canopied bed. His fingers undid the sash on her dressing gown, and she lay there in nothing but her light, almost transparent, muslin shift.

A strange sense of peace stole over her. Somehow it would be fitting for their marriage to be consummated here at Beresford, where all her needless fears had been centered.

He dragged her shift down to her waist, fully exposing her small breasts, and rained kisses on their soft curves. Writhing against him, she clasped his head in her hands, her fingers splayed through his crisp, dark hair.

She felt his weight upon her and, although he was still dressed in his shirt and small clothing, their bodies moved together in the same rhythmical motion, the sweet, ecstatic tension building, building . . .

Then, all at once, it was over almost as soon as it had begun. Having lit the fire that threatened to consume them both, Francis rolled off her body and, without another word, left the room, crashing the door shut behind him.

Once again she was left frustrated, aching with desire. She lay on the bed, her own hands moving over her body where his hands and lips had been. But it was not the same. Turning her face into the pillow, she wept.

* * *

When he came to escort her downstairs, Francis was silent, at first merely squeezing her hand before slipping it into the crook of his arm.

"Are my eyes red?" she asked him in an aggressive tone.

He looked. "A trifle pink, that is all."

"Good. I had Mary put pads soaked in witch hazel on them."

He halted at the top of the wide oak staircase. "Forgive me, Belinda. I should not have gone so far. It is only that I find you so devilishly alluring that I cannot resist you, although I know I must."

Belinda was not quite sure whether to believe him, but she was flattered that he should find her, a little dab of a female, alluring after having spent some time in the company of the beautiful Lady Rosaline.

It was, therefore, a smiling and seemingly content Lady Kenmore who was presented to the small company of a dozen or so guests in the Great Chamber, a magnificent room paneled in oak with a high, painted ceiling.

For a while, Francis remained by her side, remarkably attentive. Even after they had separated, he sent her secret little signals across the room, raising his eyebrows and smiling, so that she felt confident and secure in this new environment.

Her short stay in London had added a great deal of town bronze, but she could not help uttering a gasp when she was introduced to a frail little man, who peered at her shortsightedly.

"Mr. William Wilberforce?" she repeated incredulously. "The famous abolitionist?" Realizing, too late, how gauche she must sound, she could have bitten her tongue. "Pardon me, sir," she muttered. "I meant . . ."

His eyes twinkled at her. "My dear Lady Kenmore, I cannot imagine a more flattering greeting." He indicated the sofa on which she was sitting. "Would it be possible for us to have a little talk together before dinner, do you think? I have been hoping for an opportunity to do so."

"Really?" Belinda was mystified. What on earth could the famous philanthropist want with her?

"I leave you in good hands, Lady Kenmore," said Mr.

Courtenay. He turned to Mr. Wilberforce. "But I would again remind you, my dear friend, that your brief visit here is supposed to provide you with a short respite from business."

"Pray be seated, Mr. Wilberforce," said Belinda, as Mr. Courtenay moved across the room to speak with Francis. "You know, my sister Marianne will be green with envy when I tell her that I have met you. She is a great admirer of yours and reads all the reports about you in the newspapers." She turned to Mr. Wilberforce as he lowered his crooked little body slowly onto the sofa, as if any movement pained him greatly. "Why should you wish to speak with me, Mr. Wilberforce? I fear that when it comes to politics, I am woefully ignorant."

He smiled his gentle smile. "How refreshing, my dear lady. I am delighted to hear it. I cannot tell you how wearying it is to be ever surrounded by politicians. Fortunately I have six young children at home to keep me from becoming a crashing bore. When one is weighed down with work, a game of cricket or blind man's buff is a powerful refreshment for the weary mind."

Belinda was enchanted by this engaging little man, but she was still extremely curious to know why he should wish to speak with her.

"But you must be anxious to know what it is I wish to speak to you about," he said, reading her mind. "As it is nearing the hour for us to go in to dinner, I shall not waste time. I wish to sound you out, as it were, regarding your husband's feelings about slavery."

"Slavery?" repeated Belinda with a frown. "Ah, now I comprehend. But should you not be speaking to Francis himself about that?"

"Yes, yes, I intend to do so. But it is most helpful to know in advance whether I am meeting a strong adversary, so that I must be prepared to exert the utmost diplomacy, or an ally, in which case I sincerely hope to recruit your husband to our ranks."

"Might I enquire, to do what?" asked Belinda, even more bewildered. Somehow, she could not imagine Francis immersing himself in politics. "I thought your work was drawing to a close now that the slave trade has been abolished.''

"Oh, my dear, my work has only just begun! And I have been engaged in the battle for thirty years.'' He leaned forward, his thin hands placed squarely on his knees. "You see, now that the war with France is almost at an end, we hope to persuade France—and the rest of Europe—to abolish *their* slave-trading practices. Although abolition in Britain was a fine achievement, the practice continues elsewhere. My ultimate goal, of course, is not only the abolition of the trade itself, but also emancipation of all slaves.''

His eyes shone. Belinda understood how this great man's oratory could sway so many to his cause. With his melodious voice and tremendous enthusiasm he might capture any man, even Francis.

She tilted her head to one side. "Emancipation?'' she prompted.

"Yes. The freedom of all slaves. I fear, however, that I shall not live to see that day. But there will be others to carry the torch after I have gone. What I am most in need of now are allies in the House of Lords to support us in this move to persuade France toward abolition. If France agrees, then all of Europe will follow. Now, perhaps, you will comprehend my reason for wishing to speak with you. When I heard that Lord Kenmore would be here, and was to act as godfather to my dear friend Courtenay's child, I saw it as an act of divine providence.''

"But why Francis? Are there not many other active members of the House of Lords? To own the truth, I am not at all certain that Francis ever goes there!''

"Doesn't,'' said Mr. Wilberforce succinctly with a boyish grin. "Found that out. You see, Lady Kenmore, to recruit your husband would be a double victory because he himself is a slave owner.''

"Ah,'' she said, "*now* I understand.''

"Exactly so. To have a plantation owner with numerous slaves on our side would be of tremendous significance in our campaign, don't you see?''

She did see, but was loath to admit that she could not

share Mr. Wilberforce's buoyant optimism about Francis. "I am not certain that he would be interested, sir. When I asked him only recently if it were not wrong to own human beings, he told me that his slaves were treated far better than are most indentured servants."

"I do not doubt it. In many cases, that is true. But it does not alter the fact that to own another human being is abhorrent in our enlightened age."

With any other person she might have sprung to her husband's defense, but Mr. Wilberforce did not appear to be in any way judgmental on the subject.

"What do you think?" he asked her, blinking rapidly. His fingers drummed restlessly on the arm of the sofa. "Shall we give it a try?"

She felt as if she had been enrolled in a conspiracy, but at the same time she was convinced that this was a conspiracy to accomplish some good, not evil. "Why not?" she exclaimed, suddenly excited by the idea. After all, Francis was a man who did not hesitate to come to the aid of a female in distress, was he not? Perhaps the cause of slaves would also rouse his chivalrous instincts.

"You look as if you were hatching some sort of plot," said the subject of their discussion.

Belinda started, the blood rushing to her cheeks.

"Your servant, Wilberforce," said Francis. "No, please don't get up, sir." He held out his hand to the older man. "We were introduced two months ago, at the Theatre Royal, I believe."

"Ah, yes," said Mr. Wilberforce, with his gentle smile. "I have not forgotten."

Before any further exchange could be made, dinner was announced. Although the topic of slavery was the subject of general discussion at the dinner table, no further mention was made of the wooing of Francis. The discourse was informal, at times even heated, with the ladies freely joining in and openly proffering their opinions.

Belinda marveled at this. She herself was content to sit and observe, not feeling confident enough to contribute to the conversation, but she envied the women. As she listened, she vowed that, one day, whatever happened and to whomsoever she was married, she, too, would be capable of joining in such a discussion.

When Mr. Wilberforce began to speak, most of the actual discussion lapsed; the company was content to sit and listen. But Francis spoke up, challenging him, arguing with him, while Belinda marveled at the delicacy with which Mr. Wilberforce dealt with him. She had the feeling that Mr. Wilberforce was drawing information from Francis without his realizing it, and without antagonizing him in any way. It was a masterful performance.

She was delighted to see, as the Countess led the ladies from the room, that Francis went to take the chair beside Mr. Wilberforce, evidently eager to continue their discussion.

When they had sat for a while in the drawing room, Lady Rosaline came to her side. "I am going to the nursery for Baby Robin's feeding," she said quietly. "I hesitate to sound like a doting mama, but would you care to see my little treasure? The rest of the ladies have seen him already, and I doubt that Francis will be overenthusiastic about becoming acquainted with his godson before the christening. But do not let that concern you; it is always different when it is the man's own child, you will see."

Belinda was happy to accept her invitation. Although the other women, most of them wives of prominent politicians, were not at all condescending in their attitude toward her, she was painfully aware of her own inadequacies, and began to wish that she had listened to Marianne more closely when she had read items from the newspapers to her. But her mind had always been on such important matters as wondering if their threadbare sheets could stand one more turning, or whether she could persuade the local ironmonger to extend their credit yet again.

She therefore welcomed this opportunity to escape. Besides, although she was a trifle in awe of the beautiful and majestic Countess, she was also determined to discover more about the relationship between her and Francis.

chapter
<u>17</u>

The nursery was a delightful suite of two small rooms opening into one another: The first, a playroom in whose corner sat a dappled rocking horse with wild black eyes and a worn red leather saddle. Upon a table stood a doll's mansion with several windows made of real glass and a pillared entrance; a little girl's delight. The other room, a bedroom, contained the child nurse's bed, a small white-painted wardrobe and a large cradle of weathered oak, festooned with a lace canopy.

The nurse was sitting in a rocking chair, trying to soothe the irate baby, whose indignant screams were almost deafening in the small room.

"Oh, my poor little Robin. Forgive me, Lady Kenmore," said the Countess. "I had hoped to stave him off for a little while longer. Will you excuse me?"

To Belinda's surprise, Lady Rosaline delicately turned away to undo the bodice of her dress, sat down in the rocking chair, and accepted the red-faced baby from the nurse, discreetly enfolding him against her breast with a shawl.

The baby's screaming died to a whimper which, in turn, became an ecstatic grunting and sucking sound.

"Sit down beside me." Lady Rosaline indicated a small tub chair.

Belinda sat, enthralled by the picture of contentment made by the mother and child.

"Are you shocked that I suckle the baby myself?"

"No. Merely surprised."

"Ah, 'tis the Irish peasant in me, I suspect," said Lady Rosaline with a musical laugh. "My mother was an actress from Dublin, you know."

She leaned her head back to observe Belinda with her vivid green eyes. "Are you happy?" she asked unexpectedly. "With Francis, I mean."

Belinda liked her direct manner. "Oh, yes," she replied eagerly. "He is the kindest man imaginable."

Lady Rosaline's eyebrows, which were darker than her hair, rose. "I am glad to hear it. Yours was a brief courtship, I believe."

Belinda blushed. "It was. Fairly brief." She proffered no further explanation.

"But you do love Francis, do you not?"

Belinda looked down at her locked hands and then at the Countess. "I love him with all my heart," she said vehemently. Embarrassed, she turned her head away to look about the room, wishing to escape those searching eyes.

"I cannot tell you how happy that makes me!" Lady Rosaline leaned across the baby to touch Belinda's hand. "Has Francis ever told you what he did for me, for us?"

"The duel? Yes."

"Were it not for Francis I probably would not be alive. My treacherous cousin was extremely resourceful in trying to eliminate me so that he might become the Earl of Beresford. And had Richard been the one to kill him in the duel, it would have put an end to all his political aspirations. We shall be eternally grateful to Francis."

This was Belinda's chance. "Had you known each other long, you and Francis?" she asked in a light, conversational tone.

Now it was Lady Rosaline's turn to blush. "Ah, so he has not told you that part of the story. You must ask him one day, perhaps when you have been married a little longer.'' The full lips parted in a smile. ''Suffice it to say that I was disguised as an actress when I first encountered Lord Kenmore, and, at that time, he did not carry a very high opinion of actresses' morals.''

''Oh,'' said Belinda. ''Oh, dear.''

''Precisely. Unaware of my true identity he . . . ah . . . laid siege to me. The unfortunate thing was that when he did discover who I was, he came to the realization that he truly loved me. But, alas, I was already in love with Richard. Poor Francis. But all this happened a very long time ago, you must realize.''

Belinda sat up very straight, her hands gripping one another. ''Does he still love you, do you think?''

Lady Rosaline's eyes widened in surprise. She waited until she had moved the baby to her other breast before replying. ''No, my dear Belinda—I may call you Belinda, may I not? I do not think so,'' she said firmly. ''I saw how Francis was looking at you before dinner. But why do you ask? Were you concerned that he still imagined himself to be in love with me?''

Belinda nodded.

A chuckle escaped Lady Rosaline. ''Francis does not like to be thwarted. I believe his parents were excessively indulgent when he was a child. As a man of the theater, he is also given to enacting melodrama in real life. Until he met you, I believe he saw himself as the lover who had lost his one true love. It may take a little time for him to realize that it was nothing but a dream, that his marriage to you, his obvious love for you, is the reality.''

For one wild moment Belinda was tempted to blurt out the truth, that Francis had married her to rescue her from Lord Winchell, nothing more, but she held her tongue.

Seeing her hesitation, Lady Rosaline quickly changed the subject.

''Mr. Wilberforce has spoken to you, has he not?''

''Yes,'' replied Belinda. ''Did you know that he was going to?''

''Oh, certainly. Richard is one of his chief supporters in

the House of Commons, you know. In fact, it was his suggestion that Mr. Wilberforce make an attempt to recruit Francis to the cause. You see, Belinda, when we met Francis in January, after his return from Jamaica, he vowed that he was about to become a new man, that he would take his seat in the House of Lords, and marry.''

The Countess looked down at the baby's head, a gentle smile on her lips. ''I had no doubts at all that he would do so. When he asked if he might stand as godfather to the child I was expecting, we told him that he must prove himself worthy of such a responsibility. It was then that we agreed upon the wager. But, of course, Francis will have told you about our wager.''

''Wager?'' Belinda frowned and shook her head. ''No, I don't think so.''

''Never say he didn't tell you! Ah, well, it is of no matter now, for he has won it fair and square; as I knew he would, once he set his mind to it.''

''What was this wager?'' asked Belinda, bewildered.

''Why, that he would fall in love, and marry the object of his love, before the date of our child's christening, and that the love must be mutual.''

It took a moment for the words to penetrate Belinda's puzzled brain. As they did, an icy pall began to wrap itself about her, starting at her chest and slowly enveloping her entire being.

''. . . we both felt that with a good marriage and a new way of life, Francis was capable of great things,'' the Countess was saying. ''So, you see, my dear Belinda, your husband has won his one hundred guineas. I have never before been so eager to give such a sum of money away!''

It had been a wager. Not a chivalrous impulse, a wager. Not kindly concern for a female in distress. He had proposed this arrangement of theirs solely to win the wager, nothing more. And the Bad Baron had won his wager!

''Is something the matter?'' she heard Lady Rosaline's voice say from afar.

''No, no. Nothing at all. I am just a trifle dizzy, that is all. If you will excuse me, I think I should retire to my room.''

Lady Rosaline was all concern. "You are probably fatigued from the journey. Mrs. Grainger shall go down with you to—"

"No, thank you. I shall mange to find my own way," said Belinda agitatedly. "I should be grateful if you would make my apologies to your other guests."

"Certainly, I shall. Good night, my dear. Forgive me for not rising."

Belinda's fingers brushed the baby's tiny head in its soft linen cap. "He is beautiful," she whispered, blinking back tears.

"One day soon you and Francis shall have a child. A child is God's greatest blessing."

"Yes." Belinda turned away abruptly, almost running from the nursery, her eyes now blinded with tears.

But by the time she reached her room she was cold with fury. How dare he deceive her thus! How dare he make her believe that he had married her out of chivalry! He was an accomplished actor, indeed, to catch her in his web and woo her so that it would appear to others, in particular the Countess and her husband, that she was deeply in love with him.

What an utter fool she had been!

She thought of all those times when they had come so close to consummating their marriage—or so she had thought; it was all contrived, no doubt, to keep her off balance, to increase her love, her physical desire for him.

Love? She loathed and despised him. And she would have her revenge. Oh, yes! She stood in the center of the silk-draped room, her eyes glittering. Tomorrow, just before the christening, she would publicly denounce him in front of his "one true love."

She laughed harshly. "We'll see how the proud baron will like that!"

Yes, tomorrow the Bad Baron would lose, at one and the same time, his wife, his good name, and his one hundred guineas.

chapter

<u>18</u>

"So, Kenmore. You have won the wager." Richard Courtenay smiled good-naturedly at Francis as he handed him a balloon glass of cognac.

The two men stood alone in the library together, having repaired there to see the portrait of Rosaline's mother, in her role as Portia, which was displayed above the mantelpiece.

"Is that an intimation that I have passed the crucial test?" asked Francis, with his mocking smile.

"So it appears. Rosaline is convinced that you and Lady Kenmore are happily married and love each other."

"And you?"

"As long as Rosaline is convinced, that is all that matters."

Francis was content to leave it at that. The relationship between himself and Courtenay was still tenuous. How could it be otherwise? "I must own that I had been wondering how you would contrive to reject me as godfather to your son at the very last minute."

Courtenay smiled again. "Oh, we have our spies in London. They had already given us excellent reports on your marriage."

"Ah, of course. I had forgotten that you were acquainted with Dorothea Calvin."

"And Lady Jersey."

"Ah, yes. Lady Jersey, the town crier of London society."

Before any more could be said, Rosaline hurried into the library. "Ah, so you *are* here. I must return to the ladies or I shall be considered an extremely negligent hostess. And now I find that you, too, have deserted our guests, Richard." She turned to Francis, her eyes glowing. "You have an utterly charming wife, Francis."

"So my marriage has received your stamp of approval, my fair Rosaline?"

"It has, indeed. It is quite evident to me that you are both deeply in love with each other."

His eyes glinted with amusement. How ridiculous women were with their romantic notions!

"You need not smile, my lord. Belinda will know very well that it is not fashionable to display one's affection in public, but I can tell that you are happy together."

She gripped his arm, sending a tingling warmth up it. She still held the power to excite him. "Take great care of her, Francis. She will need all your guidance and support to ease her into the role you will expect her to play as your wife. But try not to eradicate that freshness and lack of prevarication that is her charm."

He made her a bow. "I shall look to you as her mentor."

"No, Francis. The last thing your wife needs is to have me as her mentor," she replied in a serious tone. "We are two very different women."

Her eyes met his in a long look. His were the first to fall away.

"Now, we must return to our guests," she said briskly. "Tomorrow you shall have your one hundred guineas, Francis. Tonight I expect you to meditate on the heavy responsibilities you are about to assume as young Robin's godfather."

"Oh, lord. Don't remind me. I have already been made to feel totally unworthy by Wilberforce. Over our port he read me a lecture on the grave responsibilities of a godparent." He gave a whimsical smile. "Tell me, Courtenay, did you invite Wilberforce to act as co-godfather to ensure that your child receive adequate religious guidance from one godparent at least?''

"Something like that," said Courtenay, with a rumbling laugh. "Come, let us join the ladies."

"Oh, Francis, that reminds me," said Rosaline. "Belinda was feeling not quite the thing and has asked me to make her excuses."

Francis frowned. "What is the matter, do you know?"

"I think she is merely fatigued from the long journey. She said she felt dizzy." Her eyes widened. "Do you think she could be—"

"Hardly, after only one month," said Francis dryly.

"For heaven's sake, my love," said Richard. "You will be putting Francis to the blush." With a shake of his head and a rueful smile at Francis, he took his wife's arm.

"I believe I should go up and see Belinda before I join you," said Francis.

"Good idea," said Richard, and with a firm hand on his wife's elbow, he escorted her from the library.

For a moment Francis remained, trying to impress the memory of Rosaline's beauty upon his mind, so that he would always remember it, but his concern for Belinda intruded, and he quickly made his way upstairs.

He had to knock twice on the door of her bedchamber before Denton admitted him. "Where is Lady Kenmore?" he asked.

"I am here," said Belinda from the bed. She was not actually in bed, but lying on top of the covers. "Thank you, Denton. You may tell Mary to bring me some hot milk in about fifteen minutes. I shall ring when I am ready for it."

As soon as Denton had closed the door, Belinda slid from the bed, tightening the sash of her rose-pink lace dressing gown as she walked to the center of the room. Her entire body seemed to be drumming to the heightened beat of her heart.

"Why are you here?" she asked in a glacial voice.

Francis frowned. "Rosaline said you were unwell. Fatigued from the journey. I came to see if you were in need of anything, that is all."

"Oh," said Belinda with a catlike smile. "I thought perhaps you had come to show me the one hundred guineas you have won from the Countess and her husband."

Francis did not move, neither did he speak, but his eyes bored into hers like steel gimlets. "Who told you?" he demanded, after a long pause.

"Why, Lady Rosaline, the beautiful Countess herself, told me." Belinda strode forward, her dressing gown swirling about her. She halted a few paces from him, to confront him, hands on hips.

"By God, Belinda, you look magnificent when you're angry! I can see you on the stage now, a passionate, diminutive Viola, clad in tights, with a sword swinging by your side!" The mocking smile was there, but something else lurked behind his eyes.

"You can cut the bluff now. There is no longer any need for you to perform the role of admiring husband, my dear Baron."

"How can I fail to admire you when you attack me like a wildcat, your eyes glowing like sapphires?" His eyes ran over her appreciatively. "I prefer this to a milk-and-water wife."

Her fingers curled into claws. "You . . . you are loathsome, despicable," she spat at him.

He leaned his shoulders against the closed door, sliding his fingers up and down the crimson ribbon of his eyeglass. "Perhaps you will eventually come around to telling me why your opinion of me has changed so drastically," he drawled.

"You know very well why. You led me to believe that you were marrying me for chivalrous reasons—to rescue me from Lord Winchell—when all the time you were doing it to win this . . . this ridiculous wager with Lady Rosaline." As she spoke her name, she aped the Countess's rich voice.

"My dear Belinda, if you cast your mind back to the time before our marriage, you will recollect that it was not I who in any way attempted to deceive you; it was *you* who jumped to the romantic conclusion that I must be marrying you solely to save you from Lord Winchell's clutches.

Under those circumstances, you hardly could have expected me to tell you the truth, now could you?'' he said in a persuasive tone. ''And as it suited both our purposes to have you invest me with a cloak of gallantry, I chose not to enlighten you. Can you in all honesty blame me? After all, one of my reasons for marrying you was, in fact, to rescue you from Winchell.''

Belinda's breast heaved. ''You are a . . . a villain,'' she told him. She immediately wished she had not chosen such a melodramatic word, for it made his lips twitch, which only left her more exasperated.

She glared at him, biting her lips to stop the tears of disappointment and rage, at the same time overcome by a great sense of loss.

He stepped forward to clasp her limp hands in his. ''A villain indeed to make you so unhappy, my little one,'' he said in a low voice.

She longed to feel his arms about her, to rest her head against him, but that was all over now. She snatched her hands away. ''I may be unhappy, but I shall have my revenge,'' she snarled, her eyes narrowing. ''Tomorrow, at the christening of Lady Rosaline's precious little treasure, I intend to denounce you! Everyone there shall know that our marriage is a charade. You will lose not only your precious wager, my lord, but also your good name.''

''That I lost a long time ago.'' His face was like a mask, drained of all color. ''But for the past week I had thought that I might, I just might, have found the means of regaining it.''

Belinda opened her mouth to utter a scathing retort, but then closed it again.

''Something held me back, however,'' he continued. ''I am not certain what: a fear of commitment, perhaps? Or a dread of becoming bored? Your spirit greatly attracted me, but at times you seemed subdued in my presence. Now I believe I understand. You were in awe of me, am I right?''

''In awe of you?'' she growled. ''I thought of you as some great hero, a saint. Ha! Some saint!''

"Poor Belinda. And now your idol has come crashing down from his pedestal."

She continued to confront him, wary of him in this new role.

"It will not be necessary for you to denounce me tomorrow," said Francis. "I intend to speak to Courtenay immediately. I shall inform him that we are leaving the castle first thing tomorrow morning."

"Oh, so you are afraid to face the music!"

His eyes met hers. "No. Although I agree that you might deserve the opportunity of humiliating me in public, I do not intend to have a solemn occasion ruined because of my folly and your desire for vengeance. The embarrassment and unhappiness such a denunciation would cause would hurt many others, not me alone."

Belinda's heart sank. He was right, of course, damn him!

"I shall go directly to inform Courtenay that we shall be leaving tomorrow." Francis turned toward the door.

"They will have to find another godfather."

Francis turned back to respond. "That will not be difficult. There are at least four candidates from amongst their friends who are here at present, and many more will be arriving in the morning." He gave her a wry smile. "It may cause you some amusement to know that the reason I was chosen was that Rosaline also saw me as something of a hero. 'Ah, what fools these mortals be.' There are others here who are far more worthy than I to act as the child's godparent."

"She will be so disappointed." The words were dragged out from somewhere deep within Belinda, surprising her.

"Rosaline, you mean? Yes, she will be. She will be even more disappointed, however, to discover that I am not the reformed character she had hoped for. What fools *women* be," he misquoted bitterly.

"You still love her, don't you?" said Belinda bleakly.

"I thought I did." He drew his fingers across his forehead in a gesture of uncertainty that was not at all like him. "I was certain I did. All the time, during that year in Jamaica, I was kept from falling into utter degradation by the hope that she would tire of Courtenay, that their marriage had been a monumental error. They could not possibly be suited to each other. Then I returned to England to find that theirs was quite obviously a supremely happy marriage." He smiled wryly. "Now I find them happier still with their firstborn child. It was the end of a dream."

Belinda swallowed. She was determined not to let him know she was moved by his words, but she was aware that she was seeing Francis Kenmore as few people had ever seen him, open and vulnerable.

"Once we return to Luxton I shall be going home to Denehurst as soon as I am able to make the arrangements," she told him.

He was about to quit the room, but slowly turned back. "We are both forgetting one rather important factor."

"Oh? What?" she demanded, prepared for some devious tactic.

"Your sister, Marianne."

Belinda's hand flew to her mouth. "Oh, dear God," she whispered. "I had completely forgotten that she and Bertie were due to arrive a week or so after our return! Oh, Francis, what in heaven's name are we to do?" she cried, turning to him from force of habit.

It was all too much to bear. She swayed, her head spinning. Then his arms were about her in a supportive embrace. The longing to lean against him was irresistible.

"Shall we sit down and talk this over like two rational people?" he suggested.

She nodded, willing to do anything that would clear away this muddle in her head.

He sat her down on the grecian-style sofa in front of the marble fireplace. Then, flipping aside the tails of his evening coat, he sat beside her. "For the past few weeks, Belinda, you and I have been taking part in a masquerade. We have convinced our relations and our close friends that we are a happily married couple."

He took her limp hand in his, drawing his fingers down the back of it. She made no response, not even that of drawing her hand away.

"I may be suffering from acute self-deception," he continued, "but I have frequently been under the impression that we ourselves have been happy together in this so-called marriage of ours, apart from the certain constraints that were imposed upon us!"

He halted, hoping this might elicit a slight reaction from her, but, seeing that her expression did not change, he pressed on.

"I am in full agreement with you that it is time we put an end to this arrangement of ours, Belinda. My solution to the entire problem is that we make the contract a permanent one."

She started, certain that she had misheard him. "Are you asking me to be your wife?" she demanded.

"Yes. A strange proposal, I know, considering the fact that you are already my wife, but it is, nevertheless, a sincere one."

Her mouth fell open in astonishment. "Never!" she declared, her eyes blazing with indignation. "I would rather die than live permanently with you!"

He shrugged. "Very well. It seemed the perfect solution. What do you intend to do about Marianne, then?"

"Lord, I wish I knew," she sighed. "This could be the only chance she will ever have, not just of a possible suitor, but of coming out of her shell. If I return to Denehurst as soon as she arrives, I may never be able to coax her out again."

"Exactly."

She turned to him eagerly, for a moment forgetting her own predicament. "Do you think it might work, with the Earl of Ainsworth, I mean?"

"I don't know," he said frankly. "I haven't yet considered how I shall entice him out of his home. Marianne was my first concern, if you recollect."

Belinda sat thinking, her fingers picking at the beadwork on the skirt of her evening dress. Then she drew in a deep breath. "Would you be willing to continue this deception for a few more weeks, while Marianne is with us at Luxton?"

She was prepared to flare up at the least sign of mockery in his expression, but his face was a mask of innocence. "But you have just informed me that you would rather die than continue to live with me!"

"This is not a laughing matter, Francis! Answer me, this instant."

"I was not laughing. My answer is yes; although, if you continue to treat me in such a high-handed manner, I may come to regret it!"

"It is far less than you deserve!"

"You are right, there; indeed, in future you shall always be right, my love."

"Oh, do try to be serious, Francis," she said with a sigh. "I am too weary to be crossing swords with you anymore. Do you really mean it? You will continue to play my husband—"

"Your *loving* husband. And I might remind you that I am not *playing* your husband, my dainty Ariel; by law I *am* your husband."

"Apart from . . ."

"Apart from . . . yes, just so. I regret to say," he added, his mouth tilting into a devilish smile.

"And you give me your word that you will do everything in your power to have the Earl and Marianne meet?" she said hurriedly, choosing to ignore his remark.

"With your assistance, of course. I cannot do it alone." A frown creased his forehead. "Though, how the devil I'll get Ainsworth out, I don't know."

He sat, staring into the fire, stroking his chin with his thumb. Then a slow smile spread across his countenance. "I have a glimmer of an idea."

"What?" Belinda demanded.

"No, no, I cannot say anything yet, but it came from something you said about Marianne a while back." The old excitement was back in his voice. "Tell me, my brave spirit, if I succeed, what will be my reward for all my endeavors?"

"Reward?" she cried indignantly, rising to the bait. "Oh,

you really are a devil, aren't you?" she said, seeing his satisfied smile.

"Regrettably, yes. Definitely not a saint—or a hero."

"No."

She was not prepared to admit that living with a sainted hero had not always been easy. She was beginning already to enjoy the heady power of being able to unleash her temper and berate him.

"Your reward will come before we return to Denehurst," she told him. "Now, in fact. We shall remain for the christening."

His ready smile faded. "My God, Belinda, that is extraordinarily generous of you," he said in a subdued tone.

"I like your Rosaline and Richard. I would not wish to see them hurt because of our mistakes."

"And that is to be my only reward?" he asked, with a resumption of his former teasing manner.

"For the moment, yes. It is I, after all, who should be receiving a reward or, rather, compensation for your deception."

Belinda received her secret reward the following afternoon, when she saw Baby Robin, in his lace gown and cap and blue velvet mantelet, held firmly if a trifle awkwardly in the arms of his handsome godfather.

As he relinquished the precious treasure to his nurse, Francis caught Belinda watching him and flashed her a warm, intimate smile. She looked away, a pain about her heart at the thought of the short time they had left together. But she would not think of that now. For Marianne's sake, she must prepare herself to act the part of the happy bride for a few more weeks.

chapter
<u>19</u>

During the last stage of her journey to Luxton, Marianne Hanbury's apprehension had increased to alarm. Although her eyes were fastened on the copy of Dr. Johnson's _Life of Pope_ that lay open in her lap, not one sentence of the pages she had been reading had penetrated her brain.

She must have been out of her mind to embark upon this journey, to leave the safe environs of Denehurst and venture forth into the whirling, bustling world of yelling ostlers and crazed coachmen, who challenged every coach they passed to a hectic race along the Bath road. It was fortunate that Lord Kenmore's coachman resisted the impulse to accept the challenges. He was, however, frequently forced to pull the four spirited horses onto the side of the road to permit a yellow-bodied stagecoach, hotly pursued by a carriage driven by some numbskull of a coachman—or, more likely, his master—to race past them.

Every nerve in Marianne's body jangled from the scrape and rumble of the carriage wheels, and from the irritating dust that stung her eyes and seeped into the folds of her clothing.

Bertie had chosen to ride. "You'll not catch me cooped up inside a carriage," he had declared. Marianne could now understand why. She had a raging headache and, although Lord Kenmore's crimson-and-black chaise was extremely well sprung and upholstered in the softest charcoal-gray kid leather, her stomach was queasy from the continuous swaying motion.

Bertie reined in his horse and drew up to the carriage window. "Just around this next corner," he shouted, "and you'll be able to see Luxton."

So soon, she thought, her heart sinking, but she managed to conjure up a smile. "Good," she shouted back to her brother, and he disappeared, cantering on ahead.

Nervously she gathered up her belongings with trembling hands, waves of panic threatening to engulf her. *Stop it, this instant!* she told herself. After all, she was not alone; she would have Belinda and Bertie. And she must not forget that she had come because Belinda was in need of her.

But there would also be strange servants to contend with and, most of all, Lord Kenmore. She would insist upon taking all her meals in her room, of course, but supposing she were to meet with him in a corridor? Or in the gardens? She would just have to remain indoors, that was all, and send her maid ahead to ensure that no one was about before she left her room.

She drew down the thick black veil from the brim of her bonnet, so that her first view of Luxton was seen through a curtain of black net. Nonetheless, she thought the low, spacious building with its gothic battlements appeared extremely inviting, its large windows sparkling in the sunlight and broad terraces sweeping down to landscaped gardens.

The carriage passed a pool in the center of which stood a statue of a nude female. Marianne wondered what in the world Papa would say if such a statue were to be raised in the carriageway at Denehurst, and smothered a giggle at the thought. This was no time for laughter, however. Her ordeal was about to commence.

With her legs shaking beneath her, she took the footman's hand and descended from the carriage.

"Marianne!" Belinda's small form came racing unceremoniously down the short flight of steps to hug and kiss her. Tears sprang to Marianne's eyes at the sight of her beloved sister, who was fashionably clad in a round gown of white muslin trimmed with bows and a sash of poppy-red ribbon.

"Oh, how good it is to see you, my darling Lindy," Marianne whispered. "How I have missed you!"

The sisters clung to each other, until Marianne realized that they were being surreptitiously observed by the outdoor servants. "May we go inside?" she begged, instinctively ducking her head. She was terrified that the sunlight might penetrate her veil.

"Certainly," replied Belinda. "Francis is waiting in the hall to greet you."

Marianne shook her head, shrinking back. Dear Lord, it was going to be even worse than she had expected. She had hoped, at least, to reach the haven of her room before anyone else saw her.

Belinda did not appear to notice her reluctance, but continued to draw her along by the hand, uncaringly chattering away about the weather and the fine display of roses in the garden. It was not like Lindy to be so insensitive to her feelings.

There was no escaping Lord Kenmore, for he stood directly in the entranceway. With his well-formed figure, dark, waving hair and dark brown, almost black, eyes, he was quite the most handsome man Marianne could have imagined.

He stepped forward. "Welcome to Luxton, my dear Miss Hanbury. Might I call you 'Marianne,' do you think?" he asked, with a most engaging smile.

She nodded and held her hand out to him, uncomfortably aware that to greet her new brother-in-law without raising her veil was the height of incivility. But when he clasped her hand and his dark eyes met hers, she knew instinctively that Belinda must have told him about her face. Although, in one way, it was a relief, she was also acutely self-conscious and ducked her head to avoid his regard.

To her astonishment, he put one hand to her chin, lifted it, and, before she realized what was happening, kissed her veiled cheek. "A brother's welcome to his new sister," was his explanation.

"Come, I'll take you to your room," said Belinda to her

stunned sister, as her husband turned to welcome Bertie and to bear him away to the library. "I have already ordered a tray of tea and cakes to be brought to us there."

Marianne followed her sister up the crimson-carpeted staircase with its graceful baluster of scrolled wrought iron.

"This is all so beautiful, so bright and airy," she said to Belinda. The sun shone in the arched windows, casting pools of light across the hall floor. "You must love it here, Lindy."

"I do," replied her sister, but she did not expand upon the subject.

Perhaps it was her imagination, but it occurred to Marianne that there was a tinge of sadness in Lindy's response. But then Belinda's letter had been melancholy. That was why Marianne had come to Luxton, after all. It was up to her to give Belinda the companionship she craved.

The ensuing conversation in Marianne's room consisted of a recital of all the happenings at Denehurst, which to an outsider might have appeared insupportably dull, but to Belinda was enthralling. She, in her turn, regaled Marianne with a lively account of her debut in London and her presentation to the Prince Regent. In addition, she lightly touched upon the christening she and Francis had recently attended at Beresford Castle.

Throughout her entire account, Marianne could not rid herself of the notion that something other than loneliness was troubling her sister. Lindy had always been excitable and impulsive, but now there was a frenetic quality about her, as if she were an overwound clock, striking the hours too fast.

Taking advantage of a lull in the conversation, Marianne broached the subject. "You sounded so melancholy in your letter, Lindy. It was that which persuaded me to come here. Was it only that you were missing us and Denehurst, or is there something else that is troubling you?" She fixed her striking blue eyes on her sister's.

"Certainly not!" Belinda tossed her head. "In truth, I must own that I grossly exaggerated my loneliness so that I might entice you here. I could not think of any other way." She hastily changed the subject. "You will never guess whom I met at Beresford Castle, Marianne. Mr. Wilberforce! He was the other godfather at the christening.''

Marianne's eyes brightened. "Oh, *do* tell me all about him. Did he talk to you about his campaign against slavery?''

"He did, indeed. Can you believe that? What is more, he is hoping to engage Francis's interest in it—because of his plantations in Jamaica, you know.''

"How utterly fascinating! Bertie was telling Papa and me all about Jamaica and Lord Kenmore's estates there.''

Belinda frowned. "He was? I had no idea they had even discussed them.''

"Oh, yes. I was quite amazed at how much Bertie knew about the West Indies, and sugar crops and suchlike. Indeed, I have never before seen him quite so animated about anything.''

"Oh, I am surprised to hear that.''

Francis never ceased to amaze Belinda. Thank heavens the topic of Mr. Wilberforce had steered Marianne clear of her suspicions. Belinda had forgotten how well her sister could read her! She must remember to be continually on her guard with Marianne.

Their conversation continued over tea and hot scones with jam and golden-topped clotted cream, until Belinda glanced up at the clock. "Heavens, I must go and change for dinner. What will you wear, Marianne?''

She went to the wardrobe to examine the extremely meager collection of dresses the maid had hung there. "We must send for the dressmaker and have some more dresses made for you as soon as possible,'' she said, without turning to face her sister. She braced herself for Marianne's response, knowing very well what it would be.

"I have no need for any more dresses, Lindy. It is just a waste of money, as you well know. As for dinner, I shall put on my nightgown and robe, as I always do.''

Drawing in a deep breath, Belinda slowly turned to confront her sister. "I very much fear that even Francis might be a trifle shocked at such dinner attire.''

A little frown creased Marianne's forehead. "Francis? What in the world can you mean, dearest?'' Then Belinda's meaning slowly dawned on her, and her scarred face grew rigid. "You know I always take my meals in my room," she said breathlessly, her fingers picking at the braiding on her traveling dress.

"Yes, I do know that, but it is my opinion that while you are staying in Luxton you should do us the courtesy of dining with us." Belinda spoke in a crisp, no-nonsense fashion, but her heart cried out at the expression of dismay on Marianne's face. Nonetheless, she made no move toward her.

"Oh, Lindy. How could you!" Marianne's voice broke, and she turned away to bury her face against the wing of the chair in which she was sitting.

Although Belinda longed to go to her, she steeled herself not to. "Be strong," Francis had warned her. "Do not, on any account, yield to her. Keep reminding yourself that you are acting for her own good."

Easy enough for him to say! He didn't have to cope with a distraught sister.

"If you say one more word on this subject, I shall go home this instant, even if I have to take a stagecoach to do so!" Marianne's face crumpled and she dissolved into heart-rending sobs.

Belinda rushed forward to enfold her sister in her arms. "Oh, my darling, don't cry. *Please*, don't. You shall have your dinner here tonight. Perhaps tomorrow you might try to come downstairs?" she suggested in a coaxing tone, but she knew in her heart that it was a forlorn hope.

"Dearest Lindy. I do love you so," cried Marianne, as she pressed her face against her sister's.

A few minutes later, Belinda left her sister and walked disconsolately to her room. She had failed miserably. At the least sign of resistance she had caved in.

"Well?" asked Francis, when he came up to change for dinner.

Belinda shook her head. "I tried, Francis. But I just couldn't bear to see the look of betrayal on her face. And I do so hate to see her cry."

"I thought you might find it beyond you to remain adamant. Your sister has been coddled far too long." His face held a set, determined look. "I should like you to go to your sister again, but this time I shall accompany you."

"Oh, no, Francis. It would be too much for her."

"Shock tactics are the only way in this instance. If you have her best interests at heart, you will do as I ask." His expression softened. "I shall be firm, not cruel, I promise you. Will you do it? Remember, it is for her."

Inwardly quaking, Belinda straightened her spine, mentally preparing herself to do battle with her tender sister once more. She marched down the corridor, followed by Francis, and knocked at Marianne's door.

"Who is it?"

"Lindy. Let me in."

The door was unlatched. It swung open to reveal Marianne, already dressed in her old powder-blue robe with the frayed cuffs. Belinda turned to signal to Francis. Before Marianne had time to realize what was happening, her brother-in-law was inside the room, closing the door behind him.

She cried out, flinging her hands up to cover her face, but not before he saw in the dim candlelight the scars and pockmarks that disfigured her; not an inch of skin was left unscarred. Although he had been warned, he found it almost impossible not to flinch from the pitiful sight.

Marianne turned to flee from him, but Belinda stepped before her, barring her way. She was trapped, deceived by her own sister! She stood, hands covering her face, her body racked with sobs.

Her brother-in-law approached and, with infinite gentleness, drew down her shielding hands. "Forgive me, my dear Marianne. But you cannot hide yourself away from me forever, you know. You must remember that I am now a member of the family."

She made no move, her body limp with resignation. Slowly the sobs died away, but the shuddering still ran through her slender form.

"Come, sit by the fire." Francis drew her to the fireplace and sat her in the wing chair, wrapping her shawl about her knees, while Belinda knelt to chafe her cold hands and kiss her averted face.

"How can you bear to look at me?" cried Marianne. "I am hideously ugly. It makes people sick to look at me!"

Francis sat on the corner of the little blue chintz-covered loveseat. "I do not find you hideous at all. You have exquisite eyes. Indeed, some might say that they are even more beautiful than your sister's," he added with a smile, "although I cannot do so. As to your face: yes, it is a shock to see it at first, but, even now, I am growing used to it. By tomorrow, no doubt I shall have forgotten you look different from anyone else."

Marianne swung around to confront him, her hands dropping from her face. "How can you say such a stupid thing?" she demanded heatedly. "If a thousand years were to pass, it would not alter the fact that I am incredibly ugly."

"Well, yes, it would," said Francis. "For you'd be nothing but bones."

Marianne's eyes flashed. Belinda could not remember ever having seen her look so furious. Then, to her amazement, her sister's mouth quivered into a smile.

"There, that is better." Francis took Marianne's hand in his. "And now I find that you are also of an easier temperament than your sister, for she would not have given in with such good grace!" He cocked an eyebrow at Belinda, who gave him a comic grimace in response. "Now, my dear Marianne," he continued. "I realize that you would prefer not to have to encounter the entire household on your first night here. But as I am most anxious to become acquainted with my new sister, might I make a suggestion?"

Marianne inclined her head. It occurred to Belinda that her sister was so bemused by this entire scenario that she was too stunned to offer any protest.

"Why do you not take your dinner here in your room with Belinda, while Bertie and I become reacquainted over our dinner? Then we shall all repair to the little parlor on this floor to take tea and, perhaps, a few hands of cards together. No servants, I promise you. We shall all be cozy together, just the family."

Belinda knitted her fingers together as she watched her

sister's face. It was almost impossible to recall how Francis had deceived her, when he was displaying such a wealth of tact and sensibility with Marianne. He seemed to know exactly the correct words and manner to employ with her; his demeanor was that of an amiable and caring relation. She marveled at how well he played the role, considering he had so few relations upon whom to practice it.

Marianne sat, nervously twisting the sash of her robe into spirals. "Would it truly please you to have me join you after dinner?" she whispered, still gazing into the leaping flames of the fire.

"It would please me greatly," acknowledged Francis. "I understand that, unlike your sister, you take great pleasure from books. It would be a relief to have someone at Luxton with whom I can discuss literature."

He sounded so wistful that Belinda was forced to repress a giggle.

Marianne turned eagerly to him. "I have tried so hard to get Lindy to read, but, alas, she is far too impatient and must always be busy at something or other."

"A great pity," said Francis, shaking his head.

Belinda, catching his sly, amused glance, had to bite back the rejoinder that she had always been too busy managing the household at Denehurst to have the leisure to read books and plays. But when Marianne continued speaking, she was glad she had remained silent.

"But then, you see, Lord Kenmore, Belinda has had to work so very hard caring for all of us that she has never had any time for herself." Marianne gazed earnestly into his face. "That is why it makes me so extremely happy to see her the mistress of such a lovely home and married to such a good man." Her countenance flushed pink and she ducked her head, but a small smile curved her lips.

"I thank you for those gracious words," said Francis, rising to his feet. "Tomorrow I shall personally escort you on a tour of Luxton, my dear sister. For now, I must quickly change or your brother will be thinking he has been deserted."

He gave the sisters a cheerful smile as he left. "I look forward to rejoining you both later this evening."

As soon as the door had closed behind him, Marianne grasped Belinda by the arms and pulled her down beside her. "How fortunate you are, my darling sister! Lord Kenmore is the most amiable and charming man imaginable."

Charming, he was, thought Belinda. For he had charmed Marianne right into his pocket. "I know it," she muttered.

"Oh, Lindy, how I envy you!" Marianne's eyes filled with tears. "I had never realized that such men existed."

"Well, none of 'em is perfect, you know," was Belinda's brusque rejoinder as she scrambled to her feet. "Every one is as flawed as we are, only more so," she added darkly.

"Ah, but one should be able to forgive their flaws if they are as kind and as sensitive as your husband is, dearest."

Belinda gave her sister a perfunctory smile and soon found an excuse to leave the room, uneasily aware that, in her sister's eyes at least, the hero was back on his pedestal once more.

Later that evening, they all sat down to a game of Speculation. Belinda had never seen Marianne quite so carefree and relaxed. Francis had just the right sort of light, teasing manner to banish her shyness and draw her out of herself. For all her excessive sensibility, Marianne had an excellent sense of humor and, before long, her laughter was pealing out in a way that gladdened Belinda's heart.

She flashed a glowing look of gratitude at Francis across the card table and received in return a look so filled with warmth and tenderness that she blushed and fixed her gaze on the cards in her hand. Intercepting the exchange, Marianne smiled at her sister.

"I have the distinct feeling that Bertie and I are *de trop*," she whispered to Belinda when she poured some more tea into the delicate porcelain cup.

"Nonsense!" snapped Belinda.

"Belinda, Bertie, I should like to propose a toast," said Francis, standing up and holding his cup high. "To our sister, Marianne!"

"To Marianne," repeated Belinda and Bertie, both grin-

ning at their sister's evident discomfiture at being thus
singled out.

Francis resumed his seat and leaned back in his chair. "I
also wish to announce that I intend to throw a ball for my
bride, so that I may present her to my neighbors and friends
who live in the vicinity."

"Capital!" cried Bertie, who was always game for any
social pleasure.

Belinda held her breath for a moment as she watched her
sister's expression. Then she said heartily, "What a splendid
notion!" as if it were an utter surprise to her. In a manner of
speaking, it was. When they had discussed the ball, Francis
had said he would broach the subject when the time seemed
appropriate.

Marianne did not join in the general approbation of the
scheme. Her fingers were employed in plaiting the azure-
blue ribbons on her best dress, into which she had changed
after dinner. Her lovely eyes clouded over as they met
Belinda's.

"You need not come if you do not wish to," said Belinda
gently. "But it is to be a masked ball, you know."

Silence.

Now Belinda was certain that Francis had sprung the idea
far too soon. She cursed him for not having waited. "Of
course, it will take a great deal of time to arrange," she
hurriedly interposed, "weeks, in fact."

"A masked ball," said Marianne, as if she were in some
sort of dream. "Can one . . . would it be possible to obtain a
mask that covers the face completely, do you think?" A tide
of red flooded her face. She hastily rose, walking away to
gaze at a china display cabinet filled with Sèvres porcelain,
in the corner of the room.

Blinking back tears, Belinda jumped up from the table to
stand behind her. "Yes, dearest, it would be," she told
Marianne.

"I think we should make it a costume ball, with an
Elizabethan, a Tudor theme," declared Francis. "Then all
must wear the full or half-face masks they wore in those

days for masques or routs. We could even include characters from the plays of Shakespeare."

"I say, what fun!" exclaimed Bertie. "I think I shall be Sir Walter Raleigh, complete with pipe. Who will you be, Marianne?"

Captured by the spirit of the moment, she pondered, then declared: "I shall be the Princess of France in *Henry the Fifth*. Then I shall not have to say much!"

"What about you, my pensive wife?" asked Francis of Belinda.

"I have no notion at all," growled Belinda. "I know nothing of history and such flummery. As for Shakespeare, I know of only one character."

"Ah, yes." Francis's eyebrows rose expressively. "Ariel the delicate Ariel. No, no. I hardly think it would be suitable to present my bride clad in a pair of tights delectable as she might appear in such a costume."

Belinda glared at him, but then dissolved into a grin "Who, then?" she demanded.

He surveyed her for a moment. "Juliet," he said eventually. "The young Juliet, in a sumptuous renaissance gown of rich blue velvet embroidered with gold."

And so it was all settled, and everyone went to bed Bertie, with thoughts of shipwrecks and pirates exciting his mind; Marianne, dreaming of herself in a beautiful costume dancing the waltz with some man dressed in doublet and hose; Belinda, happy yet fearful for her sister, and, for herself, restless and trying not to think of the uncertain future.

As for Francis, he sat up late, staring into the dying embers of the fire in his bedchamber, swirling a glass of his favorite armagnac, his mind mulling over a great deal more than just his plans for the ball.

chapter
20

Throughout the day of the ball, guests from Bath and places even farther afield had been arriving at Luxton. Bandboxes, valises—even trunks—had been carried in. Belinda felt as if she had spent the entire morning doing nothing but greeting, and being presented to, hordes of people.

"I had no idea you had so many acquaintances," she gasped to Francis after lunch, as they snatched a moment in the hall to speak to each other before another carriage drew up.

"Nor had I," said Francis with a wry grin. "I have never been so besieged with covert, and frequently quite blatant, requests for an invitation." He pinched her cheek. "You have become all the rage, my love."

"Gammon!" declared Belinda. "They are all coming out of sheer curiosity, having heard that Lord Kenmore has made a dreadful misalliance." She laughed up at him, but the laughter died on her lips when she saw his serious expression.

"Not so. Each day that passes I become more and more convinced that you are the woman for me, Belinda. I give you fair warning, I do not intend to lose you without a fight." He put out his hand, but Belinda pretended not to see it.

"Any news yet?" she whispered, casting a hurried look about to see if there were any servants within hearing distance.

"News of what?" He appeared to be lost in thought.

"News of the Earl of Ainsworth, of course. For heaven's sake, what other news would I be referring to?"

"Ah, yes," he said, coming to his senses. "Alas, nothing has arrived from him yet. I had been hoping that Ainsworth would have sent some sort of reply, even a refusal, by now."

"What exactly did you say in the invitation?"

"Is it necessary for us to stand out here in the hall amidst all this chaos to conduct this conversation?" He stepped back as two footmen marched by, carrying gilded music stands into the mirrored ballroom.

"Yes, we must," said Belinda firmly, "for I am on my way upstairs to see to Lady Sadler. Does she have to bring those wretched pugs with her? I dread to think what they will do to our carpets."

"Never travels without 'em," Francis informed her. "By the bye, I didn't send Ainsworth an invitation to the ball."

"What!" Belinda let out a scream that turned the heads of all the servants. They hurriedly resumed their duties when they caught their master's baleful eye upon them.

Francis took Belinda's arm, drawing her into a doorway. "I said I did not send him an invitation to the ball. To do so would have been useless. He would never have accepted it."

"Then why in the world are we bothering ourselves with all this?" cried Belinda, flinging out her arms at the activity in the hall.

"The ball is being given for you, my love. You may recollect that it was also designed to give your sister a taste of society. After all, if we can contrive to bring these two recluses together, we do not wish to have them shut themselves away again, do we?"

"But I do not understand." Francis was being so obscure

that Belinda felt like slapping him. "How do you intend to lure the Earl here tonight when you haven't even sent him an invitation?"

"Told him Wilberforce desired to meet him."

"Wilberforce?" Belinda was beginning to think that Francis was going out of his mind from all the strain of the past few weeks. "But Mr. Wilberforce won't be at the ball, Francis," she said in the patient tone of a mother humoring an infant. "Don't you remember that he was returning directly to London after the christening, so that he might have a meeting with the Tsar while he was in England? Why in the world would you tell the Earl that Mr. Wilberforce was going to be here?"

"Because I had to find an excuse to entice him here tonight."

"But why Mr. Wilberforce?"

"You were my inspiration for that. Sometime or other, I heard you say that because of her disfigurement, Marianne was more sensitive to the plight of others who were disadvantaged. It occurred to me that the same might apply to Ainsworth."

"Perhaps you were wrong to think so," Belinda said impatiently.

"No, I was not. My spies, meaning Besley, in the main, have ascertained that the Earl is greatly in sympathy with Mr. Wilberforce's aims, and follows all the parliamentary reports of the debates on abolition and emancipation most keenly."

"Very well, but how do you intend to explain Mr. Wilberforce's absence to Lord Ainsworth once he arrives?" demanded Belinda, her tone decidedly acid.

"I shall think of something, never fear. Besides, if I do not hear from him soon, I shall not have to concern myself on that score."

The reply from Lord Ainsworth arrived in the mid-afternoon. To the great relief of Francis, and delight of Belinda, it was in the affirmative.

Francis called for Besley to give him his instructions.

"Lord Ainsworth will be arriving at ten o'clock tonight, Besley. I have advised him to come to the terrace side entrance, so that he may avoid meeting the other guests. You are to station yourself directly beside the door and, when he arrives, escort him up the back staircase to the small library, which is to be kept locked until then or until I myself open it. You will inform Lord Ainsworth that I shall be joining him there."

Besley had not been taken entirely into his master's confidence, but he had guessed at most of it and, although he frowned upon belowstairs gossip, so had most of the household. During the past weeks he and the other servants had seen poor Miss Hanbury's ravaged face and also been captivated by her shy, gentle manner. "Shall I leave his lordship alone, my lord? That is, after I have offered him refreshment?"

"You will offer him nothing. Merely show him into the room, but do not enter it yourself. The refreshments will already be there for him. If he wishes, he may help himself. Do I make myself clear?"

"Perfectly clear, my lord. I am not to go into the library with his lordship. I am to leave him there alone," intoned the butler.

"Just so." Lord Kenmore's eyes glinted. "Although it is my sincere hope that he will not, in fact, be alone."

"Yes, my lord." Besley's lined face bore as stony an expression as one of his master's statues. "Very good, my lord."

No expense had been spared to ensure that the Elizabethan costume ball at Luxton would be a huge success. A group of mummers and several musicians playing ancient instruments had been engaged to wander through the throng of guests and put on impromptu performances for them.

The ladies in their stiff silks and brocades and velvets, and the gentlemen in their doublets and hose and Roman togas, joined in with gusto, eager to attempt the branles and galliards that occasionally replaced the more familiar allemandes and waltzes.

To Marianne, whose memories of watching the balls at Denehurst before her mother died were very faint, it all held the semblance of a strange dream, in which she took the role of observer rather than participant. She had been taught to dance by Belinda and Bertie, but dancing with her brother to the accompaniment of Lindy's attempts on the tinkly nursery piano was quite different from being whirled about by strange gentlemen who flirted and flattered in a manner to which she was entirely unaccustomed.

It was a distinct relief, therefore, to find her brother-in-law making an elaborate bow before her and soliciting her hand for a waltz. Francis looked extremely dashing in a crimson doublet with slashed sleeves faced with gold, his well-shaped legs encased in golden hose. He wore a half-mask of a fox's head, which did not cover the lower half of his face.

"Are you enjoying yourself?" he asked her, as they spun about the ballroom.

"Oh, yes," she replied, trying hard to appear enthusiastic.

"Not entirely, I collect?" he said gently.

She shook her head. She was miserably aware of the tension in her body as she tried to concentrate on the steps, her head ached from the noise and, most of all, she had been continually anxious all evening that her golden mask, which was formed in the image of a sun with sparkling rays, might slip in the exertion of a dance and reveal her face.

"It is only that I am so unused to having so many people about me; that, together with the dancing and the music and the crowds . . ." she tried to explain, eager that he should not consider her ungrateful.

"You have my entire sympathy, my dear sister. Even my feet are growing deuced sore in these square-toed shoes. If it's any consolation to you, though, you are definitely one of the most beautiful women here."

She was not at all amused by this and gave him a frowning look.

"I am not funning," he assured her. "Several gentlemen have begged me to reveal the identity of the young lady with the chestnut hair in the dress of gold tissue trimmed with pearls.''

When the dance came to an end, he was about to lead her back to her seat, but paused. ''Would you prefer to rest for a while? I myself am finding this heat a trifle overwhelming, particularly in this mask. We must remember not to have a ball in June next time.''

Actually, he was thoroughly enjoying the evening. Anything unusual or with a theatrical aspect always stimulated him.

''Could I rest a little, do you think?'' asked Marianne.

''I know just the place.'' He steered her expertly to a far corner of the ballroom and, before she knew it, they had slipped out the small door behind the musicians' platform.

''Lindy may wonder where I have disappeared to.''

''I shall make a point of telling her as soon as I have you settled.''

All the public rooms downstairs were filled with people; eating, dancing, playing cards—some even sleeping, for the wine was flowing freely. Francis led Marianne past them to guide her up the back staircase to the first floor.

''It will be a great deal quieter for you here,'' he said, halting before a recessed door at the far end of a corridor. He motioned to the footman, who had accompanied them upstairs, to light the candlesticks on the mantelshelf and the branch of candles on the desk. Immediately, the little room sprang into view.

''What a charming room!'' cried Marianne, who had not seen it before. It was a small library-cum-study with a flocked wallpaper of gold leaf upon a ground of olive green.

''This is my sanctum,'' said Francis. ''I frequently sit here late at night, either to work or to read, particularly if my house is full of actors and I need to escape from them.'' He smiled. ''I thought you might like it.''

He gave instructions to the footman in a low voice, and then turned back to Marianne. ''I regret I must leave you now to return to my guests. I shall inform Belinda that you are here. I have also ordered that refreshments be conveyed to you. You have my assurance that you will not otherwise be disturbed.''

''You are very kind, my lord.''

'' '*Francis*,' not 'my lord,' remember?'' admonished her brother-in-law. ''When you are ready to come down again, you may order John to take you down or tell him to come and fetch me, and I shall escort you downstairs.'' He looked about the room. ''Are you certain you have everything you need?''

She surveyed the room, taking in the shelves of books and the comfortable winged chairs and the crackling fire, and nodded, her eyes sparkling behind the ornate mask. ''Oh, yes. Now *this* is my idea of heaven!''

Laughing, he walked to the door. ''No removal of masks until midnight,'' he reminded her. ''So you are safe until then.''

She nodded, inwardly vowing that she would be back in her bedroom long before that time.

Francis went out, closing the door behind him.

Marianne went immediately to the bookshelves, not knowing where to look first. Although the eye-slits were widely cut, the mask hampered her sight a little, but she dared not remove it. The footman would be returning soon with the refreshments and, despite Lord Kenmore's assurance that no one would disturb her, there was no absolute guarantee of that.

The Renaissance in Italy. Life of Petrarch . . . She ran her fingers along the spines of the leather-bound books, relishing the very touch of the different textures: some with covers smooth as marble; others, roughened by time. She breathed in the much-loved aroma of leather and ink, far more precious to her than the most exotic of perfumes.

Eventually, being in a reasonably light-hearted mood, she decided on a volume of Mr. Wycherley's comedies. She sat down in the comfortable chair by the fire, set her feet on the tapestried footstool, and proceeded to lose herself in *The Country Wife*. Even the appearance of the footman bearing the refreshment tray scarcely disturbed her, so immersed was she in the decidedly ribald adventures of Mr. Horner.

A sheet of paper written in Lord Kenmore's bold hand, and various markings throughout the pages, told her that this must be one of the plays that Lord Kenmore had mounted in his own baroque-style theater.

She was chuckling to herself while reading a scene between Mr. Horner and Margery Pinchwife when the door opened and then closed again. She was not certain that someone had actually entered the room. Realizing that she was hidden from view by the high back of the chair, she remained as still as a fear-frozen rabbit, hoping that whoever it might be would leave again without knowing she was there.

She heard footsteps on the polished oak flooring, and a gentleman came into view. She shrank farther into the chair, glad that she had taken her feet from the footstool and curled them beneath her, as she usually did when she became engrossed in a book.

Now she was able to see that the man was fashionably but plainly dressed in a dark blue coat and silver-gray pantaloons, which were of a comfortable fit on his slender form, rather than the tight fit Bertie preferred. He had dark gold hair, which he wore a little longer than the Corinthian cut Lord Kenmore favored. She could not see his face.

He walked to the bookshelves that faced her and began to run his fingers along the spines of the books, perusing their titles, as she had done.

Marianne held her breath, knowing that as soon as he turned around he would see her.

He selected a volume, slid it from the shelf, and turned around. Their eyes met across the room. Immediately, his face flushed scarlet. His expression was that of some poor trapped animal. Indeed, he appeared even more terrified by this encounter than she.

He inclined his head in a hasty bow, but the words that hovered on his lips somehow remained unspoken.

Marianne hastily sat up, making an attempt at a sociable smile through the cut-out mouth of the mask. "Forgive me for having startled you," she said. "I fear I must have fallen asleep.'' A lie, but it would help to explain her silence when he had entered the room.

To her surprise, he made no response, but remained staring at her, as if transfixed. She began to grow uneasy, wondering if she were trapped in the room with a madman. Slowly she stood up, trying to assess, at one and the same time, the distances between herself and the poker and between herself and the door.

At last he managed to get one word out: "M-m-mask?''

She gathered from the upward inflection of his voice that he was asking her a question about the mask she was wearing. "My mask?'' She put her hand up to her face-mask. "Did you not realize that Lord and Lady Kenmore were throwing a masked costume ball tonight?''

He shook his head and, with great effort, said: "F-forgot.'' Again, he flushed bright red, and this time made for the door.

"Wait, please.'' Marianne did not know why she detained him; perhaps because her sympathies lay with any human being who shrank from social contact with others.

"Please do not leave on my account,'' she said. "I was only resting awhile from the noise and throng of people downstairs. I am not used to them.'' She smiled again at him.

To her surprise, the man smiled in return. The smile lit up his lean, tanned face, making him appear most attractive. Now it was Marianne's face that grew warm.

"Will you not sit down and read your book?'' she suggested. "The tea is still hot, if you would care for some, or I believe there is sherry and port.''

He indicated the silver teapot and sat down in the chair near to hers, still clutching his book. When he set it down on the small table beside him, she saw that his hand was stained from the red morocco binding.

She poured the tea and gave it to him, and then handed him one of the linen napkins. "The red from the book has come off on your hands,'' she explained.

He glanced at his hand, giving her a rueful smile before scrubbing it with the napkin.

"I was concerned that it might rub off on your clothing."

"Thank you, m-ma'am," he stammered.

They sat, the silence stretching between them. All that could be heard was the rather embarrassing sound of tea-sipping.

Eventually Marianne could bear it no longer. She smiled across at her silent companion. "Pray forgive me for not removing my mask or introducing myself, but apparently the rules are that one must not divulge one's identity until midnight."

He appeared amused. "That d-does not apply to me." He rose to make her a graceful bow. "Ainsworth, ma'am. Nigel, Earl of Ainsworth." He got the words out with great difficulty, and then subsided into his chair again, mopping his forehead with his handkerchief.

She had not believed it possible to meet someone who was far more ill at ease with people than herself. Yet, somehow, his paralyzing shyness made her feel less nervous. Her newfound courage made her determined to help him feel more comfortable with her.

"Are you an acquaintance of Lord Kenmore, my lord?"

"Neighbors." He indicated a direction by waving his hand vaguely toward the window.

"Never tell me you own that wonderful old house I have seen from the park, the E-shaped one with the mullioned windows! Charnwood, I think Lord Kenmore told me it was called."

He nodded, smiling with pleasure at her enthusiastic appreciation of his home.

"One cannot see much of it, of course," she added, "but it appears extremely beautiful and must be quite old."

"Elizabethan."

"Oh, how perfectly marvelous! How I should love to see it!"

Marianne could not believe her own ears; had she actually spoken the words?

For a moment he looked confused. Then he said, enunciating each word very slowly but clearly: "It would give me great pleasure to show Charnwood to you."

Marianne's eyes met his. "And I should gain much pleasure from seeing it."

A pact had been made, a pact she would be forced to break, but she would not think of that now. It was as if she were two Mariannes: the one in the mask, to whom all things were possible; and the one behind the mask, who would shut herself away from the world again at midnight.

"Do you live alone at Charnwood?" asked the bold, masked Marianne.

He nodded. "Bar servants, of c-course," he added.

He leaned forward to throw another log on the fire. As he did so, she felt the strangest desire to touch the hair that curled at the nape of his neck. He caught her looking at him as he straightened up. This time his eyes kindled into quite a different expression, one she had seen only once before, in the eyes of Lord Kenmore when he was watching Lindy. She knew instinctively that it signaled that this man found her attractive, desirable even.

Dear Lord, she thought, if only he knew what lay behind the glittering sun-mask! If she were to remove it now, he would shrink back in horror from her.

"Are you waiting to meet someone here?" she asked hurriedly, her voice trembling a little.

He nodded. "K-Kenmore. Wishes to present me to Mr. Wilberforce."

She frowned. "Mr. Wilberforce? But I don't . . . that is, I am not certain that Mr. Wilberforce is visiting Luxton at present." Although she knew he was not, she did not wish to disclose her identity to Lord Ainsworth by telling him so. "I certainly do not recollect having seen him here tonight."

"Very odd," he said with a frown. "Kenmore told me he wished to meet me, to discuss the ab-ab . . ." His entire body tensed with the effort to get the words out. Then, in despair, he closed his eyes, leaning his forehead on his clenched hand.

Marianne's heart turned in her breast, so strong were her feelings of compassion for him. Instinctively, she leaned forward to touch his hand.

His eyes flew open. She did not remove her hand. Slowly,

very slowly, he turned his palm upward to clasp her hand so tightly that she could feel the band of his signet ring pressing into her soft palm.

For a long moment they sat thus, hands tightly clasped, their eyes locked. Then Marianne drew her hand away and took up her book.

"What is it?" he asked, indicating the book.

She showed him, and he laughingly raised his golden eyebrows in mock surprise that a young lady should be reading such a racy comedy.

"And yours?" she asked, adopting his own abbreviated manner of speech.

He held up a copy of Horace Walpole's *Historic Doubts on the Life and Reign of King Richard III* and, before she knew it, they were deeply immersed in a lively discussion about the last Plantagenet king. Marianne soon noticed that, although Lord Ainsworth continued to speak in abbreviated sentences, when he became involved in a discussion he rarely stammered.

She had never before encountered a mind as lively as, or even more intelligent than, her own. Only now did she come to realize what she had been missing, for most of her knowledge had been gleaned from the inadequate, and sadly depleted, library at Denehurst, or from the books Lindy had obtained for her from the lending library at Tunbridge.

It was the striking of the clock on the corner bureau that brought them back to reality. "Good heavens. Eleven o'clock," exclaimed Lord Ainsworth. "What can have kept Kenmore and Mr. Wilberforce?"

"Who showed you up here?" asked Marianne.

"Besley. Butler. Perhaps he forgot to tell Lord Kenmore I was here."

"No, I am certain that is not so. He appears to be extremely efficient," she added hastily. She was beginning to wonder what exactly was afoot.

"Not that I m-mind waiting," Lord Ainsworth hurriedly assured her.

"Do you frequently call at Luxton?" she asked, in an effort to start a new conversation.

"No. Rarely pay visits to anyone." His gray eyes held a proud, defiant expression.

"I see."

The belligerent expression faded. "Easier that way," he explained.

"I can see that also," she said softly.

"Can't you take off that mask?" he asked suddenly. To her surprise, he sprang to his feet and stood over her, as if he was sorely tempted to tear off the mask.

"No, I cannot." She stood up, and saw that he was several inches taller than her. "It is time that I went downstairs again. I shall inform Lord Kenmore that you are waiting here for him." She held out her hand. "Good night, Lord Ainsworth."

He took her hand, but did not release it. "You c-cannot leave yet. D-don't even know your name. Haven't seen your face. Won't you return at midnight, when everyone has unmasked? You are forgetting, we have yet to p-plan your visit to Charnwood." In his desperation, his words tumbled out over each other, some almost inarticulate, others remarkably clear.

Marianne swallowed the lump in her throat, stifling her tears with great difficulty. "Yes, I shall return directly after midnight," she assured him. "But for now I must go, my lord."

Before he could detain her further, she had slipped from the room.

Long after Lord Kenmore had come to convey his abject apologies, with the explanation that Besley had not informed him of his arrival and that, alas, Mr. Wilberforce had had to postpone his visit at the last minute, Lord Ainsworth waited in the small library for the lady in the sun-mask to return. The chimes of midnight struck in the small bureau clock, to be echoed by the great boom of the long-case clock on the half-landing. From below came a great shout and gales of laughter, and then the music resumed.

Eagerly, he watched the door, but it did not open. Occasionally he ventured out into the corridor to check the rear staircase, but there was not a sign of the lady in the golden dress, with vivid blue eyes and hair the color of ripe, polished chestnuts.

Five minutes after the clocks had struck one, Lord Ainsworth rose stiffly from the chair by the dying fire, and stole down the rear staircase. Silently, he took his cloak and whip and hat from the footman, and slowly rode home, across the fields to Charnwood.

chapter
<u>21</u>

The sky above the Mendip hills was flushed a delicate pink by the time Belinda began to climb the stairs. She heard Francis bidding "Good night, or should it be good morning?" to an exhausted Besley, and she turned to wait for him, poised on the third step.

"Weary, little one?"

She nodded, too weary, in fact, even to speak.

"Tell you what, I'll carry you."

"No, indeed you will not! I've no desire to be tumbling all the way downstairs!"

"Nonsense! You're as light as a feather. You're surely not suggesting I'm foxed!" he said, feigning horrified indignation.

"No. But if you're as weary as I am, it would be very easy to drop me."

He slipped his arm about her waist, supporting her until they reached the head of the stairs. Then, ignoring her protests, he swung her into his arms and carried her to her bedroom. They passed a footman, who hastily concealed his grin as he opened the door for them.

Denton jumped up from a chair as they entered and went to shake Mary awake.

Belinda gave them an apologetic smile. "If you will just

211

hang up the gown, so the velvet will not crease, and undress my hair, I shall do the rest, so that you may get to your beds." She turned to bid Francis good night.

"Delay going to bed for just a little while, would you?" he whispered. "I shall return in ten minutes."

"I cannot promise that I shall be awake when you return," she said, yawning widely, "so you'd better make haste before it's too late."

Although she was in her dressing gown when he returned, she was still in the throes of having her hair undressed. He slumped into a chair to observe the removal of the swatch of false hair and the string of pearls that was wound into it.

"Oh, that is so much better," said Belinda blissfully. She rubbed her head with her fingers and then took the brush from Mary's hands to brush her hair back into its usual mass of curls.

"Ah, now I can recognize you," said Francis. With her elfin face scrubbed clean of all face paint and her hair *au naturel*, she looked very much more like the girl he had first encountered three months ago at the theater in Tunbridge Wells. Yet there was a subtle difference about her now; a new poise, a sense of maturity. He gave the servants a dismissive nod.

"Was it a success, do you think?" she asked him anxiously, when the servants had gone.

"The ball, or the plan for Marianne?"

"The ball." She drew off her sapphire-and-diamond ring and laid it in the jewel chest. "The other was an abysmal failure."

"Ah, now that is what I wished to ask you about. The last thing I knew was that, after I had apologized to Ainsworth, he asked if he might remain in the small library for a while longer so that he might finish the book he had been reading. I thought that was an extremely auspicious sign. I collect I was unduly optimistic?"

"I have no idea what transpired between them. Marianne sent for me at a few minutes after eleven. She was already in her bedroom. All she told me was that she had one of her raging headaches and was going to bed." Belinda gave

Francis a sad little smile. "So you see, all our plans came to naught."

"And she said nothing about having met Ainsworth?"

"Not one word. And I could hardly ask her about him, could I? Had I done so, she likely would have guessed that it had been a plot." Her mouth quivered. "Oh, Francis. I am so very disappointed. When you told me that they were actually there, together, in the library I felt sure your plan would succeed."

Tears welled in her eyes. Furious with herself, she dashed them away.

Cupping her shoulders with his hands, he bent to plant a kiss on her curls. "Come, my dear one. You must be overcome with fatigue."

She felt herself cradled in his arms, being carried to her bed and gently laid upon it, the bedclothes tucked snugly around her. But when he made a move to go, she opened her eyes and caught his hand.

"Please stay with me," she whispered.

He hesitated.

"I am so very miserable," she pleaded. "Please, Francis."

"Miserable, after such a huge social success? It was, you know." He looked down at her with a warm smile in his sleepy eyes.

"Miserable . . . and cold."

She was shivering; there was no doubt about that. "Poor darling. Never mind, I shall soon have you warm again," he said lightly.

He threw off his dressing gown and climbed in beside her. "When you wake again, everything will seem much brighter," he said, taking her into his arms. "And we shall devise a new plan."

She nodded, but made no response, apart from burrowing her head against his chest. Gradually, the shivering subsided, her body grew warmer, and she slept.

Francis lay wide awake, however, submitting himself to the daunting prospect of having to lie still for several hours, perhaps, while his entire body throbbed with desire for the woman who lay sleeping peacefully in the circle of his arms.

By the following afternoon, all their guests having departed, Belinda was indeed feeling a trifle more optimistic. When she went to Marianne's room, however, she found, to her dismay, that her sister was looking wan and sick, and certainly not in the mood for conversation.

"Are you still feeling unwell, dearest?" asked Belinda.

Marianne sighed. "Please do stop fussing over me, Lindy," she begged. "It is only one of my nauseous headaches, that is all. You know they do not last." Pushing aside the large shawl that was wrapped about her knees, she rose to pace across the room, halting at the window. "It is raining," she said in a dull tone.

"Yes, the lovely weather has broken. Such a pity." Belinda came behind her, to stare through the sashed window at the rain-drenched lawns and shivering trees.

She put her arms about her sister's waist. Marianne's body trembled as she pressed back against her. "Oh, Lindy," she said in a quavering voice.

For a moment Belinda thought she was about to confide in her, but then Marianne's body tensed and she pulled away. "I am going out for a walk," she announced.

"In this?" said Belinda. "You'll be soaked to the skin in less than five minutes."

"Nonsense! You know how I love walking in the rain."

"I shall come with you, then."

Marianne's eyes flashed. "No, Lindy. I wish to go alone, if you please."

The steely edge in her voice warned Belinda not to insist. "Very well," she said with a sigh, knowing how intractable Marianne could be when she was in one of her rare stubborn moods. "But be sure to dress warmly."

"I'll take my heavy walking cloak and stout boots." Marianne gave Belinda a tight-lipped smile. "What a little mother you are to me, Lindy." She held out her hands and drew Belinda to her in an embrace. "And what a burden I have been to you all these years," she said in a choked voice.

"Fudge!" retorted Belinda. "I won't stay to hear you talk such fustian."

Marianne was forced to smile. "Forgive me. I am a trifle blue-deviled this afternoon. It must be the change in the weather."

"Take one of the dogs with you," suggested Belinda. "They're needing some exercise."

"I'll take Pepper." The brindled spaniel was Marianne's favorite.

A short while later, Marianne stood at the west door, wrapped in a heavy serge cloak with a large hood. As the footman opened the door for her, Pepper, the spaniel, halted in the doorway, daunted by the heavy splosh of water that fell from the lintel onto his head. He looked up at her, his eyes full of reproach, as if to say, "You surely cannot expect me to go out in this!"

"Getting lazy, he be, ma'am," said the footman.

Marianne smiled. "Come on, Pepper," she said briskly, and led the way out into a sodden world.

The roses in the garden shivered and drooped, their blossoms heavy with water. She picked her way around the puddles on the flagstone path, but within minutes the hems of her skirts were sopping wet. She was not concerned, for she had on thick woolen stockings and stout leather boots, eschewing the wooden pattens that made one mince along as if on stilts. She preferred to stride out, as men did, when she went on her solitary walks.

She loved to walk in the rain, to feel its touch, like a lover's caress, upon her face. The rain was kind to those who preferred to walk alone. Few people chose to venture out in it on foot, and, even if they did, the rain served as a curtain, hiding the face of one person from another.

She passed only one man, a laborer mending a paling, who lifted his hat as she passed. Pepper ran to inspect him, but the man evidently passed muster for, having received a perfunctory pat, the spaniel galloped back to her. After that, he stayed close beside her, as if her slender form afforded some shelter from the incessant downpour that soaked his fur, making him appear half-drowned.

When they entered the small coppice of hazel trees, however, Pepper raced on ahead, pausing only to shake his coat free of some of the water, before dashing off again to nose out one of the poor shivering rodents or rabbits who took shelter from the rain beneath the mounds of wet leaves or under the low branches of bushes.

When she first came out of the wood, she could not see the spaniel. The rain was even heavier now, and the wind had increased, blowing it uncomfortably into her face. "Pepper," she cried. "Come here, Pepper!"

She saw a stile in the tall hedge to her right. Gathering up her wet skirts, she clambered over it, beginning to wish that she hadn't walked quite so far from the house. As she jumped down from the bottom step of the stile, her hood fell back so that in an instant, her hair was drenched.

She did not see the man until it was too late for her to retreat. He was standing just beyond the stile, fondling Pepper, a shotgun cradled comfortably in his left arm. There was no time to draw the hood across her face, no chance to turn and flee, for the stile was at her back.

Despite the heavy rain, she saw all too clearly the swift succession of expressions on the face of the man she had met at Luxton the previous night. She saw, as if in suspended motion, the look of joyous recognition dissolving instantly into horror and disbelief as he beheld her ravaged face.

She let out a cry of anguish and, turning, stumbled back to the stile. Somehow she managed to scramble over it. Ignoring the pain of scrapes and bruises, she began to run, with an alarmed Pepper barking at her heels.

As she ran, she could hear Lord Ainsworth's shouts. "Stop! Stop! For God's sake, wait!"

Hampered by her sodden skirts, she ran heedlessly, blindly, across the field and into the wood. Even there, impelled by her one desire to escape him, she continued to run, blundering into tree stumps, wet branches slashing at her face. More than once, she tripped and fell heavily; the third time, her ankle twisted painfully so that she could no longer run as fast.

She was almost out of the wood, when the Earl caught her. She felt his hands grasping at her cloak.

"No! No!" she shrieked. She struggled like a mad thing, one arm flung across her face to hide it from him.

"For the love of God," he shouted. "Stop, or you'll inflict some terrible injury on yourself!"

"Get away from me!" she yelled, close to hysteria. "Get away!"

"If I give you my word not to come near you, will you stop running?" he shouted, himself panting for breath. Gasping and sobbing wildly, she nodded, aware that she was no longer capable of running. Aside from the stabbing pain in her ankle, she had a stitch in her side, and she was not even sure in which direction the house lay.

Her shoulders heaved as he released her cloak. "Take my arm," he commanded.

"No. I beg of you, just leave me alone." She turned her back on him and began to walk across the lower park, now limping noticeably.

"You are hurt," said his concerned voice from behind.

"Please, please go away," she begged, without turning. *"Please."* Her tears mingled with the rain upon her face.

"No, I cannot leave you in such a state."

She tried to quicken her pace, but she could still hear the squelch of his boots behind her. The park seemed to stretch interminably ahead of her. She had a sudden longing to lie down, to curl into a ball and let the rain wash her away. Despite this fanciful notion, she pressed on, the searing pain in her ankle and her side slowing her to a lurching walk.

Then he was beside her, his arm taking hers. She had no strength left either to protest or to fight him off. He said not a word, but became her support as they slowly progressed across the park. Marianne had an almost intolerable desire to halt and turn her head against his chest, to feel his arms about her. *Oh, God*, her inner voice cried, *if only I could always have worn a golden mask!* How different matters might have been then.

When they reached the lawn beyond the rose garden, she disengaged herself from him. "Thank you," she whispered, her face averted. "I shall be able to manage by myself now."

"I am coming in."

"No."

He took her arm in a painful grip. "Don't you understand? I c-cannot leave you here, not knowing how badly you are hurt. I shall not leave you until I know you are being attended to; nor until I have learned your name."

"Why?" she screamed at him. "Why would you wish to know my name?"

He made no reply, but took her arm to mount the terrace steps. Pausing in the doorway, she turned to face him. Slowly, she drew back her hood and lifted her face, fully exposing it to him.

Beneath the shadow of his wide-brimmed leather hat, she saw his jaw tighten. His gray eyes were full of compassion now, not horror. But she hated compassion even more than she hated horror.

Without another word, she opened the door and, having dragged off her cloak, with the assistance of the attendant footman, she limped across the conservatory, leaving a trail of mud behind her.

Lord Ainsworth watched her go, and then turned to the footman. "I wish to see Lord K-Kenmore."

"Yes, sir . . . that is, my lord. It is Lord Ainsworth, isn't it?" the footman asked anxiously, afraid that he might have mistaken him.

Lord Ainsworth nodded.

"I'll advise his lordship immediately that you are here, my lord."

"Will you then see to the dogs; Miss . . . the lady's spaniel and my two? They are outside."

They were, indeed, barking indignantly at being abandoned. "Certainly, m'lord."

Lord Ainsworth grasped the footman's arm as he was about to leave. "Can you t-tell me the lady's name?" he asked, his face flaming as he spoke.

"You mean Miss Hanbury, my lord?"

"Ah, so she is Lady K-Kenmore's sister?"

"Aye, sir. Miss Marianne Hanbury, Lady Kenmore's elder sister. And a sweeter young lady you'll never find," he added in his broad Somerset accent, determined to do his bit toward the promotion of the romance.

For a horrible moment he thought he might have gone too far, his lordship's eyes turning the color of slate, but then the Earl gave him a faint smile. "I believe you. Now, go tell your master I am here."

In less than five minutes, Lord Ainsworth had been bustled into the library where he now stood before the fire, steam rising from his clothing to his great embarrassment.

"Are you certain you will not take a change of clothes?" begged Lady Kenmore, for the third time. "You and Francis are almost of a height."

"No, I thank you b-both. It is about your sister."

"Marianne?" One hand flew to her mouth. "Has something happened to her? Tell me quickly!"

"No, no. She—she . . ." The sight of her anxiety caused him to stutter, so that it took a moment for the words to come out, causing him acute embarrassment, and Belinda even further anxiety.

"Take your time, old man," said Francis calmly.

Lord Ainsworth closed his eyes, took a deep breath, and then began again. "Miss Hanbury met me," he said, addressing Belinda. "She is ex-extremely overwrought."

Belinda frowned. Then realization dawned upon her. "You saw her face?"

He nodded miserably.

"Yes," said Belinda. "I can see why that would have upset her. She is, as you can imagine, extremely sensitive about her face. This is her first visit away from her home since her illness."

An expression of mingled pain and anxiety filled his eyes. "She ran from me. Hurt her foot, I think. Should go to her." In his apprehension, he made no attempt at the niceties of speech.

"I will, immediately." Belinda took his cold hand in hers. "Thank you, my lord."

He hesitated, then said, "I'd like to wait, if I may; to-to see how she is."

She gave him a warm smile, liking this shy man more and more every minute. "I shall be down again as soon as I have satisfied myself that she is comfortably settled."

Left alone, the two men exchanged glances. Then Francis clapped the Earl on the arm. "Come and get changed. I'll not take no for an answer. My wife will not be down for a while. We shall have time for a glass of claret and a small cigar before she returns."

Lord Ainsworth hesitated, then smiled and nodded. "Should, I suppose. D-dripping on your carpet."

By the time Belinda came down again, the gentlemen had not only downed two glasses of fine claret, but Lord Ainsworth had also smoked his first cigar. He had also had all his questions about Miss Hanbury fully answered.

"Oh, you wretched men," was Lady Kenmore's uncere-monious speech upon her entrance. "*Must* you smoke those horrid things in here, Francis?"

Francis raised his eyebrows at Lord Ainsworth. "You see how it is, Ainsworth? A married man cannot be master in his own house."

But Lord Ainsworth did not hear him, for he had turned eagerly toward Belinda when she entered.

Reading his anxious expression, she gave him the news he desired. "Marianne is resting and tolerably comfortable. A swollen ankle and a few bruises, that is all."

His relief was tempered by his anxiety as to the state of Miss Hanbury's mind. "Is she recovered from the shock of meeting with me?" he asked, enunciating his words slowly.

Belinda sat down, motioning him to be seated on the sofa beside her. "Not entirely. Forgive me for prying, my lord, but you see I have no idea what occurred between you both last night. I do not even know if you exchanged any conversation or..."

A flush of red crept up from his neck, but he did not try

to avoid her searching eyes. "Spoke for a long time," he informed her.

"I see. Then I would suspect that the sight of Marianne's poor face was even more of a shock to you, as you had, ah, become quite closely acquainted."

"She said she'd return at midnight." He sat, twirling the stem of his crystal glass round and round. "She never came. Now I know why." He met Lady Kenmore's brilliant blue eyes, eyes that were almost as beautiful as her sister's. "Will she see me again, do you think?" he asked in a low voice.

"Do you wish to see her again?" asked Lady Kenmore.

He nodded, his eyes fixed upon the glass in his hand.

"Despite her face?" she asked in a voice pitched as low as his.

He hesitated, the memory of the disfigured face vivid in his mind. He blinked to shut out the image, and nodded quickly.

Belinda hid the smile of triumph that threatened to sweep across her face. "Then you shall see her again, I promise you."

"You truly think so?" A spark of hope glinted in his gray eyes.

"I *know* so."

Lord Kenmore laughed. "And when Belinda is certain of something, I warn you, Ainsworth, nothing will gainsay her."

For an instant, Lord Ainsworth felt a qualm of fear, a longing to be back, alone and safe, at Charnwood. Was he insane to be embarking upon such an exciting departure from his normal, dull routine? Then he thought of Marianne Hanbury shut away in her room upstairs, and he remembered her anguished flight from him . . . and his fears retreated. He turned to Francis. "Might I p-persuade you and Lady Kenmore and her sister to visit Charnwood tomorrow, for luncheon, perhaps? Miss Hanbury might like to see the library there," he added.

"I am sure she would," declared Belinda, bestowing a bright smile upon Lord Ainsworth.

* * *

It was a good thing, thought Belinda, as she and Francis watched the Earl's departure, that Lord Ainsworth had not overheard the conclusion of her earlier conversation with Marianne, or his expression might not have been so hopeful nor his step so buoyant as he left.

"I shall never see that man again. Never, never, never!" Marianne had declared in a low, vehement voice, as Belinda had been about to go downstairs. "And I intend to go home to Denehurst first thing tomorrow morning!"

chapter
<u>22</u>

"I cannot budge her," Belinda told Francis later that afternoon, after another talk with Marianne. "Although she has agreed to remain at Luxton a while longer, she is adamant that she will never meet with Lord Ainsworth again, and she certainly will not visit Charnwood, even if he were to promise that he would not be there! Oh, I could strangle her, she is so stubborn," she said through gritted teeth.

"A Hanbury trait, I collect," said Francis dryly.

"It is no laughing matter." Indeed, Belinda was close to tears with frustration and disappointment. "Here we have two people who are patently suited to each other, and my sister digs in her heels and refuses ever to meet with the Earl again."

"Come, my sweet, do not be so impatient with Marianne. Can you truly blame her? She views Ainsworth as a handsome, wealthy nobleman with a vast estate and an ancient lineage, not as a lonely man who is desperately in need of love. On the other hand, she views herself as hideous, repulsive, not worthy of love. In other words, she is thinking of her own feelings, not of his, and I have every intention of reminding her of that."

Belinda had never before seen him in quite such a

determined mood. "I don't think you should try to speak with Marianne now. Why not wait until tomorrow?"

"Because tomorrow will be too late. Is it your wish to see your sister happy?" he demanded.

"Of course!"

"And you like Ainsworth?"

"I do. I believe that behind all his reserve and his fear of people, there's a strong man eager to escape."

"Very poetically put, my sprite. I am inclined to agree with you. So let us waste no more time in disagreement." With this, he strode from the room and ran upstairs, taking the steps two at a time from the sound of it.

It occurred to Belinda, as she picked up the accounts book she had been perusing, that Francis was positively wallowing in all this plotting and intrigue. She wondered how he would keep himself occupied once she and Marianne and Bertie left Luxton. That reminded her: Where in the world was Bertie? She had not seen him all day, apart from giving him a quick resumé of the latest news about the "conspiracy."

Deciding that she was too weary to concentrate on Besley's shaky handwriting, she tossed the accounts books aside and went in search of her brother. She found him in the library, poring over a map that was spread out on the large round table by the window and making notes in a calf-bound notebook.

"What are you doing, Bertie?"

He gave a nervous start. She wondered at the guilty manner in which he covered the notebook with his arm. "Just looking at a map of the Kenmore estates," he said nonchalantly, at the same time removing his hand from the map, so that it rolled up into a cylinder again. "Where is he, by the way?"

"Francis? Gone upstairs to see Marianne. Come and sit down, Bertie, and tell me what you and Francis have been talking about these past few days, when you have been closeted away in here together."

He shrugged. "It is nothing much." When Bertie wished, he could be as stubborn as Marianne; far more so, in fact.

"If you won't tell me, I shall ask Francis," she threatened.

"Do so," he said. Picking up the notebook, he stuffed the map back into the map rack, and stalked from the library, leaving Belinda fuming with vexation—and curiosity. Honestly, Luxton was fast becoming a veritable hotbed of intrigue!

Marianne was exceedingly reluctant to admit Francis, let alone speak with him.

"Will you come downstairs then, so that I may speak with you there?" he asked her at the door.

She shook her head. "I am not properly dressed."

"Then we can sit in the small library in privacy, without fear of interruption. I do not care where we go," he said impatiently, "so long as you permit me to talk to you."

Sensing that this new, stern-faced Lord Kenmore would not take no for an answer, she drew a shawl around her shoulders, over her dressing gown, and reluctantly followed him to the small library.

As soon as they entered, the sweet memories of the previous night flooded over her. She paused in the doorway, reluctant to move right into the room, her mind filled with the picture of a man with golden hair, clasping her hand. Then the spell was broken, as Lord Kenmore called loudly for someone to light the fire, it being "damnably cold in here!"

The fire had already been set and, as there had been a fire lit the previous night, it took but a few minutes to draw. As the flames leaped up, Francis motioned to Marianne to be seated. Again, she was reminded of the previous night; but this was no reserved, golden-haired Lord Ainsworth who stood before her, but her restless, dark-haired, and unusually serious brother-in-law.

He paced impatiently about the room, until the servant had finished tidying the hearth and had departed, and then stood, leaning his arm on the gilt-and-white cornice of the mantelshelf, fixing his dark, glittering eyes upon her.

"Would you kindly be seated, my lord—"

"*Francis!*"

"Francis. Would you sit down, if you please?"

He gave her a quick, wry smile and perched on the arm of the chair where Lord Ainsworth had sat. "I wish to speak to you about Lord Ainsworth," he began.

She stiffened. "I do not wish to discuss the subject any further," she stated flatly.

"But I do."

She bridled visibly at this, quite unused to having her wishes opposed. "I think I shall return to my room, my lord," she said, rising.

"Sit down," he barked, making a move toward her. She collapsed back into the chair, her eyes widening. "It is high time you began to think of others beside yourself, Marianne."

Her blue eyes flashed, but she made no move to rise from her chair again. "Are you alluding to Lord Ainsworth, sir, or to the members of my family?"

"Both. In particular, to Belinda."

Marianne's fingers twisted together and her mouth quivered. "I have not meant to act in a selfish manner toward Lindy," she whispered, deeply hurt by such an accusation.

"Naturally you have not *meant* to do so! But, nevertheless, by shutting yourself away from the world, you have forced her to assume full responsibility for every member of the family, including yourself."

Her eyes swam with tears. "I know it," she said in a tone of anguish. "Do you not realize how much I regret that?"

"I believe I do. But, as her husband, I cannot permit such a situation to continue. After all these years of considering the welfare of others, it is time she was able to live her own life, with only her own immediate responsibilities to concern her."

"I fully agree. That is why I wished to go home immediately to Denehurst, but it seems that you and Lindy oppose me in that wish."

"Certainly we do!" he acknowledged scornfully. "To go home, to shut yourself away again after all you have achieved here, would be tantamount to ignominious retreat! An utter waste."

He sprang up to pace about the room and then moved to

stand by the mantelpiece once more. "When you return to Denehurst it must be the new Miss Hanbury who enters, facing the servants squarely, looking them in the eye, as you have done here. Not slinking in side doors and scurrying up back staircases!"

She trembled with indignation at the scorn in his voice and expression. "That is easy enough for you to say," she began.

He held up his hand. "I know very well how difficult it has been for you to make the change at Luxton," he owned, in a softer tone. "We all realize what courage that must have taken. But you must now progress, not retreat, and employ that newfound courage to help others."

"Do you mean Lord Ainsworth?"

"Just so. Lord Ainsworth. Nigel, Earl of Ainsworth. Did you know his name was Nigel?"

"I . . . I believe so." She lifted her chin. "If it is your intention to compare Lord Ainsworth with me, I must tell you now that I do not consider there to be any comparison whatsoever between our situations."

He perched again on the arm of the chair nearest hers, and leaned forward. "Then we are in agreement," he said softly. "Lord Ainsworth's situation is a thousand times worse than yours."

"Worse!" she cried. "He has a slight speech impediment, that is all. In fact, when we were speaking together last night, he barely stammered."

"I am delighted to hear it. A miracle, wrought by you, I might add, my dear Marianne. Permit me to give you a little of the Earl's history."

"Have I any choice in the matter?" she asked, stirring uneasily. Her eyes met his defiantly.

He smiled. "Actually, no. But I am glad to see that you are beginning to display signs of your sister's spirit."

He took up his favorite stance by the mantelpiece once more, one thumb hooked in the upper pocket of his gold-colored waistcoat.

"Because Lord Ainsworth is a few years younger than I, our paths rarely crossed. He had a fairly normal childhood;

as normal as it could be with an evil-tempered tyrant for a father and a flighty flibbertigibbet for a mother. One Christmas, when Nigel was fourteen, he came home from Eton for the holidays. To spare you the harrowing details, I shall tell you only that the father, a habitual drunkard, accused the mother of adultery. A fearful quarrel ensued. The violent end to the quarrel came when the Earl took up a gun, shooting first Nigel's mother and then turning the gun upon himself.''

Marianne shrank back into the chair, her hand pressed to her mouth in horror. "Oh, God," she groaned.

"I omitted to mention that the entire episode occurred in Nigel's presence. From that day forward, the boy was unable to speak without an appalling stammer. He shut himself away, refusing to return to Eton, although his education was continued by excellent tutors. His guardians saw to that. He has a brilliant mind, at present utterly wasted.''

Ashen-faced, Marianne sat staring into space. Then her face crumpled, and she began to sob. "Oh, that poor boy, that poor, poor boy," she whispered, rocking back and forth.

Francis went to her and took her hands in his. "Forgive me, but I had to tell you, don't you see?"

She nodded, her tears falling on his hands.

"Perhaps, now that you know his story, you will comprehend my reason for having strongly advised you to accept Lord Ainsworth's invitation," he said, his gaze so intense that there was no escaping it. "I might add that it is the first invitation he has issued, other than reluctant ones to close members of his family, since the death of his parents."

"How on earth could you know that?" Marianne challenged him.

"Ah, the insatiable curiosity that marks the Hanburys! I know it because of the tale-bearing and gossip that goes on between the servants of our two households. Despite his dour appearance, my butler, Besley, is an amazing source of information regarding every aspect of the neighboring families. He tells me that Lord Ainsworth's butler and staff are ecstatic at the change in their master and at the thought of having guests at Charnwood after all these years. So, you see, you will be disappointing a great many more people than Ainsworth if you refuse his invitation.''

She bent her head, so that her chestnut ringlets fell forward about her face. "You and Lindy could go," was her murmured suggestion.

"So we could. Now why did I not think of that before?"

Surprised, Marianne gave him a startled look. She found herself the brunt of the cynical mockery in his eyes.

"Naive you might be, my dear sister, but I had not taken you for a fool. It is *you* Ainsworth wishes to invite. 'Miss Hanbury might like to see the library at Charnwood,' he told me; not, you will notice, Lady Kenmore or myself. We were not included in that particular invitation.'' He squeezed her hands and then shook them a little. "Come, Marianne, enough prevarication. Lord Ainsworth wishes to show you his home; what is your answer? You will remember to take into account what I have told you of his personal history.''

Marianne drew away her hands to run her fingers down her cheeks. "It is unfair to remind me of it," she told Francis in an anguished undertone.

"Unfair or not, you must take it into account before making your final decision.''

The movement of her fingers upon her face became more frenzied. "He will see my face in full daylight, and so will his servants.''

Francis sprang up, throwing his hands in the air in his impatience. "Then wear a veil. I don't care what you do, so long as you do not decline the invitation.''

A glowing light crept into her eyes. "I must own that I should love to see that beautiful house.''

"Then it is settled," cried Francis. "I shall send Belinda up directly. You ladies may spend some time on making those decisions of paramount importance regarding what you intend to wear, whilst I go and find Bertie. He is riding to Bath to carry out some business for me there. Have you any commissions for him while he is in Bath?''

His question went unanswered. Marianne had risen to

walk to the small bay window and was standing at it, staring out across the park, a tremulous little smile playing about her lips.

Francis crept out, softly shutting the door behind him.

chapter
<u>23</u>

As the carriage swung into the long avenue lined with poplar trees, Marianne leaned from the window, eager to see the house of which they had been catching tantalizing glimpses throughout the short journey. It had been the intention to ride over to Charnwood, but the rain was still falling, although not so heavily as before, and Marianne had been anxious to arrive looking her very best, not bespattered with mud.

As they rounded a large ornamental lake she caught her first full view of Charnwood. "Oh, Lindy," she gasped in awe. "It is magnificent."

Belinda leaned forward as the great house came into her view. "It is even larger than Carlton House," she informed Marianne.

The imposing E-shaped building was three stories high, built of mellowed red brick, with perfectly symmetrical mullioned and transomed windows. Its roofline was edged with a balustrade of white stone. It was by far the largest and most beautiful house Marianne had ever seen.

The carriage drove into a rectangular courtyard that was paved with red and white bricks, set out in a regular pattern.

As they descended from the carriage, the vastness of the house seemed to dwarf them, so lofty were its walls.

As Marianne followed her sister and brother-in-law up the steps of the south entrance, her heart began to beat so fast that she thought she would expire right there in the entrance. Then she felt Lindy's hand squeezing hers and she took a deep breath to compose herself before entering the great hall.

The butler and three bewigged footmen dressed in blue livery came forward to welcome them and take their outer garments. Marianne did not remove the pretty leghorn straw bonnet, which was trimmed with clusters of artificial forget-me-nots and puffs of blue satin ribbon, nor did she put up its full blue veil.

She looked about her, at the soaring timbered roof and the oak-paneled walls and the minstrels' gallery. It was easy to imagine an Earl of Ainsworth of ancient days striding across the flagged floor to seat himself at the head of the massive refectory table, his lady at his side.

So caught up in this picture of bygone days was she that she failed to see that the present Earl had come to greet them, and was standing almost directly in front of her waiting to speak.

A tide of color swept from Lord Ainsworth's neck, above the modest but fashionable neckcloth, spreading across his countenance as Marianne held out her hand to him.

"Forgive me," she said, ducking her head to look at the uneven stone floor. "I was imagining how this all must have looked in the olden days. You will be thinking me exceedingly ill-mannered."

He mumbled something, but it was unintelligible. The color drained from his face, leaving it unnaturally pale. He had not taken her hand. Her eyes flew to his face, but this time she did not look away again. Very slowly, she raised the blue-net veil, willing her hands not to shake, and turned it back over the poke of her bonnet. Still, he did not speak.

"I must humbly beg your indulgence today, my lord," she whispered. "I fear I am totally unused to social gatherings."

"I, too." They exchanged shy smiles, and he took her

hand, holding it a moment longer than was necessary before releasing it.

Lord Ainsworth led his guests into a beautiful room with a green damask wallpaper and green-and-gold damask furnishings. Silently, he indicated that they be seated.

Marianne could see that he was miserably ill at ease. Her heart went out to him as she noticed how his hands opened and closed at his sides. Yet, at the same time, he looked handsome in the well-fitting blue coat with the new slightly puffed sleeves, fawn pantaloons and shining hessians.

His butler moved to his side, and there ensued a brief exchange between servant and master.

"His lordship wishes to offer you refreshments, my lady, my lord, Miss Hanbury."

Marianne's heart beat even faster as she watched the flush of shame at his inadequacies as a host rush up into Lord Ainsworth's face. He looked as if he might suddenly bolt from the room at any minute. Unable to bear the sight of his agony any more, she sprang to her feet. "Nothing for me, I thank you," she said. "I, for one, am longing to go on a tour of the house," she added brightly, well aware how unpardonably rude her behavior might appear. "Will you come?" she asked her sister.

Belinda received the message clearly, as Marianne had hoped she would. "Not I," she responded. "Forgive me, Lord Ainsworth, but Francis and I are still a trifle exhausted from lack of sleep after the exigencies of the ball. Perhaps we could tour the house after luncheon? Meanwhile, why don't you show Marianne the library, as you had intended?"

Lord Ainsworth appeared slightly bewildered at being manipulated with such efficiency, but so great was his relief at the thought of being alone with Miss Hanbury that he did not care how it was accomplished.

Nevertheless, it was fortunate, perhaps, that the door had closed, so that he was unable to overhear Lord Kenmore's drawled remark to his wife: "Not exactly subtle, my love, but deuced effective!"

* * *

As Marianne walked beside Lord Ainsworth, she was acutely aware of his arm brushing against hers and of the fresh aroma of the cologne he wore. They did not speak until they reached the library.

Marianne's first utterance was a gasp as she gazed about her. She had never seen so many books; from the gleaming mahogany floor to the plasterworked ceiling, bookshelves took up every available inch of space on the walls, apart from the full-length windows draped with green velvet, at opposite ends of the room.

"It is beautiful," breathed Marianne, surveying it with delight and awe. Everything in the library seemed to bear a rich patina, even the books themselves, bound in golden calf and deep-red morocco, their spines tooled with gilded lettering and ornamentation.

"Glad it p-pleases you," Lord Ainsworth managed to blurt out. He turned away, ostensibly to invite her to be seated close to the fire, but Marianne realized that he was so overcome with nervousness that he was unable to speak.

Dear God, she thought, recollecting what Francis had told her about Lord Ainsworth's history, it would be the end for him if this day were to prove a disastrous failure.

She steeled herself, knowing that she would have to be the one to lead the conversation, to set him at his ease.

"I should prefer not to sit, thank you. I should like to see the entire library, if I may."

"Your ankle?" he asked, with a vague gesture in that direction.

She gave a light laugh. "Oh, that. It is aching just a little, but I am able to walk upon it, if that is what you mean."

Gradually, as he showed her his magnificent collection of books and prints and ancient maps, he began to relax and, as he did so, his power of speech returned.

Eventually, Marianne plucked up courage to speak of their previous encounters, knowing that the memory of them lay like a barrier between them.

"I have to beg your forgiveness for so much," she said, as they were bending over a folio of Leonardo da Vinci drawings.

"Mine?" he repeated, startled. "What on earth for?"

"For not returning to you when I had promised to do so . . . during the masked ball, I mean." She ran her fingers delicately over an exquisite drawing of the madonna and child. "You know now why I did not."

"Yes."

Is that all you can say—"yes"? she felt like screaming at him. "And yesterday—"

To her surprise, he interrupted her. "That, too, I comprehend."

As she sat at the large mahogany table by the window, he was bending over her, so close that she could have leaned her head against his arm. She could even hear his labored breathing.

His hand, with its long, artistic fingers, lay flat on the table. The other gripped the back of her chair. Slowly, she turned her head and looked up at him. Their eyes locked in a long, unblinking regard, and then, very tentatively, he lifted his hand from the back of the chair to touch her hair.

When she did not move away from him, he continued to stroke her hair, and then drew his fingers down her cheek, and across her parted lips, an expression of wonderment upon his countenance.

Her eyes never leaving his, Marianne pushed back her chair and slowly stood up. He straightened, but did not step back from her. His trembling hand lifted to brush the nape of her neck, beneath the luxuriant weight of her hair. Then his fingers twined in her hair, and, fearfully, he bent his head to hers.

Marianne closed her eyes, to feel the gentle, almost imperceptible brush of his lips upon hers. She sensed that his next move would be to retreat. The laws of propriety demanded it.

Even as he began to draw his mouth away, she put her arms about his neck, boldly pressing her lips against his, allowing her instincts to take control.

His response was intensely gratifying, but also rather frightening. "My God, Miss Hanbury," he groaned low in his throat, and crushed her against him, his mouth hungrily seeking hers, like a man long deprived of nourishment. He murmured her name against her lips: "Marianne, my dearest Marianne."

Then, with a sudden, swift motion, he put her from him, setting the width of the table between them. She was not quite sure how it had been done. All she knew was that they stood confronting each other across the table, both of them trembling and breathing heavily.

He stared at her, wide-eyed with horror. "My God, Miss Hanbury, what have I done?" he said in a tone of anguish, his fingers running through his ruffled hair. "I d-don't understand what c-came over me. C-can you ever forgive me?"

She closed her eyes for a moment and took a deep breath, striving to control her wildly pounding heart and the waves of strange feelings that she was still experiencing—feelings that both thrilled and terrified her.

"Forgive you?" she said, opening her eyes to gaze at Lord Ainsworth. "What of me? You will be thinking me the most wanton, the most immodest female in the entire world." Her voice trembled. "I cannot think what came over me, either," she whispered, a nervous hand at her throat.

"Immodest?" he cried. "Never. My God, how can you say such a thing?"

She gave him a shy smile. "My conduct was no better than yours."

The smile was sufficient invitation for him to move around the table, but he made a point of not standing too close to her. "I have never before kissed a woman," he said. "That is my only excuse for my appalling conduct." His gray eyes glowed like polished pewter.

"Nor I a man," admitted Marianne, "so I claim the same excuse for my behavior."

Their mutual shame faded as their eyes feasted upon one another. Then they exchanged smiles, but almost immediately Lord Ainsworth's expression changed to one of serious intensity.

"I love you, Miss Hanbury . . . Marianne," he added.

"And I love you, Nigel." She searched his eyes, noting how her use of his name made his expression grow even more intense. "Can it be possible, do you think, after such a brief space of time?" she asked him. "I know it happens thus in novels, but in real life?"

"It must, for it has happened thus to me."

"To us," corrected Marianne.

"To us." He paced away and then returned to stand over her. "How can you possibly love me—an inarticulate fool who stumbles over his words and lacks all the social graces?"

"Very easily. I see a mind of such intelligence that it soars way above mine; the warmest of hearts; and a face—"

She stopped short, putting her hands up to her cheeks. Dear God, she had forgotten about her face. How was such a thing possible?

"What is it, my dearest?" he asked anxiously. "What is the matter?"

She shook her head and walked away from him across the room to sink into a chair by the fire, her mind so filled with the utter impossibility of it all that she barely heard his words.

". . . and I intend to call upon your father to ask for your hand in marriage," he was saying.

"Marriage?" she repeated dully.

"Yes, of course." He frowned down at her. "What else?" Then he smiled. "Ah, I should have g-gone down on my knees. See how lacking in the social g-graces I am!" He promptly fell onto his knees before her.

"Don't be absurd," she cried, caught between tears and laughter. "Oh, my lord—"

"Nigel. I prefer 'Nigel'."

"Yes, yes," she said, nodding impatiently. "How can I possibly marry you with my face as it is?" She pressed her fingers to her quivering mouth.

He scrambled to his feet. "I see nothing in your face to prevent us marrying."

Almost pushing him aside, she sprang up to pace about the room. "Do you not?" she cried. "Then you must be lacking not only sight, but also sense! Think of it. Think of all the social entertaining the incumbent of a house like Charnwood must do."

"I detest social entertaining."

"But we would have to do some entertaining if we were

married. Think of the expressions on the faces of your guests when they see me!''

"And their disdain when they discover that I cannot converse with them!'' he cried. "Now it is you who is being absurd. Hell and damnation, who gives a damn what people think of us! If they d-don't like the look of us, they needn't c-come.'' He gripped her hands and drew them close to his breast, pinning her there. "All I care about is the fact that I love you, Marianne; that I need you and I wish you to be my wife.''

She gazed into his eyes and saw such an abundance of love and conviction there that she was overwhelmed by it and felt extremely guilty for not feeling as optimistic about the future as he did. "Although I am fully aware of the honor you have bestowed upon me by asking me to be your wife, would you grant me just a little time to consider it?'' she begged.

His evident disappointment tore at her heart. "If you must. But only a very little time, for I fear that the longer you take to consider it, the more likely you are to change your mind about me.''

"About you? Never!'' she said vehemently. "Only about my worthiness to be the wife of the Earl of Ainsworth.''

His gray eyes gleamed. "My God, I cannot believe my good fortune,'' he declared, as if he had not heard the words she had spoken. "To think that only two days ago I was utterly alone, condemned to living the rest of my life in solitude. Now I have you, the sweetest, the most adorable woman in the world. I feel as if I have reached up to the heavens and plucked down the brightest star. So you may stop talking all this flummery about your face and your worthiness, Miss Hanbury, for willy-nilly, I mean to have you as my wife.''

It was the longest speech Lord Ainsworth had ever made, and not once did he stumble over his words.

chapter

<u>24</u>

"A most determined suitor, the Earl," Francis said to Marianne several days later, as she stood in the morning room, waiting for the carriage that was to take her home to Denehurst.

Marianne looked from him to Belinda. "Are you certain that I am doing the correct thing?" she asked them, speaking in a low tone, for fear Nigel should come in and overhear her.

Belinda threw up her hands in exasperation. "Oh, Marianne! How many more times will you ask us that question? It is something you must decide for yourself. Besides, you are not being married tomorrow, are you? Nigel has to obtain Papa's permission first."

Francis came forward to take Marianne's restless hands in his. "He is a good man, my dear, and will make you an excellent husband," he said, seeking to reassure her.

"You know I have no doubts on _that_ score," was Marianne's lofty rejoinder. "I only wish I could be certain that I am the right wife for him."

"Can you for one minute doubt it," demanded Francis, "when you consider the change that has taken place in him in little more than a week?"

As if to illustrate his point, the object of Marianne's concern strode into the room at that moment. "All ready," announced Lord Ainsworth. His eyes dwelled on Marianne. "Deuced fine hat," he said of the bonnet of ruched satin with a veil of pale-pink net. "Set a new fashion."

"You're being absurd," said Marianne lovingly. She looked anxiously at her sister. "Is it truly all right, Lindy? I . . . I still prefer to wear a veil while traveling."

"An excellent idea," said Belinda. "Nigel is right. It will soon be all the crack. I can see the advertisement in the *Morning Chronicle* now: 'Keep your complexion free of dust and grime—wear veiled bonnets for traveling.' "

Marianne broke into a smile. "Now *you* are being absurd," she informed her sister.

"The horses are at the ready," Lord Ainsworth gently reminded her.

"Yes, I am coming." Marianne turned to Belinda, blinking back tears. "Dearest Lindy, I am going to miss you so!"

"Fudge! I shall be home again very soon, well in time for us to prepare your trousseau together."

"But you cannot leave poor Francis alone for that length of time," Marianne protested.

"Francis has work to do in London, so I shall be able to spend a great deal of time at Denehurst," hedged Belinda. She had already decided that the news of her separation would have to come gradually, for it was going to be a great shock to her sister.

Marianne went to Francis, holding out her hands to him. "How can I ever thank you enough for all you have done?"

Francis gave her his wry smile. "By being happy, my dear Marianne. Besides, it is your sister you should be thanking, not me."

"I know, but I believe that you had a great more to do with it than you will admit, and I thank you with all my heart . . . my dear brother." She put her arms about his neck and kissed his cheek. He hugged her to him, his eyes meeting Belinda's over her head.

Now Lord Ainsworth was standing beside Marianne, but the words he wished to say to Francis—being extremely important—would not come. With a rueful grin he held out his hand and Francis shook it heartily. "Safe journey," he said, clapping the Earl on the shoulder. "Take care of them both, won't you? And be sure to keep an eye on young Bertie; if you're firm with him, he'll heed you."

"Never fear."

"And you will bring Bertie back from Denehurst with you?"

"Happy to," said Nigel.

"Good."

After the gentlemen shook hands once more, it was time for Marianne and Belinda to make a final parting.

"Oh, Lindy," said Marianne, her voice breaking.

Belinda put her arms about her sister. "You are going to be so very happy, my dearest, I can tell," she said, looking up into Marianne's face. "Give my love to Papa, and you may give whatever you wish to Angelica."

As they moved into the hall, Bertie burst in. "Are you coming?" he demanded impatiently. "The horses are growing restless."

"Not only the horses, it appears," said Belinda. "Aren't you going to say goodbye to me, brother mine?"

"Oh, sorry, old girl." Bertie gave her an abashed hug, hurriedly releasing her as if she were a fiery-hot stove.

Francis held out his hand to his brother-in-law. "*Au revoir*, Bertie. You are to return with Lord Ainsworth."

Belinda gave Francis a puzzled look. This was his second reference to Bertie's returning to Luxton. Francis shot her a quick frown in response to her look of enquiry, effectively silencing the words that hovered on her lips.

"This letter is for your father, Bertie." Francis drew forth a sealed letter from his coat pocket. "Please tell him to direct any questions he may have to me. I trust that I shall be able to answer them to his satisfaction."

"Which will be to mine, also," said Bertie, his face glowing. "I cannot thank you enough, sir," he said shyly.

"If you prove yourself worthy of my trust, that will be thanks enough. Now, get along with you. Do not forget all the advice I gave you when you embarked on your last journey.''

''I shan't, sir, I give you my word.'' Bertie dashed out again, his restless energy not permitting him to remain indoors one moment longer.

There was nothing more to be said. Belinda and Marianne exchanged one last swift embrace. Lord Ainsworth kissed Belinda's hand, the warm expression in his eyes being all the thanks she needed. Then Francis ushered them all outside.

Two vehicles waited in the carriageway: Lord Ainsworth's black-and-gold traveling chaise with his coat of arms in gilt on the side panel, and one of Lord Kenmore's heavier carriages for the servants and luggage.

Nigel handed Marianne into the chaise, where her maid helped her to dispose herself comfortably. ''My first j-journey in many years,'' he told Belinda, as he prepared to enter the carriage himself.

''May you enjoy it,'' she said.

''That is my intention,'' was his smiling response as he climbed in to seat himself opposite Marianne.

Marianne let down the window. ''Goodbye, darling Lindy. You will come soon to Denehurst, won't you? And Francis, too, of course.'' She thrust her hands out to both of them. ''You realize that the most wonderful thing about all this is that we shall be living so close to each other. Imagine, our children will grow up together, and we shall be comfortable grandmamas together, as well!'' She hurriedly drew in her hands as the entourage began to move off.

Belinda waved to them, but she could see very little through the haze of tears that filled her eyes. As the carriages drove around the fountain and started off at a brisk pace down the straight avenue, she turned away, wishing only to escape, to shut herself away in a darkened room.

Francis gripped her arm. ''Let us not go in for a moment.''

''I wish to go to my room.''

''And I wish to speak to you before you do so.''

''Please, Francis, I beg you, let me go. Can you not see how overset I am?''

"I can, and I know very well that it is not only Marianne's departure that is troubling you. That is why I wish to speak with you."

It was ridiculous to be arguing outside on the steps before the interested gaze of several servants.

"About your business," Francis roared at them, and they scattered like a flock of frightened starlings, recognizing the folly of hesitating even for a moment before obeying their master's orders.

Francis took Belinda's arm in a firm grip and guided her along the flagged pathway to the back of the house. She was too weary, too dejected to try to resist him.

It was a glorious, warm June morning. The heady fragrance of lilac blossoms hung in the air, and from the lavender bushes that lined the pathway came the drone of bees. At the rear of the house, two gardeners were scything the stretch of green lawn to maintain its velvety smoothness.

Francis took Belinda's limp hand in his and walked her across the lawn, the flounced hem of her blue-sprigged muslin dress brushing up the cut grass as she went.

On the terrace, observing the scything, stood Billy, their young page. Francis lifted a finger, and the boy came tearing across the lawn to him. "Mornin', Massa, Lady Kenmore."

"Billy, I wish you to go into the house and tell Besley to bring two bottles of champagne to the summerhouse in the rose garden."

"Two bottles champagne. Summerhouse. Very fine, Massa." Billy dashed off as fast as his small legs could take him, racing up the terrace steps, to be halted there by a footman.

"Remind me to give Billy something for his pains," murmured Francis.

"Why in heaven's name would you ask for champagne at ten o'clock in the morning?" demanded Belinda, so intrigued that she had ceased crying. She blew her nose in her dainty handkerchief and put the soggy ball of lace in her pocket.

"Why not? It is a day of celebration, is it not?"

"Yes, yes, of course it is," she replied with a wan smile. "Oh, Francis, they looked so happy, didn't they?"

"Indeed, they did." He grinned like a schoolboy, evidently very pleased with himself. He took her hand in his again, swinging it as they walked, breathing in the scent of new-mown grass.

Then he began to sing in his rich baritone voice: " 'Merrily, merrily shall I live now . . .' " breaking off to observe, "You know, my Ariel, I am beginning to see why all these philanthropists feel impelled to carry out good works. Making people happy can be extremely stimulating."

"Yes," replied Belinda, deeply resenting his mood of contentment when she was feeling so desolate. Indeed, she reflected, casting a sideways glance at him, his mood was strangely carefree altogether. Dressed in breeches, a plain loose shirt with only a yellow-spotted tie knotted at his throat, and his dark-green nankeen coat slung casually over his shoulders, he displayed an attitude of relaxed abandon.

The roses in the garden were in full bloom, almost decadent in their utter profusion. Delicate white blossoms, voluptuous yellows and oranges, blowsy pinks—they opened themselves to the sun, their petals still moist from the previous day's rain. Petals were strewn across the flagstone paths, as if they had been deliberately scattered there.

"Talking about making people happy," said Belinda, as they slowly wended their way through the garden, "why was Bertie so chipper today?"

"Ah. That is a secret between him and me."

"You are not permitted to have secrets from your wife," she said severely.

A spark lit his eyes. "Just so," he said, darting a look of triumph at her. He swung her hand a little. "And so, when we are comfortably settled in our Chinese summerhouse, sipping our champagne, I shall share Bertie's secret with you, little wife."

She was agog with curiosity but would not now have long to wait, for they had arrived at the summerhouse: a whimsical, Chinese-style folly with sliding doors that looked ou over the rose garden. This was the first time Belinda had been inside it, for it was usually kept locked.

The interior was furnished with scarlet-and-gold lacquered furniture, ornately decorated with Chinese scenes done in black and gold. At the rear of the room stood a circular double couch that looked more like a bed than anything else, to Belinda's eyes. It sported a heavy cover of scarlet silk, with a huge golden dragon embroidered on its center. A canopy floated above it, like the dome of a Chinese pagoda, with silken draperies of scarlet and gold hanging from it.

The sensuous perfume of flowers permeated the entire room. To Belinda's surprise, jars and vases of lilac blossoms and roses had been placed on every surface. Two tall blue Ming vases stood by the entranceway, filled with white lilacs, their waxy blossoms exquisite against the vibrant blue of the vases. She was reminded of the roses in the breakfast room at Kenmore House, and wondered what mischief Francis was up to now.

He stood, observing her reaction, a strange, self-satisfied smile upon his face. Then he began to sing again.

"Merrily, merrily shall I live now,
Under the blossom that hangs on the bough."

"What is that song you keep singing?" demanded Belinda, who was growing more and more exasperated by his strange mood.

"Ariel's song from *The Tempest*: 'Where the bee sucks, there suck I. In a cowslip's bell I lie.' "

"Song? You mean if ever I were to play the part I would have to sing?"

"Indeed you would. Ariel is forever bursting into song."

"Well, that settles that idea, at least," she said, with finality. "For I cannot sing a note in tune."

Whatever rejoinder he might have made was interrupted by the arrival of Besley and John, the footman.

"Aha, the champagne has arrived," shouted Francis.

The servants bore in a silver bucket with engraved handles containing a magnum of champagne, and a wicker basket containing two crystal glasses, a bunch of lustrous black hothouse grapes and some early strawberries, their glowing red a splash of color against the pristine white of the linen napkin.

"Perfection," said Francis. "You have surpassed yourself, Besley."

Besley bowed, his cheeks reddening slightly at this uncommon praise from his master. "Will there be anything more, my lord?"

"Nothing, thank you, Besley. And may I impress upon you that we are not to be disturbed for any reason whatsoever?"

"Yes, my lord." He bowed again, jerked his head at the footman, who was gazing open-mouthed at the flower-filled summerhouse, and they both departed.

"It occurs to me," said Belinda, a few minutes later, as they sat together on the cushioned divan sipping champagne, "that this would be an excellent setting for a clandestine meeting."

"Never," said Francis, raising his eyebrows in mock horror. "You have a highly suspicious, not to mention lurid, mind, little one."

"Yes, I have. So tell me quickly about Bertie, if you please."

"Could it not wait until later?"

"No, I wish to hear your story now."

He gave an exaggerated sigh. "Very well, if you must." He crossed one leg over the other and leaned back against the bolster of the divan, his arm lying along its back.

"I intend to make this as brief as possible. I think you will agree that although Bertie needs to live a little, he must also learn to shoulder his responsibilities. I am becoming very interested in Mr. Wilberforce's aims regarding the emancipation of slaves. He advocates that the freeing of slaves will be a benefit, not a detriment, to the plantation owners, you know."

"What in the world has that to do with Bertie?" she asked him, utterly bewildered.

"I have sent a letter to your father to ask his permission

to send Bertie to Jamaica for six months so that he may compile a report on my slaves."

"Bertie in Jamaica? Oh, Francis, how could you encourage such lunacy! He will be utterly ruined there."

"It is time Bertie was trusted with some responsibility. And the journey itself will toughen him up, I can assure you. I speak from experience."

"If it doesn't kill him!"

"Nonsense! How like a sister to make such a remark. Your brother's far tougher than you think. It will do him good to see another side of the world. I have also impressed upon him the importance of such a report to Mr. Wilberforce. I believe he will feel extremely proud to find himself an active participant in Mr. Wilberforce's campaign."

For a long time after he had finished speaking, Belinda sat, running her finger up and down the cold glass she held in her hand. "So, you have brought both order and happiness to my family," she at last whispered.

"Not entirely. I regret to tell you that I have no intention of taking on either your papa or your dear stepmama."

"I should think not," said Belinda indignantly. "They are old enough to take care of themselves. Besides, I shall be at Denehurst to look after them."

"Ah, now there we have the very crux of the matter, do we not? When do you intend to leave Luxton, my dear— tomorrow? Next week? I wonder that you did not suggest leaving with Marianne and Bertie. That would have saved me the expense of providing you with my second traveling chaise to carry you back to Denehurst."

She gazed at him, wide-eyed, wondering if he could possibly be serious. To her dismay, she saw the mocking smile and glittering eyes of the old days.

The sun went behind a cloud, casting shadows across the rose garden. She shivered and drew her azure-blue vigonia shawl about her shoulders. Francis quickly rose to slide the doors closed, turning the latch to lock it.

Belinda drew the fringe of her shawl through her fingers. "I thought . . . that is, I felt that as Marianne had grown so close to you, and Bertie also, there might be some way of breaking the news to them gradually.''

"Better that way,'' he agreed, sitting down beside her again.

"When she spoke of our being neighbors and of our children growing up together, I thought my heart would break.'' She turned her face from him, unable to stifle a little sob.

"A touching moment, indeed.''

She turned on him, her eyes wild with fury. "How can you sit there, making fun of me, when you know how dreadfully unhappy I am!''

He grasped the hand that was raised to strike him. "Because, my dearest little goose, I have no intention whatsoever of having our marriage dissolved or annulled! Because I intend to ensure that Marianne shall have all her wishes fulfilled. She *shall* live close beside her sister, although both of you will have to be prepared to accompany your husbands to London for the Season, for it is the intention of said husbands to take their seats in the House of Lords—where we shall be in full support of Mr. Wilberforce, by the way; and your—that is *our*—children *shall* grow up together.''

The hectic color drained from Belinda's face. "You are forgetting—''

"If you mean that damned wager with Rosaline, then I wish to inform you that, to my mind, I have fully repaid any obligation I might have owed you, by what I have done for both Marianne and Bertie.''

"I agree,'' she said in a low voice. "It was not that.'' Her fingers twirled the fringe round and round. "You do not love me.'' The words appeared to be dragged from deep within her. "You married me for . . . well, for other reasons, not for love. It was Rosaline you truly loved.''

He sat up straight. "My God, you're an impossible wench. Why must you be so obdurate? Here we are, in the most romantic love bower filled with flowers, with me about to speak of my love for you, and what do you do? You inform me bluntly that I don't love you, that I am in love with another woman. Tell you what, my dearest heart, you'll need to curb that outspokenness of yours." His eyes laughed silently at her.

"Oh, do be sensible for a moment, Francis."

"I am trying to be, my love." Indeed, a serious expression had replaced his amusement. His hand slid along her shoulders. She could feel its warmth against her neck. Slowly he drew her to him. She offered no resistance.

He lifted her chin, forcing her to look up at him. "It is you I love, my darling wife, not Rosaline. She was my first true love; you will be my last! I believe now that I have loved you from the first time I saw you, standing like an avenging spirit over Winchell's unconscious bulk. Did you know that I still have the gold ribbon you wore in your hair that night?"

"No! Oh, how romantic!" She gazed up at him, her eyes filled with wonder, unable to believe what was happening. "I love you so much, Francis," she whispered, a sob catching in her throat.

Anything else she might have uttered was lost in the wonder of his kiss. Slow and sweet, it sent shivers of ecstasy through her body.

She felt his springy hair beneath her fingers as she caressed his head. Now his hand left her face, his fingers brushing the pulsing hollow of her throat, and his lips pressed against it. Gently, his fingers traced a path to her breasts. He bent his dark head to kiss their softness through the thin muslin of her dress.

Belinda moaned in her throat, straining to get closer to him. His hands moved behind her to loosen the sash of her dress, and expertly unfastened the tiny buttons, so that the bodice fell open.

"Please, Francis, please," begged Belinda, her body pulsating with desire for him.

"With pleasure, my love. Always at your service." He swung her up into his arms and carried her to the exotic couch, laying her down on its silken cover.

He bent above her, drawing her dress down to reveal her thin chemise. To her amazement, as he undressed her, she looked up and saw, on the canopy, a large mirror. "Oh, my goodness," she gasped, and started to giggle. "I feel like a captive in a harem."

His dark eyes gleamed. "Do you indeed, my darling?" he said, unbuttoning his shirt. "Then I shall be your loving sultan and you my favorite slave."

"I am not quite certain that this is a proper place or manner in which to consummate our marriage," she said primly. "Should it not be at night and in our own bed?"

"If you wished to wait until nighttime or to be in our own bed for us to make love, then you should not have married Francis Kenmore," he told her firmly.

Deciding that any further protest would be useless, Belinda resigned herself to the great pleasure of watching her handsome husband undress, eagerly readying herself to become the wife of Baron Kenmore of Luxton, in fact as well as in law.